When the Rustle Came from Behind, She Spun Around,

her heart in her throat.

He stepped out of the shadows and stood with his feet slightly apart. Khaki pants were tucked into shin-high boots, and a khaki shirt fit him trimly, the sleeves rolled to the middle of his biceps. His hair was black and streaked with gray. A full beard covered his jaws.

April met his eyes and felt lightheaded, as though she was suspended in that first moment of takeoff after a plane's wheels have left the ground. Or was it the descent, when she always felt it would fall out of the sky.

"Hello, April," Gaines said in a tight, strained voice.

Dear Reader:

There is an electricity between two people in love that makes everything they do magic, larger than life. This is what we bring you in SILHOUETTE INTIMATE MOMENTS.

SILHOUETTE INTIMATE MOMENTS are longer, more sensuous romance novels filled with adventure, suspense, glamor or melodrama. These books have an element no one else has tapped: excitement.

We are proud to present the very best romance has to offer from the very best romance writers. In the coming months look for some of your favorite authors such as Elizabeth Lowell, Nora Roberts, Erin St. Claire and Brooke Hastings.

SILHOUETTE INTIMATE MOMENTS are for the woman who wants more than she has ever had before. These books are for you.

Karen Solem
Editor-in-Chief
Silhouette Books

The Sweet Rush Of April

Linda Shaw

Silhouette Intimate Moments
Published by Silhouette Books New York
America's Publisher of Contemporary Romance

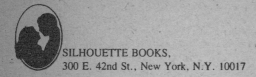
SILHOUETTE BOOKS,
300 E. 42nd St., New York, N.Y. 10017

ISBN: 0-671-46913-4

First Silhouette Books printing January, 1985

10 9 8 7 6 5 4 3 2 1

Books by Linda Shaw

Silhouette Special Edition

Silhouette Intimate Moments

Chapter 1

THE BOMBING OF THE UNITED STATES EMBASSY IN al-Qunay was only part of the problem.

At this moment the whole west wing lay in smoldering ruins. Olive-skinned cleaning crews had been working since dawn sorting the rubble. They had dragged charred timbers onto the lawn, and now they threw chunks of mortar and bricks onto a truck, every movement creating its own echo of violence—a cloudy shower of plaster, a hot haze of smoke.. They didn't look up as two open British Land-Rovers whined to a stop at opposite ends of the street. They ignored the bearded commandos who spilled out of them, and they seemed oblivious to the recoilless rifles they carried.

April Southerland didn't ignore anything. She stood on the embassy's front portico and shaded her eyes against the summer sun. Three years ago she would have said she would be home today, contentedly living as Mrs. (not Ms.) Gaines Southerland, one of those elegantly disheveled Mothers of Children, Homemakers, Gardeners, Chauffeurs and the other undesirables on the feminist list of grievances. But she wasn't; instead she was divorced—all that business about Gaines and his mysterious behavior.

Yet that had nothing to do with this, except for being the reason why she was caught here. Yesterday radicals had blown up the railway line that connected al-Qunay with the Mediterranean Sea. They had cut the telephone wires to the outside world and had taken President Nahrhim captive. No one would dare venture out to the offices and factories today. The steel and glass skyscrapers would be cordoned off, and in the outskirts of town the ancient market stalls and shops would remain tightly shuttered, faces that refused to look at the grisly sight. Only the hospitals would be open.

So, today she faced a catastrophe: she, Ms. (not Mrs.) April Southerland, the twenty-seven-year-old translator from Washington, D.C. What did she know about dealing with a terrorist?

She turned to the native assistant who stood beside her. He was watching the take-over of his birthplace with myopic, spectacled eyes.

"Shouldn't the machine guns have stopped by now?" she asked.

"Only after much fighting, madame." Bashir Id-Nasaq's reply came in mousy, accented English. He was only twenty, but he had seen this before. "And many graves."

April shuddered at the thought.

"*American, go home!*"

A wrought iron fence separated the scuffling stampede from the embassy, the boundary that marked it—in theory, anyway—as a territory in the Middle East protected by diplomatic immunity.

"*Crush Western imperialism!*"

"Down with capitalism!"
"Go home, go home!"

The yells of the students crowding the fence made April's palms sweat. Their dark, dramatic eyes hated her. They thrust their symbolic fists and took up the chant in a piercing medley of Arabic, French, Turkish, and English, all of which she spoke fluently as the special attaché to the ambassador to Orban.

"Go home, go home!"

But Ambassador Strakes couldn't go home; he was dead. And he wasn't the only one. Three others—two marines, and the vice-consul who'd been in the building. Four private citizens had been admitted to one of the city's hospitals. Only three Americans besides herself had escaped harm, all secretaries.

A man alighted from one of the armed vehicles. Doors slammed on the parked Mercedes and BMW cars of the press. Military orders rang down the street as the helmeted commandos cut a path for him through the cheering crowd. He briskly ascended the embassy steps: Ali Jassim, the forty-year-old extremist whom the Free World was already calling the most dangerous insurgent of the twentieth century.

"Only the Americans suffered casualties as a result of yesterday's coup." A newscaster spoke Arabic into his microphone as he scuttled sideways like a crab to keep up with the commandant.

"General Ali Jassim informed the United Nations late yesterday that the death of the Americans was a regrettable tragedy. He will take immediate steps for the safe return of all United States citizens."

Commandant Jassim was wearing the uniform of a fighting man. April almost winced at the rough-textured fatigues and stern, uncompromising boots. A baton was tucked under his right arm and a holster was belted about his waist. He was more handsome than in his photographs, with the beautiful, unblemished skin of his Tuscan ancestors. His thick hair was black, his eyes the color of wet coal.

Lucifer, she thought with a thrill of nerves, invincible in military dress, complete with fire and brimstone.

Jassim, towering as he filmed his propaganda for the world, lifted his hands to the crowd. The voices surrounding the embassy hushed their chanting. The work of clearing the mutilated chambers abruptly ceased. Turning, he forced April to lift her face to the ruthless sun.

"Welcome to the American embassy, Commandant Jassim," she said formally. "I regret our meeting has to be under such tragic circumstances."

"You are the chargé d'affaires, madame?" His inquiry was made in precise English and showed considerable surprise.

"Since Ambassador Strakes is dead and his staff incapacitated, you might call me the chargé d'affaires, sir. I'm April Southerland. I was special attaché to the ambassador."

"A translator?"

"At times."

"And a secretary too?"

"Secretary isn't quite the right word, sir. More like a liaison."

"I see."

He didn't see, of course, and she couldn't tell him that Ambassador Strakes had been a worsening diabetic who had kept his position only at the urgent request of the president. She could not say that she was here only because she spoke five languages and that her father was—had been—John Strakes's doctor, that sometimes the diabetes had been so bad that she was literally the ambassador to Orban herself, that she gave injections . . . something learned from Gaines . . . an intern when they married . . . his disappearance . . . his returns . . . the man she no longer knew . . . the divorce . . . coming here . . . responsibility for American lives . . . must do the right thing!

The commanding slap of Jassim's baton against his thigh jolted her to attention.

April felt a drop of moisture slide down her spine as an aide to Jassim aloofly made a notation on his pad and returned it to the breast pocket of his uniform.

"The death of the Americans is an embarrassment to Orban, madame." Jassim inclined his handsome head so that all the spectators could hear.

Pens flew. Flashbulbs popped. Cameras whirred.

"I wish to help your speedy return to America," he continued smoothly. "You will submit the passports of all wounded embassy personnel to me. I will arrange a special transport from the hospitals to . . . ah, facilitate, yes. This departure will be quickly and uneventfully facilitated."

Uneventful? With Ambassador Strakes lying dead in the city morgue?

"But what about the U.S. civilians in the economic community?" she asked. "Some will wish to return to America immediately."

Ali Jassim turned slightly, separating them from the crowd with a shoulder. "That is a more delicate situation, madame," he said carefully. "The nation's economy is heavily dependent upon American enterprise."

Disbelief formed a quivering gap in April's stomach. "Are you saying Americans cannot leave the country?"

"A most delicate balance, you understand. We would not wish to upset it too suddenly."

"Even your own people out there are shouting for us to go home."

"I am letting you leave, am I not?"

It wasn't the same and he knew it. "Sir, I must

protest. Until Ambassador Strakes is replaced, our civilians would be left without diplomatic recourse. This is
unthinkable.''

"Of course." His smile was meaningless. "I will set
up a committee to rectify this."

She could just imagine his committee! "That isn't
what I had in mind."

"Is it not?"

"And I doubt seriously that the President's Committee on Foreign Relations would approve it either."

For a moment their wills dueled rigorously. April
remained as dignified as five feet five and a threadbare
bluff would allow. Her fluff of unruly sandy hair was
clinging to her temples and the nape of her neck. Her
blurring eyes were liquid green from the sun. Could he
read her disillusionment with life in her double-breasted
blouse and simple skirt and low-heeled pumps? She
doubted it.

His inspection paused on the pearls Gaines had given
her when they married. He glanced at her ringless hands.
He was looking at her restraint, she thought, and was
guessing she was weak. She saw herself in the ambassador's office, the walls blown to bits, the plastered ceiling
falling down upon her as she rocked John Strakes's dead
body in her arms. She was many things—too shy, too
generous, sometimes too trusting. But not weak.

A blistering fury unleashed its fever through her. She
threw back her head at Jassim. *Do your worst*, she
challenged him with a look. *Declare me an enemy of the
people. Have me dragged away to prison. I will not
condone your brutal coup d'état*.

Ali Jassim was taken aback. His brows lifted like
astonished wings. He saw fear in her eyes, but he
recognized something else he had not expected—that
mysterious something that he had never yet in all his

career been able to conquer. It drove men to die before they would surrender.

"Threats, madame?" He drew out the mocking words. "Do those eyes threaten me with reprisals by the United States?"

"I have no authority to do anything," she said. "As you know, Ambassador Strakes's body—"

"The ambassador's body has been impounded."

April's breath was harsh in her own ears.

"Until the present situation is worked out between our countries," he added.

"That is unacceptable!"

The black brows snapped down. "*That* is my decision."

April's heart sank. "Then I must go on record, sir."

Trembling, she faced the cameras. "The United States demands immediate return of the ambassador and our dead. All United States citizens of the economic community must be allowed to leave immediately if they wish to." She looked at Jassim. "We are not at war with Orban, Commandant Jassim."

The commandant didn't answer immediately. He was wondering what the United States president would do if he knew that a woman of less than thirty was affecting his future foreign policy in this sector of the Middle East.

"I have noted your demands," he said at length. "Every request to leave Orban will be brought to my personal attention. You will remain and see for yourself that everything is conducted properly."

"I? But I—"

"You, April Southerland, special attaché to the deceased ambassador to Orban, will be responsible for them."

This was not what she wanted. This wasn't her reason

for being in Orban. Yet she said, as firmly as she could,
"I would want to talk with the secretary of state as soon
as communication with the outside was reestablished."

"As you wish."

"And I would want the ambassador's assistant, Bashir
Id-Nasaq, to remain. And security guards of our choosing."

"I understand," Jassim agreed with a stiff nod.

And then the inevitable question. April pressed her
hands together as if in prayer, the old Eastern gesture of
courtesy. She bowed from her waist, and her hair caught
the sun and shimmered about her face.

"And Ambassador Strakes's body?" she said. "It
must be returned with our other dead."

The silence was but an instant, a breath only, one of
those nebulous moments whose reality one later questions. With several hundred angry students and citizens
watching him, photographers and newspaper people
battling for positions as near to the fence as possible,
April saw Jassim's eyes change.

His dark gaze flicked over her stance, and for one brief
second—did she imagine it?—his eyes lost their harsh
discipline, his mouth its danger. He looked at her, she
thought, as a man looks at a woman who has unexpectedly interested him.

Horror twisted like a coil about her throat. *Dear God!*

The instant passed as swiftly as it had occurred. The
look was gone; his face was once more impassive.

"I must deny you that," he said brusquely. "The
ambassador's body remains here, April Southerland,
until everything is done according to my wishes."

"But surely—"

"I will not discuss it."

He gave her one last penetrating stare, murmured,
"Madame," in farewell, then spun hard on his heel. His

back, as he tucked his baton neatly beneath his arm, was his final word on it.

The hot street boiled over. Ali Jassim descended the steps and strode powerfully across the esplanade. Cheers and adulation rose to a furious pitch, and derision of the Americans wove through the mob in some bizarre polyphonic counterpoint. As the media people relinquished their positions, the students hurled rocks and bottles onto the cluttered embassy lawn.

"Go home, go home!"

Bashir, having anticipated April as usual, pushed his glasses back onto his nose and disdainfully thrust the passports of embassy personnel into the hands of the commandant's aide. The aide bore in his look the intolerance of one underling for another. He withered Bashir with a scowl. Then he, too, clicked his heels and briskly descended the steps.

"Madame must come inside," Bashir murmured in his solicitous English. "Please, please, no more hurt. She must come."

April glanced at the demolished west wall of the embassy, the smoldering chambers, the mangled destruction where once had been meticulous order and lavish beauty. Like her dreams, she thought, her life.

She let Bashir whisk her back inside the undamaged entryway, where the chandeliers and the exquisite lengths of carpet runners and white-walled elegance and yesterday's fresh flowers in silver vases made her feel safer. But not much safer.

Bashir opened a door and waited for her to precede him into the chamber where John Strakes had conducted diplomatic affairs. She walked to a desk and picked up the telephone.

"It's still dead," she said, shuddering suddenly and covering her face with slender hands.

Presently Bashir Id-Nasaq cleared his throat. "Madame?" He was looking to her for his orders—hardly more than a boy in the snow white kaffiyeh and prim European suit.

"I'm fine," she lied, and smiled unhappily. "Really, I'm okay, and I have many things to do. Get a message to your man with the shortwave radio. Tell him what has happened. Tell him to pass the word that the release of the ambassador's body will apparently be the crux of any negotiations."

"Yes, madame." He bowed low and began backing from the room.

April held out her hand. "Are you sure this man is reliable?"

Bashir's head came up with affront. "The ambassador trusted him completely."

But she was not the ambassador, she thought, discouraged, and the only cloak-and-dagger methods she knew she'd read in spy novels.

"Madame?" he said, hesitating, his hand on the doorknob.

"Yes?"

"This will work to the good. The people of Orban want their own democracy. We will fight for this. We will never stop."

"The country has been fighting for twenty years, Bashir."

He turned up small, blunt-fingered hands. "Perhaps another twenty." He soundlessly let himself out.

For several seconds April stood hugging herself. Then, with heavy steps, she moved to the windows and drew back the rich brocade panel.

The crowd was dispersing now. The flurry of danger was, temporarily at least, over. The sun was casting reassuring gold wedges through the windowpanes. Perhaps the embassy would have a few moments of quiet now. Not that she relished it; since the divorce she'd worked deliriously to avoid quiet.

She pushed back a damp strand of hair from her forehead and bent over her own smaller desk near the windows. From a drawer on the right-hand side she withdrew a bound packet of letters with the illegible physician's scrawl of her father across their fronts. She took a plain white envelope from the bottom of the stack, finger-stained and limp from many handlings.

Seconds lost their place as she stroked the surface of a snapshot. It was the image of a tall lean man in cutoff jeans and white Adidas. A polo shirt was tossed over his shoulder, and a tennis racket was beneath his arm. He was climbing the steps to a huge Edwardian house—laughing like a Renaissance courtier, black hair charmingly windblown about a not-too-handsome but intelligent and enormously intriguing face.

The photo wasn't large enough for the facial features to be clear, but she knew them well. His nose had been broken in a water-skiing accident, and he had Mary Southerland's astute hazel eyes. His high cheekbones were so chiseled that permanent lines engraved by the bone structure framed his wide, sensual mouth. His teeth were white and very straight, but only because his mother had given the orthodontist a small fortune. None of the Southerlands had crooked teeth, not his mother, nor Bruce, his oldest brother, nor Andrew, nor Tremaine, nor Steven. Gaines was the youngest of five boys.

"Oh, Gaines," she whispered, feeling the heavy pull of failure.

She pressed the picture to her breast and wanted to smile. One of her secret fantasies had been to have a voluptuous movie star's bosom. Gaines had always laughed when she mourned her lack, and vowed he'd married her because of it.

"Don't you know that intellectual women are always flat chested?" he liked to joke. "It's in their DNA, and you have excellent DNA, my love."

But that wasn't why he'd married her. They had thought she was pregnant.

He had taken the blame upon himself when she told him through a teary flood of self-recriminations. "Med students always think they're so smart," he'd said. "I got cocky and thought I knew everything."

She hadn't been pregnant, but they'd been married a week when they learned. By then it was too late. And even in the rush of their passion she'd always believed that in the back of Gaines's mind he had thought she'd done it on purpose. Mary Southerland had thought so too; she'd never forgiven April for it.

"Gaines was always spirited, yes," Mary was said to have remarked to one of her other sons after Gaines disappeared the first time. "But he was never irresponsible. Never cruel, never cold like he became after he married. One can't blame him. It was his way of striking out at being trapped."

The blame of the marriage was clearly on April—and the blame of its failure. That was never debatable, not even to April herself. *But you got even with me, didn't you, Gaines? Oh, how you got even!*

Shoulders drooping with fresh disheartenment, April slowly replaced the snapshot in its envelope and slipped it beneath the letters. She put it back into the drawer.

So! She was here; she couldn't change that, and she couldn't see her future beyond this one day. She was, bizarrely, a fragile link in a fragile chain and bore responsibility she didn't want for problems she had no solutions for. And Gaines? She had no idea where

Gaines was. But then, she'd known very little about Gaines after they'd married.

She had no heart to return to the window.

On Thursday night in Washington, D.C., at nine-thirty in the evening, Gaines Carroll Southerland climbed four flights of a hot, depressing stairway and fit his key into the lock of a door. He stooped low before turning the key, a quick but deliberate movement, for he was a lean, well-muscled and powerful man, over six feet tall.

He ran his fingertips down the doorframe. Wincing as it pricked him, he removed the sewing needle he'd placed there two months before. It was an old trick that had saved his life at least twice that he knew of.

Straightening, he took a deep breath like an actor taking a cue in a role that he had played too long. He unconsciously ducked his head as he stepped through the door. Stopping, shutting it, he waited for a moment, a shadow in the darkness, his head inclined, listening, evaluating.

Sucking on his finger, he flipped on the light with his other hand. He didn't look at the living room; it contained only a sofa that folded out into an uncomfortable bed, a single chair, and a portable color television set. There were no pictures, no books, no stereo, no albums, no lamps or plants. If asked, he wouldn't have known that the walls were beige. Or that the kitchen cabinets were oversize and were lined with depressingly cheerful orange paper.

Without turning on the television, where, unknown to him, the networks were wrapping up special reports of a coup in Orban only several hours old, he dragged off his tie. He tossed it haphazardly at the table, where it slithered in a spill of blue to the floor. He removed an ordinary J. C. Penney sport coat. It had been altered by an expensive tailor for twice the price of the jacket: exquisitely fitted nondescription.

After unbuttoning the collar of a plain white shirt, he unbuckled a leather shoulder harness that bore in its scabbard a .45-caliber automatic. He draped the harness over the chair. He pulled his elbows toward his spine until his biceps strained the sleeves and his back popped. Then he removed from a cabinet a bottle of J & B whiskey that he saved for occasions like this.

He'd made a mistake before coming here, and he'd known better. Seeing their home—empty, mocking, an unsealed crypt of barren rooms—always tore him to pieces. He wondered why he didn't make the break and put it on the market. Or at least rent it out. Undisturbed ghosts of a marriage? Respect for the dead? Sentimental bastard, wasn't he?

He sloshed whiskey into a glass and tossed it back. It burned all the way down. Good. Maybe this time it would work. Maybe tonight it would drown the sad, shuffling specters of his past.

Taking the bottle, he walked through the apartment and doused all the lights. He leaned his bearded head against the wall for a moment and pressed it hard in an attempt to stop the pneumatic drill from pounding between his ears. Someone from the next apartment flushed a toilet. He straightened with a sigh.

Going to the solitary chair, he lowered his long frame slowly down into it. For some time he sat staring at the darkness. Then he passed a hand across his eyes and began, as diligently as he knew how, to get drunk.

The first time April Humphries and Gaines Souther-land became aware of each other's existence was in late March, an invigorating windy day when heavy winter clothes had been put away and hurriedly dragged from the closets again. They met in the cafeteria at Mercy

General Hospital, where Gaines was taking his internship under the renowned eagle eye of his mother. Mary Southerland was the first woman chief-of-staff Mercy had ever had. Robert Humphries, April's father, was a physician on her staff.

It was Gaines's opinion that April Humphries was the most haunting woman he'd ever seen. Women had always come too easily for him; he adored them all and was never more contented than when drifting through his days with half a dozen pleasant flirtations going at once. He had once been in love with twins and had scandalized his family—to say nothing of the hospital—by taking them both on a skiing holiday to New Mexico.

On this particular day, April had lifted her head to suddenly catch him in his hospital whites, watching her. She was very smart in her mulberry-colored coat, he thought, and the hat whose brim dipped in the front to mysteriously obscure her eyes.

She stopped talking in midsentence when she saw him. With a vague nod of indifference, she touched a napkin to her mouth and, not smiling, turned back to her father.

No woman had ever turned her back on him before. Gaines took much more time to eat than he needed, but she did not look at him again.

The second time they met April was alone. Gaines was seated at a table with half a dozen loud-talking interns. He'd just come from surgery and everyone was hyper. This time she wasn't wearing a hat. Her jaw-length hair was brushed back from her face, leaving her more exposed, and she wore black: grave, high-necked, Victorian black. She surprised him by looking right into his eyes. He didn't know if she was challenging him or not.

She tilted her head as a cool, detached way of saying, "So, we meet again."

Gaines set his glass down into his mashed potatoes. They both smiled.

He looked for her again after that and was disappointed when she never returned. So, for months he began a not-so-discreet campaign of pumping his mother for information about Robert Humphries. Robert? Well, he was an excellent surgeon, Mary told him. He'd lost his wife ten years ago and had been on Mercy's staff nine years since then. He kept to himself. If her memory was correct, he did have a daughter, yes. She traveled a lot, the studious sort. Did some translating, she thought. Robert was very proud of her. Why?

Then he made a point of becoming friends with Dr. Robert Humphries. Robert's quiet, scholarly ways and spare smiles made him a difficult man to know. April was working on her master's degree in languages, he said. And the humanities. She had spent most of her teen years in girls' schools, and she was very bright. She was twenty-three. She would be in Europe all summer. Why?

Meanwhile, when April returned from Europe and learned that much of her father's summer had been spent in the company of Gaines Southerland, she began her own subtle investigation. She pried tidbits of information out of him about Gaines, then took his head nurse to lunch and discreetly questioned her.

The nurse confided in Robert; she had told April everything, good and bad: that Gaines was a rebel who argued constantly with hospital administration and championed every lost cause there was; that he had a terrible reputation with women and was a menace with a fast car.

Was there a romance brewing here? the nurse demanded of Robert. Robert shrugged. Who knew the answer to that? April had talked about getting married only once and had changed her mind. This was something much different. He should have remarried, the nurse said. He didn't know the first thing about people. He was a great surgeon but a lousy father.

By the time April and Gaines accidentally ran into each other at Fox's during the Christmas rush, the only thing left to chance was the meeting. Gaines was waiting for the elevator when it happened and April was stepping out of it, her arms overflowing with gay holiday parcels.

Her all-weather coat flared open to reveal a loosely knitted tube dress that was belted about her waist and whose big rolled neck came high beneath her chin. High leather boots disappeared beneath the hem of the dress. Gaines thought it was enormously suitable to her— different, untrendy, only hinting at the sexuality hidden beneath it.

"It's you!" he exclaimed.

"The man who likes mashed potatoes," she said.

Neither of them moved, and then they laughed softly —she gripping her parcels, he standing with his arms across his chest, hand pressing his ribs.

"Hey, lady, d'you mind?"

"Oh, sorry!" She tossed a distracted apology to the people who impatiently urged her out of the way.

"Here, let me help you with those." Gaines lifted the parcels from her arms, glad for the opportunity to brush arms and hands with her.

"Thank you. What luck meeting you here."

"Yes," he agreed happily. "What luck."

Gaines talked her into having coffee in the shop downstairs. It wasn't difficult to do. He didn't touch the cup the waitress placed in front of him, and he ordered a second only to keep April sitting there. He leaned on his fist and stared at her. He could have spent all night watching her.

"You're shopping early," he said dreamily. "It's still nineteen days till Christmas.

"I'm doing my father's shopping."

"Oh. Thoughtful of you."

"I don't mind."

He looked at her numerous packages stacked by his feet. "And thorough, too."

She smiled, as if he'd done something wonderful to earn it. "There're a lot of nieces and nephews in our family. Dad tried shopping on his own the first year after Mother died. It was a disaster. He's an incompetent once he steps out of the hospital." After a time she lamely added, "I live with my father."

"I know."

Her lips parted prettily. "You know?"

"I also know that you spent the past summer in Italy, and that you've been doing some translating for Benson Paletto."

"I'm impressed." April felt his knee move inquisitively against hers; a faint color tinged her cheeks, but she didn't move away.

"And that you're twenty-three," he murmured, "and had your tonsils out when you were seventeen."

"Sixteen."

"And you have an old fracture of the right radius."

She couldn't tear her eyes from the sensuality of his mouth. "A diving board that didn't get out of the way," she said in a near-whisper.

The minutes stretched out into an unbreathing limbo, and April couldn't think of anything to say that wouldn't make her sound like an idiot.

Imperceptibly their faces drew closer. She thought, as they dispensed with all the prerequisites and exchanged looks that would be meaningless to anyone else, that their lips would touch over the table.

"What else do you know?" she said on a wispy breath.

Recovering enough to talk, Gaines wiped a hand across his mouth. "Let's see, you once threatened to slam a desk top on the hands of a secretary at the Environmental Protection Agency if she didn't admit you to see the, ah . . . 'the man,' I think was how you put it.''

She laughed. "You've been talking to my father."

"Mostly I listened."

"He loves to tell that story. It wasn't nearly what he makes of it. I'm afraid, when it comes right down to it, that I'm fiercely self-critical, over-conscientious, and about as tough as a butterfly at full mast."

"You wander around the world. That's not exactly easy. And you wander around the capital. In anyone's book, that's tough."

"I wander around the world because it helps me in my work." She laughed again, her nervousness lending her a high color. "And I wander around the capital because no one's asked me lately to get married and have babies."

Suddenly realizing how she sounded, April sobered and jerked her head away. She worried a button on her coat as if the touch of something ordinary could solidify the melting familiarities: people wandering in and out of the coffee shop, a voice calling for the waitress, Neil Diamond's melody drifting moodily from the speaker system, silver clinking anonymously upon glassware.

She was looking over her shoulder when she heard the husky magnetism of his voice.

"Are you trying to tell me something, April Humphries?"

"And you call me tough."

With a fingertip, Gaines touched the tiny indentation in her cheek. It was no longer a dimple, for April was no longer smiling. He saw more than a cool, pretty face and the sexual beauty that he imagined beneath her clothes. He saw a certain innocence, though nothing to do with virginity, for he guessed she wasn't. But the other—the disturbing puzzle of what she thought, what she expected, what she was—somehow reached beyond him, touched something deep inside him. He didn't understand her. He wanted her. Very much.

"My father told me half the nurses at Mercy are in love with you," she said.

Chuckling, he drew her hands to the tabletop and matched his fingertips to her short, neat nails. "That isn't true."

"And that your mother has plans for you."

"A few." He shrugged mechanically.

"And you drive like a maniac, so that he barely escapes the parking lot with his life when you're around."

Gaines screwed up his face in a wince. "I guess I had that coming." He sobered abruptly. "April, I have to go."

Eyes wide and apologetic, she came hastily to her feet. "Oh, of course. I shouldn't have—"

He rose too. "My brother's wedding rehearsal. I'm the best man."

"How nice. Congratulations. I mean . . ."

"You wouldn't . . ."

She waited, strength seeping from her bones. "Wouldn't what?"

Gaines was suddenly self-conscious—fifteen again, uncoordinated, devastatingly ignorant, asking for the keys to the car. He placed her hand upon the upturned palm of his own. "You wouldn't go with me, would you?"

"A wedding rehearsal? Oh, Gaines . . ." She shook her head, her voice almost inaudible now. "That's so personal, so . . . family."

Gaines gripped her hand hard. There were times when a person knew, and it seemed he'd traveled a very long way to get there. He stepped into her until his legs were touching hers. He didn't even try to keep himself from falling deeper in love.

"That's why I want you to come," he said hoarsely. He took her by the shoulders with an incredibly gentle promise. "I'm going to marry you, April Humphries."

His statement was extravagant. To April, everything about Gaines Southerland was extravagant—his charm, his quick lightning moves, his golden idealism. And there was nothing in all of her lonely, structured past that could deny that he had stolen her heart. She had fallen in love with him.

"I know," she said softly.

Steven Southerland's wedding rehearsal was at Saint Michael's Church, where, over four decades before, Mary and Douglas Southerland had stood within its native stone walls and repeated their own wedding vows. Their five sons had been christened at Saint Michael's, and later they had married and brought their own children there to be christened. There Mary Southerland had bent over Douglas's bier in the keenest grief of her life and made him a devout promise—that she would devote the rest of her life to seeing that their sons received the best chance for success it was possible to have.

Gaines was not unaware of Saint Michael's influence upon his life, though he would have had difficulty in explaining it to April. It seemed fitting that he should bring April there, to the place where every other beginning in his life had been made.

"You're nervous," he teased as he swerved his car into a parking space and twisted on the seat to face her.

Hugging herself, April peered over his shoulder at the ancient, noble spires. People were streaming into the recreational hall. Lights flashed from behind winking doors. The sidewalks were lined with cars as food arrived for afterward. A woman stood on the steps calling back for the pâté she'd forgotten.

"I can't guess why," April said. "I've only made a decision that changes my whole life."

Gaines drew April into the curve of his arm. He could feel her pulse and hear her quick, shallow breaths. He saw himself reflected in the depths of her green eyes.

"Are you sorry?" he said huskily.

"It's happening so fast."

"There's only a second between life and death."

"I'm frightened, but I'm not sorry." She closed her fingers into his jacket and kept her eyes down. "Your face—it's been in my mind for months. I go to sleep, wake up, it's there."

"Do you love me? Really love me?"

"Yes."

They had kissed before; once, in the cold raw wind outside the coffee shop. They had laughed and raced, freezing, to the car. Now, when Gaines's mouth came down hard upon hers, meaning for it to be quick, there was nothing of quickness. Heat, molten torrents of it, submerged them in waves that could find no quenching, no resolution, no cessation of movement as they strained to be closer.

Groaning, his tongue preshadowed the offers of his body—a thrust, an entry. Gaines pulled her down beneath him. April lifted her hips to his, struggling to touch him anywhere, everywhere. It was lost. They were lost. And if she hadn't been the one to pull away and stuff her face into his neck, he didn't know if he could have stopped himself.

"Will you?" he moaned against her eyes and her ears. Beneath her coat he found her waist and her breasts, the crevice of her thighs. "I want you . . . to undress . . . hold . . . so much."

"Yes!" She clung blindly as she searched again for his mouth, which was already searching for hers.

They stopped only because they had to, and then they slumped back against the seats in stunned depletion, grappling for control and remembering where they were and heaving for every breath.

"Oh, girl," Gaines choked. He scoured a hand across his face and shifted his hips.

April didn't say anything. She was suddenly very afraid; it had just come to her—the horrendous fear of losing what one dares to love so much.

Wishing he could dispense with the wedding rehearsal, Gaines took April into the recreational hall, his arm about her waist. When they walked through the door a dozen voices rose up like a chorus in unison to demand: "Where've you been, Gaines Southerland? We've been waiting half an hour on you!"

April glanced up at the man she had just betrothed herself to—so excellent, so rakish, so confident of where he belonged.

"Mother's about to have a stroke, and the bishop's smoked a dozen cigarettes," a deep masculine voice called out.

"You should have called us," a woman's voice chimed in. "The bride is near hysterics. Oh, dear, where has she disappeared to again?"

"Are all of these your family?" April whimpered from the corner of her mouth.

"Most of 'em."

"There're so many."

Unperturbed, Gaines helped her off with her coat. "They only look like a savage tribe. They haven't eaten anyone in three decades."

Let's only hope your mother doesn't begin now, April thought, and prepared herself to brave the sea of curious people who were already circling about her, speculating behind innocent smiles and fluttering hands.

The room was decorated in white. Snowy streamers cascaded from the high vaulted ceilings and were swung back in drooping swags to white-clothed tables laden with food. Children darted in and out among the adults who stood in clusters, smoking, sipping drinks and nibbling hors d'oeuvres.

"Tribe" was a good word for his family, she decided: an elite clan, protective of its own.

"Well, tell me what to do, Mr. Southerland," she murmured as they prepared to join everyone. "Quickly, so I can make a good first impression."

He draped an arm about her neck. "You're pretty safe if you genuflect to Mother."

She tossed him a threatening look.

"Just joking. Tell Bruce, the tall dark man over there leaning on the stick, that his limp makes him look sexy. War correspondent. Got hurt in Cambodia. Tremaine, the one with the muscles, who looks like Sylvester Stallone, is a broker. He likes to talk about his race car, but don't mention it to Dorothy, his wife. They've almost divorced twice over it already. Most of these children running around like hooligans are theirs. Steven's the groom—an engineer. I don't see him, but he'll be so nervous he won't know whether you speak or not."

April mentally groaned as she tried to absorb all this sketchy but vital information. "What about Andrew?"

"He's a commercial artist. He'll be okay when you genuflect to Mother." Drawing her closer, Gaines raised his voice. "Andy, where's Mother?"

"With the bishop."

Andrew Southerland strolled toward them with a slender artistic grace, a thirtyish smile shaping knowledgeably around the stem of his pipe. He nodded to Gaines, bowed to April and removed the pipe.

"They've talked each other through the ceremony twice," he said. "If you hadn't come soon, one of them would've collapsed." His scrutiny moved appreciatively over April. "What've you been up to here, Gaines?"

Flushing, April smiled. She liked Andrew immediately and suspected that half the women in town shared her opinion.

Andrew had never met a stranger. Hazel eyes twinkling, he lifted her hand to his lips. "I have to say that I admire your courage to brave the snobbish old Southerlands, Miss . . ."

"Humphries," April supplied. "Please call me April."

"Ah, I might've known. You look like an April, all sandy-haired and green-eyed. Were you born in that month, or would that be too obvious?"

She laughed. "I'm afraid my parents were obvious. But I got even. I was a terrible child."

"Well, well, well," drawled a rich bass voice from behind April's shoulder.

Bruce Southerland was one of those fastidious, excellent princes that other men hated on sight. At forty-one he had made several fortunes already and was boredly looking around for another. Limping attractively to Gaines, he balanced himself on a shining, brass-handled stick and gave April his full attention.

"Where did you get this treasure?" he demanded. "I thought all the good ones died back in the fifties."

April inched closer to Gaines's side. Bruce was obviously a bachelor who enjoyed the freedom.

"Pay no attention to Bruce." Gaines laughed into her hair and placed a light kiss there. "He's oversexed."

Catching April's eye, Bruce winked. "You think I've

got trouble? Mother's furious with you, Gaines. Listen, I need to talk to you.''

Shrugging happily, Gaines brushed his older brother aside. "In a minute. I'll go settle Mother down." He gave a boyish, courtly bow. "Would you do me the honor of caring for April?"

Bruce would not be put off. He glanced around the room and mumbled, "I need to talk to you now, you jerk."

Then, without any warning, it happened: three things in a quick chain reaction, three very human things that were not serious in themselves but, placed in this particular setting and with these particular personalities, had the effect of dominoes that would topple against their counterparts for years to come.

April realized, because it was deeply in her nature to feel people's vibrations, that Bruce's urgency was making him draw Gaines away from her whether he wanted to be drawn or not; Mary Southerland was walking into the room like a queen prepared to hold court; beside Mary was a very lovely woman who took one look at April and stopped while Mary walked on. She looked as if she were challenging April to a showdown.

In all her fifty-nine years, Mary Southerland had not lost her beauty nor her figure. She was as exquisitely slender as the day she was married. Tonight she wore a wool crepe suit designed especially for her, and its mauve color lent her clear skin and silver hair a radiance that was both fragile and faintly arrogant. But most of Mary's charisma, April thought, was good breeding: generations of wealth, prestige, a character of impeccable correctness, and, after Douglas's death, matriarchy in the 1980s.

Mary took one look at the two women facing each other, then glared at Gaines as if he'd just betrayed her.

Bruce swore under his breath.

Comprehending, April met Bruce's gaze and saw regret there. She realized when it struck Gaines, for he moved swiftly to her and gripped her fingers hard until she thought the bones would break.

"I'll be damned," he muttered to Bruce. "When did Rosemary get here?"

Andrew removed his pipe and drew Bruce's eyes in a quick message; Rosemary was the daughter of an equally prestigious family, a woman Mary had always privately favored for Gaines. No one expected her to attend Steven's wedding. But then, no one had expected April Humphries to be at this rehearsal, either.

Gaines glanced from one to the other of his brothers. "Why didn't you tell me?" he demanded in a harsh undertone.

"I tried to," hissed Bruce. "Mother didn't warn anyone. She asked if I'd go to the airport and pick her up. And you turned up . . . late."

A ghastly hush fell upon the room.

"Well, Gaines." Mary's voice cut across the silence like a diamond on glass. "I see you decided to finally grace us with your presence."

April guessed that Mary couldn't have cared less that Gaines was late. Her temper was directed not at her son, but at the woman on his arm. Gaines, too, realized the object of his mother's temper. It incensed him, but he contained his anger beneath flawless manners.

Stepping forward, he placed a kiss on Mary's forehead. "I should be tarred and feathered," he said self-effacingly.

Mary's brows were unforgiving. "You could at least have called and . . . warned us."

April felt her color rising. Who did Mary think Gaines was, a child whose knuckles needed rapping?

"That wasn't possible, Mother," he said. "I'm sorry to have inconvenienced everyone. Hello, Rosemary."

He took Rosemary's hand and kissed her cheek and smiled. "It's wonderful to see you again, dear. I think everyone knows everyone else except for April. Mother, I'd like you to meet April Humphries, Robert's daughter, whom we've spoken of."

Mary leveled her hazel eyes on April. "I'm so happy to meet you, my dear. Please feel welcome at Saint Michael's. Gaines, would you walk with me back to the altar, please?"

Turning, Gaines met April's dismay. *Trust me on this,* he said with a look. *I love you.*

What could she do but smile through the introductions? Once April and Rosemary had gotten through the clumsy amenities, the family charged to the rescue with laughter and domestic conversational games. Rosemary was bustled off by the daughters-in-law while Bruce took April under his wing. He was a perfect host while Gaines was busy—constantly attentive, a gentleman, lending moral support though they did not speak about it. Andrew and Tremaine went out of their way to introduce her to wives and children and friends.

But beneath the laughter and gaiety, where the silence of undercurrents ran deep, something irredeemable had happened. By the time the evening was over the family had unconsciously chosen sides. They chose her, April. And April doubted that Mary would ever forgive her for winning. She knew, with a woman's unmistakable instincts, that Mary would never forget.

Even now, as Gaines sat thinking about that evening in the sweltering darkness, he knew that April had never been able to bridge his mother's resentment. She had foreseen it; she had wept bitterly about it in his arms that night.

He'd told her everything would be fine once they married, for he didn't realize that he'd sided against his mother merely by loving April. And then, kissing away her tears, he'd carried her up the stairs of her father's warm, empty house. He'd held her for a long time before he undressed her. When she stood at last before him—so fresh, so needful, lifting her lips in loving trust to his—he made his fullest commitments to her.

"I want a life with you," she confessed, and placed her palms upon the flexed muscles of his hips. "I want everything."

For Gaines, April's inexpert loving was a world that he'd never ventured into. Her pleasure of discovering him was so torturously prolonged that he suffered from it as much as he loved it. She adored him with her eyes and slipped up from behind to hug his back the moment he was undressed. She kissed his shoulders, the back of his neck, his waist, and, as she slowly sank to his feet, moving her hands over his hips with touches of silk and whispered lovewords, she kissed the backs of his knees.

He'd never had a woman approach him so before. When he turned in the circle of her arms, she was tentative in touching him—a newborn—and he did no more than place her hands there, expecting no more.

When she leaned into him and closed her mouth upon him, nothing that had gone before seemed to even exist. He taught her his pleasure on an excruciating wave of arousal until she, becoming the teacher, guided him into her. He took her wildly, gently, carefully, blindly, and then with a passion that still, after all this time, made him want to weep.

How they'd loved through those long winter months! It had been breathtaking and golden, a star streaking toward earth in slow motion. Yet when the star finally hit earth and they married and then learned she hadn't been pregnant after all, April stubbornly took the blame upon herself.

As he looked back on it, he saw it was natural for Mary to latch on to April's self-blame and attribute every slight and petty sin to it, along with the failure of their marriage, the way his life had changed. But he knew better. He was the one they should blame. He had caused it all.

April, April, my sweet love, April. It won't go away, sweet April. God help me, I can't stop loving you.

Chapter 2

WHEN THE TELEPHONE SHRILLED AT A QUARTER PAST ten o'clock, Gaines was halfway between asleep and awake and was drifting somewhere on the hazy side of sobriety. Swearing, flailing about and remembering that he'd gone to sleep in the chair, he located the telephone receiver and dragged it to his ear.

"Yeah," he mumbled groggily, and turned it right side up. "What d'you want?"

The voice on the other end was a sterile echo. "Go immediately to area A."

For a moment Gaines didn't respond. He blinked his brain awake and raked through his hair. Then he scoured his full growth of beard. He let out his breath and tried to rid his mouth of a terrible taste.

"Bug off, Wesley."

"Unacceptable."

"You heard me, Wesley. I said no."

"No names, please. We will talk when you get to area A."

Gaines pried himself off the chair and weaved painfully. He lifted a sympathetic hand to his temple. "What's the matter with you, Wesley? You deaf? I'm out. Now go to hell. And say hello for me when you get there."

"Go immediately to area A."

Click. The dial tone buzzed in his ear.

Damn!

Unable to quell a hot surge of temper, Gaines wrenched the telephone out of the wall and hurled it viciously to the carpet. The receiver tumbled end over end, and the bell gave one reproachful ding at him.

He stood for a moment in the unfriendly room. The farther away from it he got, the more he knew what a mistake it was—the pinpoint in time where he'd gone wrong. David Paris had motioned him down to his pillow in the emergency room of Mercy Hospital. A dozen or so words had married him to Wesley Durant and the CIA: bigamy, infidelity, and only April had divorced him.

It had started with the delivery of a message for a dead man, but it had grown into a malignancy. It had spread into Vietnam, Poland, Lebanon, Israel, Central America —small jobs, but important; jobs that needed a fresh face and a good head. A thousand times he'd wanted to tell April what he was doing. A thousand times Wesley had seduced him into waiting. For April's sake, he always said.

He jerked up his head. He couldn't start raking over that again. The memory of what he'd lost was unbearable . . . unbearable. . . .

By the time he had showered and changed into a pair of clean slacks and a fresh shirt his watch read eleven o'clock. Wesley was waiting for him, as usual, in a small park within sight of the Potomac River.

Gaines grimaced. Buildings made Wesley nervous. A lot of things made Wesley nervous.

It wasn't that Wes was an ogre; he was pleasant enough. He was a smiler, even when he asked a person to do something that meant almost certain death. And that made him difficult to second-guess. There were times it paid to dissemble with Wesley and times it paid to be direct. The trouble was, he was never certain which. And he never won.

As he approached, Wesley rose from the bench where he sat smoking. He ground out his cigarette with the toe of a discreet Florsheim and smoothed back his hair, not a wisp of which was out of place.

"You're late," he said as he fell into step. One always walked when talking to Wesley.

"Screw it, Wesley."

"Now, now." The agent remained unruffled at the irreverent thrust. "Is that any way to talk?"

"I never talk to you, Wesley. I listen."

"Not very well, I might add."

"So fire me."

Wesley's smile broadened until his teeth were actually showing. "I understand how you feel, son. That's why I handpicked this assignment myself."

Gaines looked out at the river. "Cut the 'son' bit, Wesley."

Cupping his hand, Wesley lit another cigarette, snapped his lighter closed and slipped it into his pocket. "Have you seen the news?"

A bone dislodged somewhere deep inside Gaines, and he stopped walking. He should have known; Wesley's gait was too smooth, the hint of kindness in his tone too unnatural.

He shook his head.

"There's trouble in Orban."

That was it!

"Bottom line," Gaines demanded, perspiration streaming suddenly down his back.

"Jassim now runs the country, just as we feared."

"Is she alive?"

"Now just a minute, Gaines."

"Is she alive?" Gaines grasped the front of Wesley's jacket, realized his mistake and, embarrassed, slowly released it.

Wesley readjusted his jacket and gave the lapels a meticulous brushing. "Yes. But there are casualties. The ambassador, that we're sure of. And the vice-consul, some of the marine guard. We think there are others, but communication's bad right now. They refuse to release the ambassador's body until certain negotiations have taken place."

"And President Nahrhim? Is he alive?"

"We think so. A thousand members of his government have already been arrested."

Gaines's mind was taking flight. He hadn't drawn an easy breath since April had taken the job with John Strakes. Nahrhim's government was too young to support as much American investment as it did; it was geographical location, not military security or political stability.

"Who's on the inside?"

"Practically everyone. But Marek and Salah would concern you."

"Has our president issued a statement?"

"Soon. The Hill's on the warpath, naturally. He has to play this one very carefully."

In the course of Wesley's talking they had begun walking again. The running lights of small boats blinked as they moved up and down the Potomac. The night air was muggy, full of salt smell and pierced with the pristine needle of the Washington Monument in the distance.

Wesley turned, smiling. "We need a new face, Gaines. I think you could handle it."

"My face isn't all that new."

"This coup won't have attracted anyone who knows you."

Gaines gave a bitter, self-mocking laugh and shook his head; he'd sworn he would never take another assignment.

"An army couldn't keep me out of Orban," he said. "You knew that when you picked up the telephone."

"We knew you'd go, yes."

Wesley ground out his cigarette. Deep in his heart he felt compassion for Gaines Southerland. Before he died, David Paris had picked his man well. Gaines was a natural. He had a near-photographic memory and the superb instincts of a gambler. His personal change had come harder than most. Yet it had come in time; the smart, likable man was now a shrewd, dangerous man who didn't appear to be what he was. He was one of their best.

He put his hand upon Gaines's shoulder. "It's going to be simple but a bit touchy. We want you to look into some American businesses."

"What kind of businesses?"

"There are six different American enterprises in al-Qunay; two of these are government contracts. Ali Jassim knows that the success of his coup will depend in great measure on whether business goes on as usual. He's temporarily restraining American investors from leaving the country. All very calm and polite, but illegal."

"He can't keep that up."

"He can cause a lot of flak if he screams 'American exploitation' and starts throwing Americans in prison."

"He wouldn't be stupid enough to do that."

"Who knows what a revolutionary will do?"

"Have American investors been ripping off Orban on the sly?"

Wesley flicked an imaginary piece of lint from his cuff. "The truth is, we're not sure. If they have been, we'll deal with it. We just don't want any surprises. And no noise."

"I'll bet you don't."

"And if there's dirty linen, we don't want it found in the government's closet. We've got to keep the lid on this, Gaines. The press . . . well, the press gets rabid at times like this. Discretion is the key here."

Gaines laughed. *Discretion* was Wesley's favorite word. "If I agree to go in and find out your dirty little information for you, there's something I'd want to make clear."

Wesley sighed. "This is your last assignment."

"I want out. You can fix it. I mean it."

Wesley knew better than to press Gaines when he was in this mood. "You've given us more than we had the right to ask for."

The compliment caught Gaines off guard and he scowled, pinching the bridge of his nose. "What about the embassy?"

"That is not our concern."

"It's *my* concern."

"The president will handle that himself."

"Well now, Wesley," Gaines drawled, "what would the Agency do if the embassy should suddenly come up short one attaché to the ambassador?"

Wesley didn't blink an eye at the question; he had hoped for it. The Agency got nervous when civilians were caught in situations like the one April Southerland was in. It wanted her out.

"As long as it doesn't jeopardize national security," he said, knowing his meaning would be clear, "it would be none of our business."

Gaines glanced at his wristwatch. "Get me set up, then. I'll use the passport I've got. Notify Marek I'm coming in."

For another fifteen minutes they discussed particulars. At precisely eleven thirty-two—Gaines looked at his wristwatch—they both buttoned their jackets and prepared to walk away in opposite directions.

"Oh, and Gaines?" Wesley called over his shoulder before Gaines had gotten three steps.

Wearily, for his consumption of alcohol was beginning to tell on him, Gaines turned back, his eyes bloodshot and narrowed. "What?"

"You have no official business with the embassy. You and I did not even discuss the embassy."

"Sure, sure." Gaines dragged a finger beneath his collar. *Assignment: Get wife back. Mission; impossible. We will disavow all knowledge, etc., etc., etc. Gaines Southerland will now self-destruct.*

Wesley Durant wasn't nearly so pessimistic in his thinking as Gaines. As he moved off in the opposite direction, he went with the smug satisfaction of having gotten what he wanted and having done something compassionate for an employee at the same time. The Agency did have a heart, despite what everyone said about it.

He, unlike Gaines, was smiling.

When Bashir Id-Nasaq placed a napkin-covered tray on April's desk at four o'clock in the afternoon and reminded her that "madame has eaten nothing since breakfast," April rose, stretching and yawning, from her chair.

"But things are moving right along," she said teasingly. "The commandant is being cooperative, and I'm only suffering from malnutrition and exhaustion."

Bashir assumed an expression that neither agreed nor

disagreed. He announced that a man who called himself Bruce Southerland was waiting in the reception room with members of the press.

"What?" Food was forgotten, Ali Jassim forgotten. April stood with her arms extended in midair. Bruce? Here?

Bashir patiently repeated himself. "He says he is brother, just arrived from States. He carries a stick."

April hardly heard a word after "brother." Oh Lord, something had happened to Gaines!

"It's a black stick," Bashir grumbled to himself, mistrusting all very tall men. "For beating servants. As in your Civil War . . ."

Swishing the wrinkles from her skirt and tucking in the pink tail of her blouse, April fluffed at her hair and flew, sandals skimming, to the reception room near the front portico of the embassy. There were three American guests waiting as she rushed into the room, two men and one woman. They all wore badges designating them as members of the international press corp.

Of the Southerland men, Bruce and Gaines looked the most alike. Bruce had picked up a few pounds since she'd last seen him, yet they seemed somehow to give him an added sophistication. He still carried the stick, to Bashir's consternation, and she guessed that he no longer needed it. It was a trademark now.

"Bruce!" she cried, tears of fondness distorting her voice as she hugged him. "Oh, Bruce, Bruce!"

Bruce caught April with his free arm and lifted her off the floor. There were times when he suspected that he was a little in love with her himself.

"Thank God you're all right," he exclaimed, laughing with relief. "We were all worried. I talked to your father just before I left."

"Is Daddy okay? Communication's still so bad over here. The telephones have just started working again."

"Robert was certain that bad news would have found him already. He sends you his love and wants to hear from you as soon as possible. But yes, he's very concerned."

Her gaze brimmed with unshed tears as she grasped Bruce's free hand in both of her own. "Have you seen Gaines?" she whispered. "Is he all right? Is he well?"

"I saw him a couple of months ago." He smoothed back a wisp of April's hair. "He's all right, darling. Unhappy right now and wearing that 'son-of-a-bitch' chip on his shoulder. But he's all right."

"You're sure?"

Bruce kissed the lines of worry from her forehead. "I'm sure."

"And Mary?"

He drew April toward his associates. "April, if my mother were up to her eyelashes in turtles, she would defy anyone to say it wasn't the proper way to be. Yes, she and her tyranny are doing fine. Now, I want you to meet my co-workers."

He energetically introduced them. "What's Jassim like?" he asked when he had finished. "A cross between Fidel Castro and Ayatollah Khomeini?"

April laughed. "More like Bluebeard and the Black Knight, I'd say. Jassim and I have a sort of arrangement—I'll stay out of your way if you'll stay out of mine."

Cynthia Hymes, a reporter for *Time*, crossed her legs in their baggy pants. She was tall and resembled a sophisticated New York model remarkably, down to the fingernails. Her shirt looked as if it had been slept in for several days, and her platinum punk haircut made the statement that she was either too brilliant to care or a slob.

"One reporter says that Jassim is probably the most charismatic figure of the decade," she said.

"They probably said the same thing about Machiavelli." April smiled. Cynthia was definitely not a slob.

Phillip Cook was a truly beautiful black man and was a free-lance photographer. A Nikon, a Leica, and a light meter hung from straps about his neck.

"According to one reporter, women are supposed to find him virtually irresistible," he said with a splendid smile.

Cynthia bridled. "The reporter was a man, naturally. But I'm wondering if his charm has any bearing on why you didn't return to the States when everyone else did, Ms. Southerland?"

Ah! April remained perfectly still for a second and pulled a leaden diplomacy over her anger. Brilliant or not, Cynthia Hymes had piranha's teeth.

"I managed to resist him," she said, and changed the subject. "Well, Bruce. The press didn't get hassled when it came into the country?"

Bruce scraped ash out of his pipe's bowl with a pipe nail and repacked it with a sweet tobacco. "Jassim is anxious for everyone to believe that the American deaths were an accident."

"The deaths were an accident. The bomb was not."

"Yes, well, the city literally opened its arms to us—within reasonable limits, we were warned."

Cynthia laughed with a smoker's raspy hoarseness. "Of course, it's the unreasonable limits we're interested in."

A clawing little worry scratched at April's instincts. The United States press—any press—was a balance of power against a usurper, but it could also be a menace: gelignite in the wrong hands.

"The courtyard's quite pleasant this time of day," she said, rising with a rustle of silk and linen. "Why don't you let me play ambassador and get you something cool to drink?"

Bashir had already poked his head into the reception room and was disappearing for refreshments.

The embassy courtyard could have been lifted out of another century and transported to the present day by magic carpet. Whitewashed walls enclosed it on all sides. Gleaming tile roofs extended over shadowy colonnades right out of *Arabian Nights*. Shrubbery was thick, private, isolating, and roses spread over the walls and arches like a Moorish veil—hot and perfumed.

Phillip immediately began snapping pictures as everyone else settled on benches that lined the arcades. They chatted as Bashir placed a heavy tray of unrecognizable confections on a table.

"Well, Bruce," April said, "these unreasonable limits you spoke of. How do you see them?"

Bruce took the glass she passed him. "Off the record?"

"Everything is off the record here."

"The president's nervous. He sees another Iranian incident in the making."

"For all his ruthlessness, I don't think Ali Jassim is stupid."

"A good part of Nahrhim's government is in prison, April."

"And there's cause to worry, but there've been no mass executions, no evidence of a purge."

"Yet."

"There's gossip at home," Cynthia said.

"What kind of gossip?"

"That some American investors had an arrangement with Nahrhim and have been milking the country dry."

April wondered if Cynthia knew how dangerous that kind of talk could be over here. "I would say that very softly, if I were you."

Bruce came awkwardly to his feet. He limped to one

of the roses, picked it, and placed it flamboyantly in his lapel. He turned with a flourish of his stick.

"April, you and I both know that unless the American public finds out for itself, Intelligence will shove everything under the table. We could wake up in five years and find out that millions of American dollars were spent without anyone knowing."

"Are you talking exposé?" April's cup froze midway from her lap to her mouth.

Cynthia lit a cigarette and snapped her lighter closed. "You say it like a dirty word."

"We intend to find out the truth," Bruce said.

"Whatever it is," added Phillip Cook.

No alarm must show on her face, April warned herself, no alarm. She traced the rim of her glass with a fingertip. "What you're talking about could ripple a long time."

Phillip said: "Our advisers think it might be good to cause a stir. You know, America taking care of its own dirty laundry. Letting Jassim know we don't want trouble even though we don't support his politics."

"Sort of defanging the cobra before it can strike." Cynthia picked tobacco from her tongue. "I'd like to meet this Jassim character."

April only observed: "One treads very carefully around a cobra, Ms. Hymes."

Laughing, Phillip winked at Cynthia. "Especially male cobras. I don't think the females have much of a bite, Cynthia."

"Shut up, you male chauvanist."

Phillip cackled with laughter. "Cyn, you know what's going to happen to you if you keep thinkin' all those ugly thoughts? That pretty face is goin' to shrivel up and get all ugly and mean, and . . . ugh! I can't bear to think about it."

Cynthia Hymes glared at Phillip for a moment, then ran her fingers through the wild disorder of her hair and laughed.

Everyone was relieved to change the subject. April played hostess to it all, but inwardly her thoughts were a turmoil.

An exposé? Well, it wasn't her business. Let Intelligence worry about it. She couldn't stop Bruce from doing his job. Yet, if Jassim was only putting up a front to the world and secretly had bloodletting on his mind, Bruce could just as easily find *himself* up to eyelashes in turtles.

She listened to everyone's complaints about the climate and tried to think of something besides trouble. How like Gaines's hands Bruce's were—beautiful hands for a man, slender, blunt-fingered with wisps of silky black hair across their backs.

A length of memory unraveled in her mind—Gaines's hands, shaking that of her father, giving her the key to the new house . . . his hands as he waited for her to walk that endless center aisle of Saint Michael's, taking hers, holding them tightly, slipping the ring on her finger, lifting her veil, taking her arm and later, much later, cupping her face, lifting the pearls out of their rich black box . . .

She came to herself with a start and focused her attention on Bruce.

"So, when will you let me take you to dinner?" he was asking.

They were walking back through the corridor of the embassy, past the Oriental fabrics draping over the divans, along the woven path of carpet. Cynthia and Phillip were already out on the portico, gazing at the skyline and pointing at the tank that still guarded the capitol square.

Dazed, for she hardly remembered leaving the courtyard, April slipped her arm lightly through Bruce's. "As soon as I can. We're very tired here. Gunfire and sirens go on all night, and I work hard during the day with dozens of people."

"Tomorrow?"

She didn't know if she could bear sitting across a table from a copy of Gaines Southerland for an entire meal. "Well . . ."

A tease twinkled in Bruce's warm hazel eyes. "If you won't marry me," he laughed down at her, "at least let me coddle you. I'm a coddler of the highest order."

"Bruce—"

He sighed fondly. "I know, I know. But I have my feelings of responsibility too. You didn't come out very well with the Southerlands, my dear. I'd like to make up."

On the street the limousine waited, still loaded with luggage from the airport. Cynthia poked her shaggy head out the window. "Curfew'll catch us before we can get to the hotel, Bruce. Hurry up."

"And I need a bath," Phillip added over her head.

Sighing, Bruce planted a quick, hard kiss on April's mouth and promised to call the next day. And he insisted upon dinner until she agreed.

"There's no way to get around you, is there?" she said.

"Now you've got it!" He tossed a charming salute over his shoulder and crawled into the car.

"Be careful," she called after him.

For a moment she waited as the black Mercedes strained to start. After a few uncertain grumbles the engine exploded into a sputter that gradually, and with a good deal of revving by the driver, leveled out into a rumble.

Bruce poked his head out the window with a doubtful

frown as a cloud of white smoke billowed out from the tailpipe.

April waved. The car jumped away from the curb and glided up the street toward the capitol square, turned left and quickly disappeared.

I'm halfway around the world, Gaines Southerland, April reflected as she watched the car until it was out of sight. *Halfway around the world, and you tell me why I can't escape you.*

April was still brooding about Gaines when she emerged, two hours later, from the small bathroom attached to her office. Tonight she wouldn't even go home; dozens of papers must be finished for the evacuation flight day after tomorrow.

She unzipped a gigantic napa-finished tote that half her personal belongings could have fit into. She removed a delicious pair of slacks and a slinky silk tunic—liquid peach, coolly delectable. She had barely stepped out of her underwear and into her change, looping the rope belt loosely about her waist and sliding into clunky wedge-heeled slings, when Bashir knocked at the door.

He wore a disapproving smile and balanced a tray precariously on his head.

"Madame should go home." His myopic eyes blinked. "She will not sleep well in this office."

"I will sleep better than you, I daresay."

She took the tray and placed it on her desk by the window. As he proceeded to draw the drapes and turn on lamps, she lifted the cover of the tray.

"Delicious. You've been reading my mind again."

"Madame will eat every bite. She will need extra strength for the trouble Bruce Southerland will cause."

April's brows flew accusingly together. She pointed a

peeled orange section at his head. "You've also been eavesdropping."

"Americans talk loudly, madame," Bashir said without a qualm as he arranged her silver.

His unruffled courtesy always floored her. Rolling her eyes at him, then shaking her head, April waved him away and ate the orange. "Sometimes I think I learn as much diplomacy from you as I did from the ambassador. What am I going to do with you, Bashir Id-Nasaq?"

Without giving her any insight into the solution of that particular problem, Bashir tucked the tray beneath his arm, inclined his head and shut the door after him.

He stood for a long moment outside the door, smiling. He had worshiped April Southerland from the moment he'd seen her bending out of the limousine and standing beside John Strakes, peering up at the embassy with a solemn, wondering awe. When the day came that she left Orban his life would be over. He would die of a broken heart.

April nibbled from her tray and arranged the evening's work on her desk. After opening one of the drapes so that the sunset could chase away her moodiness, she flicked on the television set.

The censored news reports of the coup and the outside world flashed onto the screen.

Once the oranges had disappeared, April took more time with the grilled mutton and black bread spread thickly with butter. The wine was different from American wine, more heady; it made her sleepy.

She sat twirling the empty long-stemmed glass in her hand and remembered the first night she and Gaines had spent in their big new house. It had been completely empty and they'd spread sleeping bags on the carpet before the fire. They had drunk wine and made love on

the floor . . . and then they'd gone to sleep in each
other's . . .

April thought, when she lifted her head from her desk,
that she'd slept only a few moments. She drifted
between wakefulness and the straggling cloud of a dream
and wondered if the television had roused her.

Sitting up, she rubbed her eyes. Her neck was stiff and
one of her feet was asleep. She danced about until the
sting subsided, then picked up the glass from the floor
and hobbled to the television set. She cut it off.

The room was dark now except for the eerie glow of
the streetlight from the open window. She waited a
minute for her eyes to adjust. That was when she saw the
man.

"Please, Madame Southerland," he said in a low,
sandpapered voice from beside the thick swirl of draperies, "do not make a sound. I don't want to hurt you.
Would you step to the center of the room, please?"

Not if he had threatened to shoot her on the spot could
April have moved.

He took a step toward her, a tall disorderly man in
untidy black trousers and a limp cotton shirt. His face
was the same as any other that one would see on the
streets—dark eyes and tousled curls growing low upon
his brow. He could have been anywhere from twenty to
forty, but his body strength, despite his baggy clothes,
was terrifyingly efficient.

"I won't do . . . anything," she finally managed to
say. She could see his gun now, an outlined bulge in his
pocket against the top of his leg.

He smiled. "I know."

"Wh-what do you want?"

"For you to come with me."

Icy fingers walked up April's spine. "But I—I can't."

"Do not make trouble for me, Madame Southerland," he said. His smile vanished.

April's shock diminished enough for her to apply a grain of logic to her situation. The man obviously knew who she was. He had called her by her name. That made him either a counterterrorist from President Nahrhim's people or a fanatic of Jassim's.

But why? What would either faction want with a negligible American female whose influence barely included running this embassy during the interim? Perhaps General Jassim wanted to see her but didn't want to come to the embassy. That must be it.

"Look," she said, arranging an absurd smile, "if the commandant wants to talk, all you have to do is say so."

The man pointed to a door that led to the courtyard. "This way."

"Then it *is* Commandant Jassim." She hesitated. "I really should tell Bashir—"

Smiling, he said, "Do not count on the boy, madame. I suspect it will take him a while to get out of his room."

April groped for the back of the chair. "You . . . you locked him in?" She forced herself to stand very straight. "I'm sorry, sir. You have miscalculated. I will not go anywhere with you."

"I must insist." His hand hovered over the gun, its meaning frightfully clear.

Ohh! She jerked angrily around. Her breasts moved beneath the silk, and her hand lifted instinctively to them.

"You could at least give me time to change my clothes," she said angrily. "You can see I'm not dressed to go out."

He glanced around the room and indicated her clogs beside the chair. "You may put on your shoes, madame."

She slipped her bare feet into the shoes and forced her hands to stop shaking. "May I get my bag, please?"

The man picked up the tote and rummaged through it. Small, feminine overnight items clattered with bottles and loose change and sunglasses and wallet and a fat volume of poems by Wordsworth. He held the book toward the dim light and let it fall open naturally.

He read, haltingly: "'Where beasts and men together o'er the plain / Move on—a mighty caravan of pain . . .'"

He lifted his brows at her in appreciation and let the book close. He dropped it into the bag and handed it to her, motioning her to the door.

April crushed the tote to herself and glanced miserably at the telephone. He saw that too, and with a casual gesture that she knew was not in the least accidental, his thumb caught in a belt loop just above his gun.

She channeled every gram of resentment she possessed into a look. "I don't want any of your threats," she lashed out. "Don't say one word to me!"

She mutely followed him through the door, out along one of the terraces of the courtyard and through a door half hidden in the trellised vines. With any luck, she thought, they would be picked up by Jassim's commandos.

Moving about in al-Qunay on foot during the daytime without being accosted was an accomplishment; at night it was a miracle. The sophisticated part of the capital was crowded into the streets surrounding the buildings of state. Once a person ventured beyond that, it was a network of haphazard, jerking streets and rows of boxlike houses that huddled together as if in dire need of comfort.

April had never ventured into the city alone, much less after dark. Now, hurrying along where floodlights whipped back and forth and loudspeaker commands burst out of the silence—sometimes machine-gun fire— was the most frightening thing she'd ever lived through. Land-Rovers roamed about, bristling with weapons. Roadblocks were everywhere with soldiers checking credentials, and they invariably extracted money from Americans who were unlucky enough to get stopped.

She soon forgot everything except the thrill of still finding herself alive every time she was led around a dark corner or through a twisting, smelly alley. She entertained no thoughts of escape. It would have been suicide.

It seemed hours before they reached the edge of town, but it was actually less than one. April was helplessly lost now. The only time he spoke was when she asked his name.

"Harry," he said in a bald lie.

She said an Arabic word and thought she saw him smile.

It was very dark when he indicated she should stop walking. They stood near a dingy little movie house. Posters of Ali Jassim had been slapped on its billboards.

"Are you all right?" he asked.

She was drooping with anxiety and strain. Her feet were tortured. She felt the stickiness of blood from where she'd stumbled into rocks and bricks.

"No, I am not all right!" she whispered shrilly, unable to swallow down the hysteria that bubbled in her throat. "This is an outrage!"

He held up his hand to silence her and propelled her down a short dark alley to the back of the cinema house. It was more like an added partition of sheet iron that jutted out like a rusty thumb. He stopped before a wooden door set into it. His knuckles struck two short raps. He leaned his ear against the planks to listen.

It was the first real opportunity April had had to

escape. Perhaps while this maniac was speaking to whoever was inside, she could dart around the corner.

As if he'd read her thoughts, the man's hand shot out and clamped around her wrist like a band of steel. "Please don't think about it," he said without even looking at her.

The door creaked shrilly on its rusty hinges, and April's heart jerked. A masculine voice murmured something from the inside, but she couldn't distinguish it.

"When?" asked the man.

Again, the murmur.

"Three hours," her abductor replied. "I'll be there."

April knew, with dismay, that she wasn't being taken to speak to General Jassim. The man drew her closer. A smile flashed across his dark face, and with no warning whatsoever, he lifted her hands to his lips. Head bowing, he kissed it.

In an extremely unceremonious fashion, he shoved her through the door. Before she could turn, the door slammed shut.

Oh, dear God, she prayed in agony. Was this the end? Was this the end of her life?

For a good ten seconds she dragged her eyes across the purple shadows. She didn't dare move. Something deep inside her was snapping loose. She would die here, she thought, without a single effort on the part of her captor. Her own fear would kill her.

When the rustle came from behind, she spun about, her heart throbbing in her throat.

He stepped out of the shadows and stood with his feet spread slightly apart. Khaki pants were tucked into shin-high, steel-toed boots, and a khaki shirt fit him trimly about his ribs, the sleeves of which were rolled to the middle of his biceps. Dark patches of sweat streaked the sides of the shirt, and beneath his belt glinted the butt of a handgun. His hair was black and streaked with gray. A full beard covered his jaws.

April met his eyes and thought with astonishment how strange it was that she wasn't on the ground anymore. They were both moving. They were suspended in that first moment of takeoff after a plane's wheels have left the ground. Or was it the descent, when she always felt it would fall out of the sky?

"Hello, April," he said in a tight, strained voice.

Falling, she thought hazily. Definitely falling. The window was circling around her head and the butt of Gaines's gun was no longer beneath his belt but against her cheek.

Someone—a woman, she thought—spoke as she slid down a dark tunnel where there was no light at the end.

"Gaines?"

Nothing.

Chapter 3

APRIL'S FIRST THOUGHT WHEN SHE FLOATED IN ON A wave of consciousness was that she was waking up in the house that she and Gaines had lived in when they married. They were in bed, she dreamed, curled in the drowsy cocoon of each other. Through a film of warm gold haze she could feel his familiar wall of muscle, the brush of his hair against the nape of her neck. An enchanting fantasy, it seemed to her, one she would like to indulge. She considered snuggling back and drifting off to sleep again.

Her eyes flew open. Gaines? Gaines's hair? His hair *was* against her neck! His muscles *were* a wall about her! She was lying half across a bed and half across his lap with her head draped over the side of his knee.

"Ohh," she moaned as she swam up through the rubble of her illusion.

"Easy. Have a heart, will you?" Gaines braced an arm about her shoulders. "It's me. Gaines."

"I know who it is!" April shoved feebly at his chest. "Put me down, you . . . Put me down, Gaines!"

Gaines came to his feet, and she practically spilled out of his lap. He took a step backward and widened the space between his hands, as if he were letting go of an uncertain toddler.

"I'm not sure you can stand up."

For several seconds April feared he might be right. She weaved precariously and looked around herself in astonishment.

The room could have been the set of a pornographic movie. The bed, covered with a bright spread, was flanked by a folding screen draped with pieces of sheer lingerie—garter belts and fancy bras and see-through nighties. The dressing table was a clutter of bottles and glasses and ostrich feathers and a *nargileh* for smoking hashish. One whole side of the wall was covered with photographs. Even in the shadows the various states of female undress were apparent, and several surprisingly artistic nudes. A photographer's lair? A promiscuous man's fantasy?

"Of course I can stand up," she said, and took several steps to prove it. Dizziness promptly swirled down to her knees, and she stumbled over her feet again.

"Damn it, April." His oath was muffled as he caught her. "You always were the most hardheaded woman I ever knew."

He carried her to the bed and dropped her rather ungently upon it, first her upper half, then her dangling puppet's legs.

April pulled back against the headrail and drew her legs reproachfully beneath her. Gradually, as her shock subsided, she began to exchange looks with him—half-hostile glances, fleet and guarded, with the visceral intimacy of people who have once been passionate lovers: comparing, weighing, wondering how much is remembered.

He was taller than she remembered. Thinner, perhaps, and possessing a hard, steely toughness that she would never have imagined of him, as if the older he got, the more disillusioned he grew about himself. She'd never seen him with a beard before. Trimmed close, it set the angular ruggedness of his cheekbones into prominence. He was wound very tight, like a big cat poised before the attack—muscles stretched, eyes everywhere at once, sharp, dangerous eyes, not at all the laughing ones she'd married.

"You have a lot of explaining to do," she said guardedly, and grimaced at the room. "We would've let you in the embassy, you know. You didn't have to resort to this . . . bordello."

"But it was such an adventure getting it."

"The owner must have one every time he walks in."

He lifted a shoulder. "He runs the movie house. He romances his ladies here. He leased it to me for an hour after I promised him that I wanted it for the same purpose."

"An hour?" She smirked. "Well, practice makes perfect, I suppose. What are you doing in Orban?"

"Would you believe making a house call?"

Beginning to recover from the shock now, April tried to arrange her thoughts into some sane order, tried to understand why she was there. But the puzzle had too many pieces missing.

"I don't suppose you'd tell me who that wretch was who brought me here," she said cautiously. "He told me his name was Harry. Somehow I tend to doubt that."

Gaines looked at her thoughtfully. "His name is Marek. Marek lies a lot."

She waited a moment for him to explain how he came

to know Marek, but he only grasped a chair and scraped it across the floor. Inwardly flinching, she watched as he turned it backward, tossed a limber leg over the seat, and seated himself in a slouching, masculine straddle.

"Well?" she demanded.

"Hello, April." A grin momentarily relieved the tautness of his features. "How've you been?"

April let her eyes close. After three years of divorce, he could still do that—sidestep an issue as neatly as ever.

"Oh, great!" she said, and started to swing herself off the bed. "You haven't changed a bit."

He waved her back down. "Don't run off. I thought we might have a little chat."

"A chat?" April raised her chin in a challenge. "All right, Gaines, let's have a chat. What are you doing in this country, for openers? And why this *James Bond* theatric? You get some terrible person to drag me out . . . Drag me out? Why be nice about it? You had me kidnapped." Her voice tightened with sarcasm. "Did you know that kidnapping is against the law now, Gaines? They send you up the river for that."

Gaines folded an arm across the back of the chair and stroked his beard. "Did anyone ever tell you that you're too uptight, April?"

"What?" She blinked at him.

"You really need to learn to relax. Tension's bad for your blood pressure."

"Blood pressure!"

She flung herself off the bed and sent her gaze bouncing incredulously off the ceiling. Then she froze in midmotion.

Of course! Bruce said he was here to investigate American investors who had been making profits at the country's expense. And wasn't it a coincidence that her ex-husband should suddenly appear in Orban at the moment of trouble? Wouldn't it be the ultimate irony if Bruce had come—in innocence, she was sure—to expose his very own brother?

She bent for her shoes near the window and casually slipped them on. "I suppose you know that Bruce arrived in al-Qunay today."

Over her shoulder she watched Gaines's back to see if the name of his brother ambushed him. Only a hint of reaction showed: he sat infinitesimally taller and there was a slight tension about his mouth when he turned.

"Bruce? Well, what's the old boy up to now? Reporting the street fights? Doing a profile on what's-his-name?"

"Don't be snide. You didn't know Bruce was here, did you?"

Gaines stretched his long legs out in front of him and regarded his boots. "Bruce and I don't talk much anymore."

"He says that some Americans have been making enormous profits and some may make more with the overthrow of Nahrhim's government."

He shrugged. "The people who raise the fuss wouldn't raise it quite so loudly if the money were going into their own bank accounts."

She'd been silly to think he'd admit to such a thing. Which meant that he was undoubtedly guilty.

"Did you have anything particular on your mind by all this?" she said, feeling suddenly depressed. "If you didn't, I really need to get back to the embassy."

Gaines had kept a tight grip on his emotions as he watched April moving about the room. She'd changed a lot. The years were transforming her shyness into a definite flair: classic elegance combined with a sort of unstated aggression that gave a person the impression she knew much more than she was telling. Age was also lending her a sexual maturity that he doubted she was aware of. Even if he hadn't known her, he would have looked twice.

But he did know her; that was the problem. It was easy to remember her naked: her breasts, her waist, the line of hip, the shadowy nest, the way she liked to make love. He couldn't fathom anything as utterly inaccessible as she was.

"I apologize for Marek frightening you," he said with a hesitant, blunt-edged honesty. "But I had to get you out."

She stopped suddenly as she stooped for her tote. Her head came up. "What d'you mean . . . out?"

"Out of Orban. In case you haven't noticed, there's an explosive situation here. Quiet assassinations, not-so-quiet bombings. Of course, I don't have to tell you that." He leaned sharply toward her, his words cutting like a blade. "Do I have to tell you that, April?"

History turned its ugly pages in April's mind. She wasn't about to believe that Gaines had started worrying about her at this late date—too many handwritings on her wall.

Picking up the bag, she slipped it over her shoulder. "You're fooling around with me, Gaines."

Gaines unfolded himself from the chair and threw one boot onto the seat. He leaned an arm across his knee and casually braced his weight.

"Well, it wouldn't be the first time, would it, girl?" he said, and brought things to a quick, unpleasant climax.

She threw back her head in defiance. "Oh, Gaines, that's beneath even you."

"But you still look good." He nodded in a familiar manner and deliberately captured her in a sweep from her toes to her head. "Awful good."

April tried to fling his insult back in his face, glaring

back at him but seeing nothing but blatant arousal and lazy isolence. She fumbled her way to the door and turned before she opened it.

"Gaines, I haven't pretended to understand you for a long time now. But because we once loved each other, I've chosen to believe that somewhere inside you, you have a reason for the things you do. Well, do what you must. It's not in my power to stop you or influence you. But don't try to pretend that you care about what happens to me. I can't take any more pretending. I swear I can't."

The tears she promised she would never shed again banked hotly behind her lids. She blinked furiously. "Oh . . . damn you, Gaines!"

In the anonymity of darkness Gaines's hands shook; he hadn't thought it would be so hard. He swung his leg off the chair.

"No pretenses now," he said icily. "I've come a long way to get you, April. I'm tired, and you're tired."

"What?"

"I'm taking you to Tel Aviv and putting you on a plane for home."

She couldn't believe him. "I'm not leaving Orban. I won't leave. I mean . . . I can't."

"I've got a truck for us up in the hills. We can be out of Orban by dawn."

"But you're not listening to me. Someone has to be at the embassy. I'm telling you—"

With the swift grace of three steps, Gaines was before her. His posture was irrefutable. "But you see, my darling, I'm not asking."

She reached blindly for the doorknob. It was cool and solid in her palm. She thought, *I will open this door and things will end between us the way they always have. Why does it always end in hurt?*

"Then you should have," she mumbled, and gave

him the rejection of her back as she wrenched open the door.

Belatedly April remembered the speed with which Gaines could move, and the drive of his power. He was before her in a flash, and one hand slammed savagely against the door, rattling the bottles on the dressing table.

"No!" she cried, spinning around, experiencing a real and acute fear of him now.

He towered over her, one arm extended beside her head, the other holding the door shut. "You put one foot out that door, April, and I promise you'll regret it."

From outside there came the distant night sounds of war, paroxysms of violence—a siren in downtown al-Qunay, the screech of tires, and the isolated, single report of a gun. They faded into insignificance compared to the war going on within the walls of the tiny room.

"You're sitting on a powder keg at the embassy, April." His words were brutal. "Are you so naive that you don't know that?"

"You're making too much of it." She shrank as far away from him as possible. "You think Jassim is going to start lining people up before a firing squad?"

"He could."

"Have you ever met the man?"

Gaines narrowed his eyes. "No."

"Well, he's not what you think."

Sighing, he lifted his hands and took a step backward. "He really convinced you, didn't he?"

April couldn't keep from crumpling when Gaines moved away. "Jassim's being careful. He wants American favor, and that makes him play both ends."

"What he's going to get is a nasty little civil war." He aimed a finger at her. "And you're not going to be here when the bullets start flying."

"What do you think would happen to the Americans in this country if I left? The U.S. doesn't seem in any great hurry to send someone to replace John Strakes."

"They're working on it. And I doubt very seriously whether your presence here makes an iota of difference, one way or another."

He gave her no more credibility than he ever did! Anger scorched the lobes of her ears.

"Well, I can't leave!" she declared hotly. "Jassim would . . . I don't know what he'd do."

"Run complaining to the United Nations that he had just misplaced another U.S. citizen? Not hardly." Gaines threaded his fingers through his hair. "Look, April, some of the American investors over here have been coming out a little too good profitwise. In a few days some of Jassim's interrogation rooms may show a few Anglo faces. Do you understand the trouble that could mean?"

"And that's why I have to be here."

In her agitation, April had stepped toward him, her hand imploring. Perhaps it was the pleading in her voice or the fact that she had moved closer; Gaines wasn't sure. He looked down at her outstretched hand as if she, in some mysterious, unexpectedly tender way, were offering him back his life again.

Before she could move away he took the hand in his own, opened its slender fingers and smoothed its palm as if he could read his life story in its lines. In years past, that hand had touched parts of him with the most adoring love he'd ever imagined. Lifting it, he placed it upon his beard, as if she were holding his jaw. Turning his face into it, he gently kissed its palm.

April couldn't move. She watched Gaines's hair tumble with incongruous boyishness as his head bent. How many times had she buried her face in that sweet-smelling crispness? How many times had she blown it dry, arranged it at the last minute before they had gone out?

As if she were that younger, more innocent person again, she clasped her hand about his face—a butterfly's caress. His eyes lifted. He didn't speak. He didn't blink. After some moments—she had no idea how long—she self-consciously drew back her hand.

"April—"

"You don't understand." She looked everywhere but at him.

"I understand dead bodies."

"He won't kill me."

Gaines knew a moment of total frustration. He groped in his mind for the right words but couldn't find them. "Killers don't feel loyalty for little attachés to the ambassador, for God's sake!"

The moment hung between them—hovering, agonizing.

"*Neither do husbands,*" she said through her teeth.

Her truth slashed him open like a knife. Gaines felt the slice of it, saw inside himself to the skeletal bones of his vast mistakes with her. He turned away, but when he heard her open the door he reacted instinctively. He was behind her in two strides.

"Oh, no you don't!" He grabbed her arm savagely.

April knocked Gaines's arm away with what he thought was astonishing strength. His gun was dislodged from his belt and went clattering across the bare floor. She succeeded in opening the door, even in getting her shoulder through it. Gaines grasped the willowy span of her waist with both hands. And she, bent in the middle and clinging to both doorknobs, was dragged forcibly back against his urgent, straining thighs.

They struggled absurdly, she pulling herself forward, he dragging her back for every inch she gained. He couldn't believe she was so strong. Her breathing was loud and rough, and he had to laugh at the sexual battle of it, though it was anything but funny.

"You're getting . . . weak in your old age . . . April," he huffed, sweat pouring as he pulled her hips back into the masculine angles of his body. "You'd better start taking . . . care of . . . yourself."

With a great heave he peeled her off the door and stumbled backward. Her weight was heavy against him. She screamed once, shortly, and threw herself away, barely managing to keep on her feet.

"Oh, this is stupid," Gaines heard himself say as he caught his balance. "All I want is—"

"I know what you want!"

That much was true. Desire had raged through his body at the first touch of her, so violently that it staggered him. Now heat was rushing its exhilarating stain over his face and its ache deep into his groin. All sorts of fantasies were forming in his mind.

Hardly realizing what he was doing, Gaines spun April around as if she weighed nothing at all. The momentum sent them both hurtling toward the foot of the bed. They fell without time to prepare for it, and, with his arms closing about her back, he took the brunt of it. He rolled with her, up and over the foot, and moaned as the brass rail caught him hard across his spine.

April ended up beneath him, her hands pinioned by his, her abdomen straddled and his hips pressing hard against her belly. Her tunic was twisted up beneath her arms, and she saw her breasts gleaming, naked and white, in the darkness.

When Gaines's eyes collided with hers surprise was in them: the reach for a step when there is none. She thought to cover herself, but she couldn't move. His gaze flicked from her breasts to her mouth. He paused for a second as if he didn't trust his impulse; then swiftly, fleetingly, he brushed a kiss across her lips.

She caught a startled breath.

He jerked his head back, stiffening as if she'd thrown cold water in his face. Shifting his weight onto his palms, he stared down at her nipples. They were tight and pink, blatantly aroused.

Swearing softly, he rolled off her and onto his feet.

Immediately April clambered off the bed. Her hands shook so badly she could hardly repair her clothing. From beneath her lashes she shakenly glimpsed Gaines unzip his pants and stuff his shirt inside, make an adjustment to his briefs, and then rezip them.

He walked the necessary feet to his gun, stooped and retrieved it. He slipped it beneath his belt and, sighing, smoothed down his rumpled hair. Then he laid one palm on his waist as if forcing himself to calmness.

April snatched her eyes away. She laced her hands very tightly at the center of her waist and held her breath, turning her back to him and praying that he wouldn't say anything. What was happening to her?

Presently he cleared his throat. "You're afraid," he said at last. "Is it of me?"

Afraid? "Of course not," she vowed hotly. Then, softly, more honestly, she said, "Yes. No. I don't know."

She glanced apprehensively at him over her shoulder. A hard expression was on his face, unreadable and distant.

"I fear the pain you can bring me," she admitted. "I don't want to ever go through that again."

Whether it was the erotic little room or the war-torn town or their physical moment of brushing against the past—as bittersweet as that was—she and Gaines continued standing with their backs to each other. It was as if that space were the curtain of the confessional; words came that might otherwise have remained unsaid.

"You shouldn't be afraid," Gaines said, knowing as he spoke that she would continue being afraid because he couldn't say the words to heal her. "You were the innocent one."

Her laughter was inaudible, a harsh breath. "I don't think I was ever innocent."

"You were perfect."

"You broke my heart."

"Do you think I haven't paid for that?"

An awkward silence.

"I suppose you're happy now. I mean, now that . . ." She hesitated.

"No."

The pause grew more tedious.

"Are you? Happy?" He coughed lightly.

"I don't think so." Her tears collected in a drowning pool. "I . . . never figured out what happened. I never knew why I couldn't take the . . . distance. Other women got used to it, lived with it."

"You were never other women."

April couldn't tell from his tone if he was glad or sad about that. Why didn't he ever say it was her fault? she wondered. Why didn't he yell paranoid criticisms like other husbands? She might have something to get her teeth into if he did.

"I had to get out," she said as if she could say that now, after three years. "I was coming apart."

All the times when Gaines had put the needs of his country before April came back to haunt him now: Wesley and all his glorious obligations to duty. What glory? What duty?

He stroked his mouth with his thumb, then: "Someday I want to tell you . . ."

Eagerly, eyes brimming with hope as they had a

hundred times in the past, April turned. She took an anxious, pleading step toward him. "Tell me what, Gaines?"

The current of the truth was pulling and stretching inside Gaines. He was getting out of the Agency. He wanted to tell her everything. But the timing was wrong; sometimes survival boiled down to what a person didn't know. He'd seen it happen before.

He exerted tremendous control on himself. "I—"

She didn't move. And Gaines stood without speaking until he saw the hope die in her eyes. He would tell her nothing and she knew it.

Distress tightened the flesh across his cheekbones. "The ramblings of a demented man."

"Yes," she said tonelessly. "I'm on very familiar terms with that man. I've often thought I'd like to hit his face."

"Then do it."

He thought he'd feel better if she did. But she didn't, and he had known she wouldn't. He took her by the shoulders.

"In spite of what you may think," he told her in a final surge of despair, "there hasn't been a day when I didn't wake up with a pain in my gut because of what's happened to us. I accept the blame for that. But that was then. And this is now. You might be right about your work at the embassy. You might could go about your job and nothing would happen. But it's a risk. It's one I can't take. I'm sorry."

He watched her closely for the slightest indication that she understood, that she still felt anything for what they had once had. He saw nothing except the vacancy of her stare. He couldn't even see anger.

He had difficulty with his words. He took her shoulders again, and she didn't resist. He gave her a little shake.

"Dammit, April, if something should happen to you . . ."

Like a robot, April detached herself from him. Nothing had changed, she knew. She could search and search for the tender man-boy intern who had cared so fervently about the world, who had triggered all the best part of her and dispelled her displacement in life. That man was dead. And every intelligent person knew that death was final.

She bent and picked up her bag from where it had fallen. "There is no way I can stop you from doing this, is there?"

His silence said everything.

She walked to the door without looking back. "I don't think I'll forgive you, Gaines," she said. "In fact, I'm sure I won't."

He knew the pattern, Gaines told himself. He must keep repeating to himself not what he wanted but what he must do.

"Have it your way," he said dully as he followed her out.

When Marek abducted April from the embassy, his calculations were unfortunately off on two counts. His first mistake was in thinking that locking Bashir in his room was a good idea. The second was in thinking that the small wiry national would spend a few moments being embarrassed and that he would quietly go on to bed until someone came next morning to let him out.

It took Bashir exactly eighteen minutes to extricate himself from the locked room by scrambling up through some loose planks in the ceiling of his closet. And it took him another two minutes to reach Ali Jassim's aide at the House of State by telephone.

Bashir blotted at the sweat on his upper lip. He was

slipping, to have let that misbegotten catch him un-
awares like that. He was trembling with fear of what
April Southerland could be going through at that very
minute.

"Who is calling at this horrendous hour?" Captain
Nadal's grouchy Arabic crackled in the receiver after
several rings. "The commandant is asleep. He cannot be
disturbed."

"An irregularity has occurred here at the embassy,"
Bashir replied in Arabic, and gave his name. "My
humble apologies for disturbing you."

"That's beside the point now." Nadal was a diminu-
tive man. He attributed this in great part to a lack of
proper rest because of imbecilic telephone calls like this
one.

"I wish for you to give a message to the commandant.
The attaché to the ambassador, April Southerland, has
been kidnapped."

"Idiot!" snapped Nadal, wide awake. "You should
not have wasted so much time in telling me. Stay on the
telephone. I will get the commandant."

Bashir had not expected to talk to Jassim himself.
From where he waited he nervously looked out at a sky
awash with white summer stars. The moon hung thinly.
It was a perfect night for surveillance. He had considered going after April himself, but Jassim could find her
more quickly and efficiently than he could. And then he
hoped they did terrible things to this abductor.

"Bashir Id-Nasaq?" Jassim's deep voice warned the
embassy employee that this had better be good.

Of course it's me, Oh Stupid One. "Yes, I am here."

"April Southerland was taken from the embassy?"
came the question. "You are sure about this? She didn't
just leave for some reason she didn't tell you about?"

Bashir removed his glasses and pinched the bridge of

his nose. "I was locked in my room by a strange man. I went to her office some minutes later. She was gone."

"Give me a description of this man."

The description was given.

"And you have no idea where he took her?"

If he had, he would have said so, wouldn't he? "None, Commandant."

"I understand that the embassy entertained guests from the United States this afternoon. People from the press corp. You were there, of course."

"Sir?"

"This Bruce Southerland. This is April Southerland's family?"

"The brother of her husband. Ex-husband."

"Ah, yes. The Americans do a lot of that marrying and divorcing, don't they? Yes, well, did you hear what was said between them?"

"Commandant, I did not listen."

Jassim's laughter boomed in his ear. "Everyone listens, Bashir Id-Nasaq. Let me tell you something, my little man. I would like to know more of this Bruce Southerland. I want you to hear more next time. Perhaps you will be willing to tell me this so that I won't have to bring you in to see me. It's always such an inconvenience to bring people in for questioning. They get detained; I get detained. You know how that goes."

He knew exactly how that went, Pig Face! "I am sure I will hear nothing, Commandant, but I will certainly listen. You will send someone to find April Southerland?"

"That is not your concern; but yes, we will bring her back. The new order seeks justice, you understand. It also seeks total commitment to its cause. Am I making myself clear?"

Fool! "Perfectly clear, Commandant."

After hanging up the telephone, Bashir fit his glasses about his ears and returned to his stark, monastic room in a wing completely separate from the diplomatic offices. He could predict the procedure Jassim would use. Within fifteen minutes the city would be crawling with people looking for April Southerland. In another fifteen, they would know the man who had taken her from the embassy. In another, they would have found her. Jassim's agents were very effective.

Bashir's room was behind the kitchen and opened onto the courtyard. With walls of unrelenting white and a floor of highly polished marble, it was nearly bare of furnishings. His bed was small and covered with a plain brown spread.

The only item of any interest in the room was a tapestry hanging opposite the window that looked out upon the courtyard. It was a finely stitched picture on a pale blue background. His mother had made it, and it showed the sad, bloody history of Orban. It ended when she died at the hands of border guerrillas nearly ten years ago, along with his father and three sisters.

Before the tapestry was a small table upon which was a candle. He lit the candle now and, going to a niche behind his bed, removed a small straw mat. He sent it rolling out with a flick of his wrists and dropped to his knees upon it. Facing the tapestry and bending low until his forehead touched the floor, he prayed devoutly that no harm would come to a single hair on April Southerland's head.

Chapter 4

THE TROUBLE, APRIL THOUGHT AS SHE STUMBLED grudgingly along with Gaines on the streets of al-Qunay, was that buried down there with all her complicated hatred of Gaines Southerland was a bit of leftover love.

She wasn't certain why the love had refused to succumb; all her dreams had. But she knew exactly why her hatred was there. Because Gaines could obviously live as well without her as with her. And because now he had suddenly reappeared when her life was out of control and had told her he was worried, and she wanted to believe that but didn't dare, and because her toes were bruised and hurting from the craggy eruptions of sidewalk, and because his sinewy legs and invincible endurance were vastly superior to hers, and—damn him—he was looking at her as if she were incapable of a simple thing like walking. And this whole train of thought was

ludicrous! She wished she could sit down in the street
and get even with him by dying!

"I can climb these without any help, thank you," she
said with insulting politeness when Gaines attempted to
take her arm.

Gaines stopped in the middle of the high incline of
steps and threw his weight to one leg. He braced a fist at
his waist.

April saw him watching the wind mold her tunic and
furl her slacks about her legs. He was looking at her
floppy bag, which was clutched high upon her shoulder,
and her ridiculous shoes and her rumpled weariness.
What was he thinking?

"Didn't you have any shoes but those?" he said
curtly.

She defended her shoes as if they were the real bone of
contention between them. "What interest is it of yours?
You don't have to buy them anymore."

"Then perhaps you'd do better to keep some of the
alimony I send you."

"And that's one of the great mysteries of my life."

"What?"

"Why you keep sending me money. I don't want your
money, Gaines. You're not responsible for me anymore.
I'm responsible for myself."

The whole bent of the conversation irritated him. He
rubbed the back of his neck and sighed. "I'll buy you
some shoes in Tel Aviv," he said, and motioned her up
the steps. "And some other clothes. Either that or you'll
get us both arrested."

Temper blazed like eager flames between them. "Shut
up, Gaines," she said as nastily as possible, and
stomped up the steps two at a time.

One of al-Qunay's geographical characteristics was
that it lay neatly cuddled in a misshapen bowl of hills. Its
outskirts wove a spider web of alleys and streets around

and around and up into the sides of the bowl. Curfew wasn't so stringent in the fringes of town. Even at midnight a number of people ventured out of the huddled houses and shook their angry fists about the danger of political affairs, only to disappear at the first sound of a car or strange footsteps.

To April's amazement, Gaines moved through these peasant back ways like a thief used to prowling at night. From time to time he drifted from her side, only to reappear suddenly and spirit her off in a new direction without an explanation. More than once he stopped in his stride, listened when she could hear nothing, and pulled her back into the shadows against him.

During those silent, unbreathing seconds she could feel the powerful throb of his heart against her shoulder blade and his breath stirring her hair. His arm would be across her waist like steel, swift and compelling.

It was after one of these pauses that Gaines released her and spread out a map on the ground where they stood. He balanced himself on the ball of his foot and ran the beam of a pocket light over the route Marek had designated.

She leaned over his shoulder. "Is it far?"

As he pointed, Gaines twisted unexpectedly. His arm grazed the side of her breast. Before April realized what he was doing, she had steadied herself on the tops of his shoulders—a habit long forgotten, a gesture of familiarity. He didn't move, his very stillness a recognition more volatile than words.

She straightened as if stung.

Gaines looked at her hands, then at the contradiction of her face. He knew, she thought, that something had stirred deep inside her.

"Yes, well." He came to his feet. "It's not too far." He began refolding the map.

April didn't know what to do as he stuffed the map

into his hip pocket. She was too painfully aware of physical things: his legs, taut and set apart, the wind aggravating his pants about the tops of his boots, his hair blowing wildly about his head, his biceps straining against his rolled-up sleeves. He only lacked a rifle slung over his shoulder to look the part of a mercenary, a dangerous guerrilla who answered only to the deadly rules he made himself. She saw herself caught in the vise of those ruthless arms, her head draped helplessly back, his lips searing her throat.

Shaken, she started blindly off in the direction of the sidewalk.

Gaines caught up, grasped her arm and spun her around. "Hey." His eyes saw much too much. "It's the other way."

"Oh?" She pretended to gaze around herself.

"Do you want to wind up in the boonies?"

Her cheeks burned. "You're the one with the map. Lead on."

For several blocks more they walked without speaking. They were passing the last buildings of the city now, a shambling string of ruined warehouses whose boarded fronts were partially obscured by a waist-high stone wall running along the edge of the sidewalk. The walk had become overgrown with disuse, its cracks having sprouted thistles and rustling spears of dry grass.

"Are you okay?" he asked at length.

"I'm hungry and thirsty and my feet hurt." More in control now, she lightly added: "Of course I'm okay. I do this all the time."

His brows came up. "Wander around in the middle of the night with strange men?"

"You, a stranger?"

"Hardly. I know things about you that no one will ever know."

Her pulse surged and her smile disappeared. She kept her eyes straight ahead. "Why bring up something that's dead and gone?"

He didn't answer immediately. Then, very low: "Because I'm not so sure it is."

The pretense hung stubbornly between them: frozen, but with a crack in it.

"Not dead and gone," he added, as if she had not understood.

"I know what you meant. I also know you've been undressing me for the past hour."

"Husbandly habits." His grin flashed briefly. "They die hard."

There were times when she wondered if they ever died. "Take care, Gaines." Her voice was low and rough with sincerity. "I'm not the woman I used to be."

If he hadn't closed his fingers about her wrist, April would have kept walking. He held her still as he flicked a quick inspection up and down the street. The breeze moving the leaves of nearby trees sounded like rain. The silver trail of the moon painted their faces.

She resisted him and his fingers tightened.

"Really?" He wasn't smiling now. He tried to catch her eyes. "How are you different?"

She kept her face averted as much as possible. "I've learned to laugh at myself a little, Gaines. That's all I meant."

"Interesting."

"You should try it sometime. You'd feel better."

"That's what you're doing right now, I gather? Laughing?"

Turning, she shut him out with her back. He wanted to open her up. He wanted to look inside her and see things that she couldn't even admit to herself could still be there.

"Where's the smile, April?" His taunt came softly from over her shoulder as he took her by the arms and moved closer. His breath caressed the side of her neck. "Where's the laughter, my springtime girl?"

She wanted to say something outrageous and cruel, but he wrapped his arms about her waist and fit himself to her hips. He blew her hair from over her ear and nuzzled his nose against its shell. She wondered if he was remembering how he'd done this many times before: *Do you, Gaines Carroll Southerland, take April Anne Humphries to be your wedded wife, to love her . . .*

She couldn't bear being so close. She began disengaging herself and his arm circled her neck, tipping her head back, trapping her. When she wriggled he caught her lobe in his teeth, branded her with the sweet lover's hurt. She slumped against him, moaning. She wanted to, didn't she—to take the chance, to pretend he wasn't lying, to make do and go with it? But she couldn't, and her misery sent her hurtling back to the bloody ruins of their marriage, something that was at least familiar and therefore tolerable.

She jerked away from him with a twist of despair. "Why did you leave me at Daddy's that Christmas?" she said, and buried her face in her hands. "I waited for hours. You never came. You never called."

Stunned, Gaines walked several paces away. He wiped a hand over his face. "I wanted to call," he said inadequately. "I tried to, but . . ."

"I called all the hospitals." She'd always known he'd been with a woman that night.

He said nothing.

"I called the police," she went on distraughtly. "When I called them the second time they talked to me like I was a crazy thing from an asylum."

Robert Humphries had walked her up the stairs and

put her into her own bed that night. He'd said that Gaines loved her, that something had happened that would all work out. But it had happened time and time again. She'd done well to divorce Gaines when she did, she thought.

Slumping down upon the stone wall skirting the sidewalk, she hugged her waist as if in terrible pain. Before she could compose herself, Gaines's arms came around her from behind. He dragged her roughly down with him, and she lashed against him, a whirring steel rapier, flashing, striking.

His hand clapped down hard over her mouth. With sheer brute force he shoved her hard against the wall. Her spine slammed against stone, and she cried out in muffled fury against his hand. He was suffocating her!

"Someone's coming," he whispered harshly against the swirl of hair over her ear. "Be quiet."

Still struggling, not against his imprisonment now but in a frenzy to breathe, April kicked at him. Gaines pullled his body over hers and covered her the way one covers another from the force of a holocaust.

"Lie still," he demanded. "Don't make a sound, and I'll move my hand."

Frantic, she nodded. He slowly took his hand away and she drew in a rasping breath of air.

"Okay?" he asked without a sound, and pressed his fingers against her lips.

Again she nodded, eyes stinging and wild with panic. He eased his weight a bit but remained draped over her, drawing his gun. April heard the harsh click of boots upon the street. They grew louder and louder, until the voices were no longer murmuring but clearly distinguishable. How had Gaines known? She'd heard nothing!

". . . my one regret," a man was saying. "But looks

aren't everything. People make too much fuss about a pretty face, don't you think?''

The second voice laughed. ''You worry too much.''

''Did I say I was worrying? I'm not worrying.''

In less than a minute the footsteps had rounded the last building and were drawing near where they lay huddled together. April shuddered. If they were caught now, she would be carried off to interrogation for violating curfew. And Gaines? He could be tortured before they shot him.

''It's not Sari I want,'' the first man was saying. ''She's all right, but the younger sister, Zeena, that is another story. You should see Zeena. Eyes like black coals. And legs like—''

''You dream, my friend.'' The companion laughed. ''But dream on.''

''You'll see.''

''You think so?''

''I'm a patient fellow. I'll have Zeena. Maybe I'll have both, eh?''

A hush. A scrape of boots. The clink of metal against metal. Then in a softer and graver mood: ''Things will be different now.''

''Yes.''

A hesitant sigh. ''With Nahrhim dead, everything will change.''

April's heart gave such a violent wrench at the news that her horror passed from her body into Gaines's. Her eyes raked over his face in the darkness as if pleading for him to do something, anything.

The enemy boots stepped in their direction, paused, then walked, unchallenged, to the stone wall. Settling himself in a comfortable slump, one man lit a cigarette and took a deep breath. There was the harsh scrape of a rifle being laid upon stone. The pungency of smoke drifted into the night air like slow, uncurling fingers of mist.

"Will we prosper now, do you think?" the voice asked.

The companion shifted noisily. "Don't let anyone hear you ask that. Of course we will prosper. Ali Jassim already talks of factories and building the army."

"Talk is easy."

"Everything begins with talk. I do not like the way *you* talk, my friend."

"What?" A scornful snort. "Will you turn me in? Have me executed too?"

April's fingers closed into the hard flesh of Gaines's sides.

Wincing from her unconscious cruelty, Gaines touched his nose to hers until his breath became her breath; his lips were almost touching her lips. With the force of his strength, he willed her to control herself. *Pull inside yourself,* he seemed to say. *Do not exist. Trust me.*

How bizarre this was, April thought—she and Gaines hiding on the ground, the enemy only inches away. Like standing on the embassy portico and watching al-Qunay's fall to Jassim. And now, as then, she didn't know what to do. But Gaines did. He knew how to weave through darkened streets and get trucks in strange countries. She was put in the position of having to trust him when she'd spent the last three years of her life picking out the stitches of her trust. Yet she wanted to trust. She needed to. She just didn't know if she remembered how.

"I am your friend," the second masculine voice said as the man finally slid off the wall and ground his smoke into the street. "But do not talk like a traitor. You know what happens to traitors."

"I have seen the list of traitors. A long list."

"We must go. The commandant will have all our heads if we do not find the woman."

"The trail's growing too cold. They had the man and let him get away. It's their fault, not ours."

"Now's our chance to make good. We find them, we will get a commendation."

Footsteps, receding.

". . . many yet to be purged . . ."

". . . better . . . for the future of our children. . . ."

Silence had fallen over the street like a blanket before Gaines moved. When he lifted his head to peer over the wall to make sure they were safe, April melted beneath him.

"It's all right," he whispered as tears slid silently down her cheeks. "Shh, it's all right."

"He's dead." She wept without sound and turned her face into his sleeve. "President Nahrhim is dead."

Gaines's nerves quivered in reaction. Orban's president had to have been killed in the last two hours. When he met with Marek earlier in the afternoon and arranged for him to take April from the embassy, there had been talk of an escape plan. Obviously it had failed, and either Marek had been seen leaving the embassy or something had tipped off Jassim to look for him. Which meant that now his own presence in the country was known. Marek was a top agent all the way, but even the best men couldn't fight injections. And other things.

He took April into the hollow curve of his body and drew her up until she could sit. He was not unaware of what the last minutes had cost her.

He stroked her hair, her back. "They can't hurt Nahrhim now, sweetheart. Save your tears for the living. Shh."

She continued to clutch him for a moment. Then, as if

it were improper now the danger was over, she drew away. "What will happen now?"

"I don't know."

"If Jassim dares to kill the president, he'll kill anyone. No one will be safe." She peered up at him. "They're looking for me. You heard what he said. Why would he be looking for me?"

"Who would report you missing?"

Her head dropped down. "Bashir. This Marek locked him up, and Bashir thought I was in trouble. I should go back. If I went back and no one saw me, everything would be all right."

A wave of fear curled through Gaines at her innocence. Didn't she know that Jassim's purge could include her if his new government didn't get the American recognition he wanted? By now the president had probably called a crisis team into the Oval Office. This execution would ripple across the world. Wesley was probably having a nervous breakdown at this very moment: countless telephone calls, worried faces staring at other worried faces.

He resisted the impulse to take her back into his arms. "I don't think that's such a good idea."

Suddenly she was rigid. "Bruce!" she exclaimed, alarm large in her eyes. "Bruce will get caught in the middle of this thing. If Jassim has gone this far and Bruce tries to take a television camera . . . It won't matter why he's doing it!"

That particular horror had already occurred to Gaines. "First things first," he said. "When you're safe, I'll take care of Bruce."

"How?"

He avoided answering. "I'll . . . get word to him through Marek, or something. Don't worry about that. I'll handle it."

But it was beginning to dawn on April that Gaines had

understood the Arabic the men had been speaking. He was more deeply involved in this country than she had thought at first. What kind of business did he have going?

"Let's get out of here," she said, and began drawing around herself the old and more familiar cloak of distance. It didn't fit well and she was uncomfortable with it, but it was all she had.

In the hour that it took to work their way out of the city April learned a lot about herself. Working within the embassy walls, which even in their destruction exuded wealth and luxury, it was easy to forget the extreme poverty of the country.

The camp where they went was centered around the ruins of a bomb-sheared farmhouse. Those who had tents slept in them. Those who did not were rolled up on pallets or stretched out on newspapers. Lean-tos huddled against each other as if they hoped for strength in numbers.

"Were these people for Nahrhim or against him?"

Gaines removed the clip of his gun, checked it. "A lot of them probably don't even know. The young men are probably for Nahrhim because their blood is hot and idealistic. The old men and women have seen too many revolutions come and go. They only want peace."

"You aren't planning to use that thing, are you?"

He slammed the clip home with the heel of his hand. "You don't make plans when you deal with strangers."

April kept close to Gaines as they neared the camp. Not everyone slept; some were mute shadows that appeared, then just as quickly melted into other shadows. Gaines reconnoitered for several moments.

"Wait here," he said, and took her by the shoulders. "I'll get the truck and come back for you."

Thoughts of being separated from him terrified her. She lunged after him, crushed the front of his shirt in both hands. "No!"

"It's just a few yards, April."

"Please. Don't leave me out here." More softly: "Please."

His hands came up under her chin and he lifted her face so she could not avoid his searching query. April wasn't sure what he saw. Her nervousness increased and he touched her cheek, lightly, like one of the moths fluttering around a distant light.

"Come on, little coward," he said, and pressed her into the curve of his arm.

They picked their way among the rocks and trees to the camp. When a shadow separated from a tree, materialized into arms and legs and flashed a light over them, April gasped. Gaines's hand tightened firmly about hers.

"Easy." Then he cautiously called out, "Abu Wazhir?"

The young man stepped nearer and lowered the light. He was an unsmiling but handsome young man with long dark hair and a history of mistrust about his mouth. Faded jeans and scuffed boots were all he wore. In the loop of his arm draped the predictable rifle.

"You come for the truck?" he asked.

"Yes."

Again, the Arabic!

"You bring the money?"

"Yes."

Abu Wazhir studied the tall American. He was tough, he thought swiftly. He knew the kind. A man like him wouldn't take much foolishness before he acted. It was in the eyes. They didn't threaten; they just were.

He swept his rifle barrel in a broad arc. "This way."

As they followed him, April tugged on Gaines's arm. "How do you come to know this man?"

Gaines avoided looking at her. "He's a friend of Marek's."

April thoughtfully digested his reply. This Marek was an enigma. Were he and Gaines partners in business?

"It doesn't seem quite right," she said presently when she looked at the truck. "These people probably need this. Why should we take it?"

"They'd rather have the money. The truck is probably stolen anyway, and they'll steal it again. Double the profit."

She smiled, then frowned. "I still don't like it."

A motion of Gaines's hand hushed her as Abu Wazhir swept the golden beam of his light toward the camp. From the orchard more young men ambled nearer to observe the transaction. They measured Gaines with undisguised suspicion but nodded to Abu Wazhir. They would conjecture, April guessed, that she was a spoiled American tourist caught in a bad situation who wanted only to buy her way out.

"You have to stay here," Gaines said from the corner of his mouth. "They'll never bargain with a woman."

Leaving her, he moved toward Abu with a graceful caution.

April stood hugging herself as Gaines bargained. She couldn't hear what they said. The youths made their circle tighter and tighter about Gaines. After several minutes of passionate discussion with much hand waving and noisy disapproval, they all, to a man, glanced over their shoulders at her. April felt a cold circle of apprehension in her stomach. What were they saying?

After more talking, Abu held out his hands. The matter seemed settled. He walked behind the partial wall of a house and reappeared in less than two minutes with a small white bundle, which he placed in Gaines's hand. After counting out a good many bills, Gaines waited until the young man counted them again.

Abu nodded. Gaines wasted no time in hurrying April to the truck and hauling her up into it. He slipped into his own seat and tossed the bundle into her lap. He fit the key into the ignition without looking at her.

"What happened?" she asked.

"Later," he said, and the truck started with a deep-throated roar. The vehicle jerked, and he wheeled it around hard. Tires dug in, and the steering wheel whirled free. The truck spurted down the road in a choking cloud of gray dust, a high-pitched whine and an eager grinding of gears.

April worked at the knot of the cloth as they bounced along the rutted dirt road toward the highway that would carry them to the border. With the wind whipping at her hair and the night rushing past on black wings, she peered down at hard bread and goat cheese.

"I'm surprised he sold it to you," she said gravely, breaking off a piece of bread and passing it to Gaines. She bit off a chunk herself and solemnly chewed it.

Gaines stopped the truck at the crossroads of the dirt road and the highway. The headlights caught the shifting walls of dust and glanced off the ragged slab of trees. He gave the map a final consultation and looked up.

"He didn't want to."

"The monster," she joked, and took another bite.

He looked at her for a moment, then laughed. "They were pro-Nahrhim. They're gathering munitions to fight Jassim. When they learned that I was taking a woman out of al-Qunay, they wanted to go back on their bargain."

"Obviously you convinced them otherwise."

He grinned. "I told them you were the French

mistress of one of Nahrhim's highest officials and was pregnant and sick and that I was taking you home to Paris."

"*What?*"

"They were happy to take my money and get rid of you. They sent their wishes for a safe trip."

April's mouthful of food refused to go down. She swung at Gaines's shoulder, then clapped her hand over her mouth. Suddenly it was all ridiculous and hysterically dangerous and she succumbed to a fit of nervous giggles. Between her nerves and her attempts to swallow she ended up choking herself. After some moments she recovered and, with a few more wheezing coughs, blotted her eyes on the sleeve of her tunic.

"That was terrible, Gaines," she groaned. "Wicked and scoundrelly."

"The best-laid plans." He grew silent for a moment, then poignantly said, "Do you remember that time we drove up to Canada in the dead of winter?"

She remembered only too well. In the freezing cold they had decided they'd trek up to Canada and spend the whole weekend making love at a ski lodge—all the bright holiday clothes and the roaring fires, the laughter and good food: romance in the flesh. Even before they took a room, they'd been unable to go another minute without making love in the car. It had been a battle to get the clothes unbuttoned and out of the way. To their surprise, passion dropped several degrees in the cold. They battled to get the clothes buttoned back up again. Once they took a room, a storm knocked out the power and the guests were asked to make other accommodations. They had packed up their romantic dreams and returned home to nurse the sniffles for three days.

"We did some really crazy things, didn't we?" April said, her eyes soft and glistening with memories.

Gaines gave his head a shake, and April ceased

thinking about Canada and considered how her life would be after the interlude with Gaines was over. The future was suddenly swept clear of hope, like a house with no people.

He sensed her withdrawal. He looked out at the waiting road, then at her. He slipped the gear shift into neutral, staring at it. "It wasn't all bad, was it?"

She was lost, the ghost of some other person. "Oh, Gaines."

They looked up, away.

The nocturnal space—far beyond them in the darkness, behind them in the milky white stars, between them in the seat—was suddenly a gaping chasm. Grand Canyon. Time. Words. Breaths. Heartbeats.

They looked again at the space between them.

With an effort almost as superhuman as the one it would take to bridge the Grand Canyon, they leaned slowly toward each other. The distance was gone, and, at this one moment in their lives, so was the pain they had dealt each other.

"Oh, April," he breathed, touching her face, her throat, drinking in the sight of her. "Sometimes nothing seems to make any sense."

"I know . . ."

Lips parting in wonder, they fastened to each other in slow motion. A dread welled up in Gaines as he moved his mouth upon hers, a terrible fear for when the moment would end. April's fingers trailed about his neck— butterfly caresses, hesitating as she whimpered. With a groan from some tortured place inside her, she tensed with energy. She threaded her fingers painfully through his hair and pulled his face savagely to hers.

"It could be like it used to," he whispered, and quickly shifted his weight, one hand closing desperately about her shoulder, the other spanning her back, pulling her hips toward him until she conformed to his body.

Her lap was full of food. It spilled. She never knew. She buried her fingers into his shoulders, his back.

"I'm scared of what used to be." Gasping, she pushed away, filled both hands with his beard and cupped his face to gaze up at him helplessly. "I've changed. We've changed."

"Some things don't change," he said, tasting her again with short, hungry sips. "This hasn't changed."

He slipped his hand beneath her tunic and closed it about her breast. Her flesh was warm and sweet to him. He felt her breath quicken against his mouth as she yielded, slipping her own hand between his thighs and gripping hard. With a flexing move, he trapped her there.

"If we weren't here," he whispered thickly against her ear, "would you?"

She had been wondering the same thing. She buried her face in his neck, reached about his back, straining closer. "Don't ask me that."

One kiss melted into another and another. "I'm asking."

"I don't know."

Gaines felt her opening to him. She was allowing him to venture into her deepest self, letting him touch the yearning core of her. She arched upward and he ground his physical ache against her and tried to ignore the urgency that warned him it was dangerous to stay parked there so long.

But the seconds spun by, and with a willpower he didn't think he possessed, he released her. He pulled away and caught his breath, his mouth pressed to his fist.

April couldn't speak; she could only smile and give her head a little shake. It seemed strangely unreal that she and Gaines could have this deep bond between them and could cheat each other the way they did.

Gaines bent over and kissed her mouth one final time

before he steadied himself and pulled onto the twisting ribbon of highway. April leaned back in her seat and closed her eyes. After the divorce she'd tried so hard to find someone. She had let men kiss her, hold her, and it had been just that—letting them, not sharing with them. They had thought only of their good fortune in holding a pretty woman, and she had felt nothing. No man looked desirable to her. No man aroused her. She had begun to wonder if she would feel anything ever again, and all Gaines had to do was kiss her. It was there again, that empathy, that bone-deep intuition, that burning eagerness to give and share everything and to be terribly, terribly greedy.

Gaines opened his arm and motioned to her. "Put your head in my lap. You're worn out."

The awkward space between the seats gaped again. She smiled. "This vehicle wasn't made for cuddling, Gaines."

His eyes crinkled as they had when she first knew him. "You look like a woman capable of great ingenuity."

It was good to laugh with him again. Gaines drew her into the circle of his arm. And, choosing to ignore another voice that was whispering in her ear—a warning —April pressed her cheek against his chest and let out her breath with a long, satisfied sigh.

The night blurred past them. They didn't speak but were content to experience the strange closeness that neither had expected: the fact of being. Or perhaps they feared a word might break the spell, take it all away.

April's eyes slowly closed. Innocently, as slumber crept upon her, she became pliant and slipped lower into his lap.

Gaines moved his arm upon her side as she snuggled deeply into the bend of his groin. How often did a man get a second chance? he thought. How often did a man get any chance at all? Tonight, when he'd smiled, he thought it was the first time since he'd lost her. He wanted it again; he wanted her again. Once they got out of Orban he was going to tell her the truth, that all of him—his duty, his so-called service to mankind, his grand imaginings about the good he was doing—were nothing without her.

Chapter 5

THE TRUCK COUGHED TWICE, THEN STOPPED. ROUSING, opening her eyes, April brushed her hair back from her face and pushed up to sit.

"Where are we?" she asked, and realized with a twinge of embarrassment that she had slept the entire trip nestled in Gaines's lap. She moved away with slightly more energy than was necessary and slid a brief covert glance at Gaines's profile.

The stars had disappeared. The sky was a thick, melting blackness that was slowly being seduced by the dawn. Beyond them the road unfurled along the edge of the plateau. In beautiful contrast to the high country, the valley fell off the edge and traced a narrow, piney trail for miles along the river.

He said, "We're nearly to the border."

"What happened?"

Gaines flicked a dry grimace her way and reached

again for the key. The engine turned several times, grudgingly, then refused to do anything. Whatever magic spell had made it come this far had obviously lost its charm.

"Damn it," he said fervently, and climbed out of the truck.

He stood for a moment in the open wedge of space beside the door, one booted leg on the ground, the other still in the truck, and privately cursed the genius of Henry Ford.

She stifled a yawn. "What do you think?"

"I think," he said as he walked around to the hood, lifted it and peered inside, "that it has won."

April spent the next minutes looking at Gaines looking at the engine. She felt typically female: helpless in the face of a traitorous machine. By the look of Gaines's scowl, women weren't the only ones subject to this malady.

She crawled out of the truck and bunched herself in a small huddle against Gaines's side, peering over the fender. He checked the distributor, the coil, the battery connections. With maddening absorption, he studied each mechanical part as if it were a riddle that lacked only sound male logic to figure it out.

"It's broken," she said unhelpfully, and shivered from the early morning wind.

Gaines made an incoherent sound. He investigated the spark plugs and their wires without acknowledging her. Then he checked the points.

"Do you know what's wrong?" she asked.

"Mmmmm."

"Perhaps we should walk the rest of the way."

Without lifting his head, he made a preoccupied reply of, "If I could juusst . . ."

Some things never changed. April glanced about herself and doubted they were twenty miles from al-

Qunay. She walked around restlessly, stared a few minutes at Gaines's backside as his head disappeared into the internals of the truck, then moved up beside him again.

"You don't know what's wrong with it, do you?" she said as Gaines replaced the distributor cap, clipped it into place and turned his head until his nose almost collided with hers.

A streak of grease decorated his cheek, and his right hand was black. He bent over her like a bear. "Is it running?"

She flinched. "No."

"Do you think I enjoy standing on my head inside this piece of junk?"

An old familiar laughter bubbled deep inside her. Gravely, she said: "I don't know, Gaines. Do you?"

Somewhat more gruffly, he said, "Don't you think I'd fix it if I knew how?"

"I suppose."

"Then by the process of elimination, anyone with an iota of common sense could surmise that I don't know what's wrong with it. Right?"

She shrugged with pretended negligence, seized with a sudden irresistible urge to kiss him all over his face. Unplanned, she giggled. She promptly sobered. "Do you know what I think, Gaines?"

He grinned, much more interested in how much of his wife still remained in her than he was in a vehicle that wouldn't run. He lifted a greasy hand to her face and made a claw of it.

Yelping, she dodged. "Don't you dare."

"I would dare a lot," he said huskily, "when you look at me like that."

With a quick motion, he caught her head in the crook of his arm. He locked her face beneath his with the back of his fist brought around beneath her chin.

"Gaines!" she shrieked. "Please."

It wasn't difficult to maneuver her against the fender of the truck with a thrust of his weight. Gaines bent over her until he was molded to her all the way down.

"Please, what?" He pressed deeply into her bones.

Slipping back into the easy give-and-take they'd once shared was much more alarming to April than being stranded in the hill country. She didn't need anyone to warn her that she wasn't ready to cope with this. She ended the banter by pushing a lock of hair back from his forehead and softly asking, "Are you trying to tell me that we have to walk back to al-Qunay?"

Gaines could feel her resisting, pulling away from him, keeping her breasts from pressing to his chest. "If Bruce weren't back there," he said honestly, "I wouldn't even consider taking you back. But it seems the only logical thing to do."

"You're really worried about him."

"With President Nahrhim dead, yes. Very much."

If Gaines took her to Tel Aviv and put her on a plane, she knew he would turn right around and return to al-Qunay. "Well, tell me what you want."

Releasing her, Gaines fished his handkerchief from his hip pocket and proceeded to clean the grease off his hand. "I want to keep you alive and get you home," he said without looking at her. "Whatever that takes. What do you want?"

Without hesitating, she said, "I want to go back with you."

Gaines gathered up their few provisions and her bag from the truck. He fit her bag on her shoulder and stood for a moment, his hand still resting on her arm. April couldn't have been more conscious of the weight of his hand. It was burning into her, making her remember all kinds of dangerously sweet things. She shivered and looked at her toes.

"You want my shirt?" He bent his head so that he could get a better look at her face.

She shook her head. "I'm all right." Then quickly, tilting her chin at an angle that told him she was deadly serious, she said: "You're in trouble, aren't you?"

Sighing, Gaines dropped his hand. He slipped his gun beneath his belt. He had planned to tell her everything, but if they had to return to al-Qunay he couldn't place that burden upon her.

"You were right before," he said, and looked over her head at the awakening sky. "I am involved in some dealings in Orban. They force me to go back. If not now, then later."

That didn't surprise her. And she dreaded, deep in the pit of her stomach, what his answer to her next question would be. "Were you wrong, Gaines? Have you done something bad?"

For a moment he stood with his eyes closed. Then, shaking his head, he laid their small bundle of stores on the fender. He closed his hands about her face and plunged deeply into her thoughts, trying to implant the seriousness of his convictions by the sheer strength of his will.

"There've been times I've been less than honest with you, April. I'll admit that. To protect you from myself more than anything else. But I swear to you, upon everything that I know to be honest and good, I was not wrong in what I did. I haven't cheated anyone or done anyone any hurt. Anything I have ever done, I did because I thought it was the right thing to do."

Not caring whether it was a mistake or not, April slipped her arms about his waist. She leaned against his chest. A button scored her cheek. "Gaines?" she said softly.

"Yes."

"Would you tell me something if I ask you?"

He took a quick breath. "If I can."

"Do you need me? I don't mean, do you love me? I mean, do you *need* me?"

Gaines remembered the nights he'd loved her, the long minutes of lying beside her after she'd gone to sleep, the vast satisfaction of recognizing his own human isolation even though she was not conscious: man complemented. And now he was only half a man.

He kissed her temple and realized his intolerable loneliness. "April, I don't think you can ever know how much I need you."

She began, quite suddenly, to cry. Gaines didn't trust his voice enough to speak. He simply held her in his arms and rocked her back and forth as if she were a child. Presently she pulled away and wiped her eyes with her fingers.

"I'm very tired."

He knew she was. "We can't rest yet, sweetheart."

"Just for a few minutes," she pleaded. "Let's just sit in the truck and rest for a little while."

It had been nearly forty-eight hours since Gaines had slept. But this place was too exposed. He didn't dare let her rest here.

"Come on. Give me your hand. The river is down there below us, at the foot of the hills. Help me carry our things."

Feeling the backlash of the night, they gathered their meager supplies and began the long, difficult descent to the valley floor. For the most part they walked in silence; the undergrowth grew more dense the nearer they came to the river.

The river that formed the boundary of Orban was fed by the mountains to the north. At this point it was hardly more than a stream six feet wide and waist-deep, clear, cold, clean in the sun. On the southern side stretched a sandy beach—a good quarter mile long, sunny and warm. On the opposite side bushes clawed their way up the rocky face until there was no foothold left.

It was a wild and primitive place, unspoiled by humans, a solitude that smelled of wet ferns and moss. Only the birds invaded its lost space, gulls that wheeled and dipped and ignored them to go about their fishing. And kites screaming before they flew in a wide, confident curve over the trees and disappeared.

April and Gaines dropped their supplies and walked toward the water. They drank out of their hands. Then, in the healing warmth that streamed off the wooded hills and down into the quiet, lost universe, they lay down beside the river. Lulled by the water's lonely murmur, they smiled and curled their fingers with the other's and slept.

When April awoke she did so slowly. At first a part of her didn't want to remember what had happened. It wasn't until she felt Gaines's hand resting innocently upon her that it all came spinning back.

Don't panic, she told herself, and moved her head a few inches until she could see him. He lay on his stomach, one knee drawn up against her thigh, his arm across her waist. It could have been three days instead of three years since she'd had the opportunity to see him like this, without that hard toughness, the varied masks that isolated him.

She stole quick glances at him. It was one thing to watch a man sleeping when you were married to him, or even living with him; quite another when you were divorced—the privacy that had been bought at such a cost.

Yet his face drew her: his expressive brows, the lines beside his eyes, which were etching deeper and would, with the years, give him a weathered look. She smiled at the irregularity of his nose. His mustache partially disguised the sensitivity of his mouth. His mouth never betrayed his emotions the way her own did, except in those very last seconds before he kissed her. Then it would hesitate as his eyes found hers, and it would open in that small, yearning way for hers.

It was torture to remember such things!

She looked away. The sun was high and glinting off the river, nearly to its zenith. She thought of waking Gaines, but he shifted in his sleep. He murmured something and frowned, as if he were dreaming.

Gently slipping from beneath his arm, she stood and popped the kinks from her back, then picked up her bag. She followed the steady path of the river downstream.

Her clothes were nearly ruined. Selecting a part of the river that looked the shallowest, she peeled off her tunic and stepped out of her slacks. As she lowered herself into its coldness, her teeth chattered. She scrubbed herself and her clothes and presently spread both on the sand to dry.

Lying in the sun, she let her eyes close and reveled in the rare luxury of nudity in the out-of-doors. She treasured the warmth as it seeped into her skin.

"Why didn't you wait for me?" he said.

She jerked up her head. Gaines stood at her feet, boots firmly rooted in the sand, his eyes unreadable but moving over her. His shirt was unbuttoned, and he placed a hand to the sprinkling of hair on his chest as if seeing her naked stirred an old wound to life.

"You were sleeping so soundly," she replied with a queer sense of unreality. She hadn't meant to be caught like this. She foolishly tried to feign sophistication and ignore her exposure to him. "It would have been gentlemanly for you to have made some noise before you walked up," she said overcasually.

Smiling, he dropped to the sand beside her knees.

"Gentlemanly, perhaps, but not in character. Are you hungry?"

"Starving."

"So am I."

Several seconds passed, and April had a fear that Gaines would touch her. Yet he didn't. He only looked at her with a passivity that oddly began to irritate her. Finally she drew her forearm over her eyes as if that would somehow, ostrichlike, hide her.

"You're making me uncomfortable, looking at me like that," she said.

"And you're frustrating me, lying there like that."

She sat up, hugged herself. "Then I'll go put—"

"No, don't—"

It was ridiculous to think that either one of them could keep it up. It occurred to April that they were back to the point of reckoning when he'd straddled her on that silly bed. She turned her head so he couldn't see her face.

"Look at me, April," he said quietly.

"I don't want to."

"Why?"

Because of the complexity of her feelings, the terrible, retroactive desire of them!

"Why do you think?" she said distraughtly. "You're sitting there looking at me like this and remembering when we were married and wondering if I'll do it."

Even from where she sat she felt him stiffen. "Do 'it'?" he said tightly. "What is this 'it' business?"

April's eyes collided with his. Perhaps that was what they needed to settle things between them. Perhaps they needed the clarity of argument. She realized suddenly that she really did want to punish him—for almost everything.

"Oh, for crying out loud, Gaines," she cried. "You know what I mean."

"Make love?" He wasn't looking at her body now but deeply down into her eyes. "Is that what you meant?"

She hugged her knees tighter. "Have sex is what I meant. There is a difference."

Though her cheek was pressed against her knee, she sensed the hurt go through him. A tiny flush darkened his neck, and muscles contracted all through his body. She could have bitten her tongue; she hadn't meant to say it like that.

She reached up, as if to stop him from moving away. "Gaines . . ."

He came to his feet, stared out at the stretch of the sand beside the river, the remote cliffs.

"I'm sorry." Her apology unleashed a torrent of truth from inside her. She shook her head. "It's hard for me to talk anymore. I can't . . . Sometimes I can't feel anything but a terrible, terrible anger. It eats at me." More softly: "It . . . hurts so bad."

Gaines's back continued to separate them. As if he were giving her the opportunity to say something without being stared at—

She began hesitantly. "It's been very hard for me, Gaines, learning to live without you. There've been times when I've gone into a restaurant or even walked on the street, and I've looked at the faces of people and wished that someone, somewhere could walk up to me and say that they understood. Without my having to explain. It's so impossible to explain. There aren't any words to . . . I don't know."

"You look for a friend."

Her shrug went unseen by him. "I always thought I was stronger than that. More self-sufficient."

"That's the reason marriage should be forever."

"Why?"

"Then there's someone who's lived through it with you, whatever it is, and you don't have to explain the unexplainable to them. They were there."

"I want that. I always wanted it."

"So did I."

"I thought we could have that."

"We could."

"You cheated me, Gaines."

"I didn't get the divorce."

"You were the one who made it necessary!"

April saw him accept her contempt. He fit his hands into his back pockets and stood with his legs astride. "You're right," he said. "And even my guilt is unexplainable."

His acceptance of responsibility devastated her. He had stolen her revenge, and she felt anew the reasons why she'd fallen in love with him the first time.

She stared, unseeing, at the sand. "All the guilt wasn't on your side."

He walked around a bit, scuffing at the sand. He coughed gently and said, "When you think of 'making love' and 'having love,' what do you see?"

"I don't know."

"You have a concept, surely."

"It's very intangible." She toyed with a toenail. "Anyway, you'd find it pretty childish."

"Out of the mouth of babes. Try me."

He turned around and stood directly over her head. For an instant April thought he would touch her hair, but he dropped to his knees in the sand, reached a hand outward, stopped with it poised in midair, then dropped it to his knee. The flesh across his cheekbones was tight and pained.

"Please."

Her voice twisted now and grew almost inaudible in

her attempt to explain. "It's kind of a nonphysical release, I think—a point when one mind can touch another mind and it's good and nothing can ever, ever be that good and you both know. And if you can have that and make love too, it's . . . I don't know, both of them together . . . it's perfect."

She turned away, hiding behind a profile. She let her eyes close and wondered if she could feel the thing inside her that was reaching out to him, begging to be understood.

Presently, Gaines came to his feet. He took a step away. Without looking, April knew he was studying her.

"I wish you loved me that way," he said.

He walked downstream and began taking off his clothes. April had the sensation, as he walked away, that they had come incredibly close to experiencing that nonsexual release just now. Once, a long time ago when it was new, they'd almost had it. But they had been so young then.

So why go back and look at it all again? To rake over all that pain in search of something there wasn't any guarantee of? Something that might not even exist anymore? Oh, hell, what did he care?

But he did care; that was the trouble. And she tried not to watch him as he bathed. But she did; and he, of course, knew it. He knew he was beautiful and that she had not ceased to be attracted to that beauty just because they had lost touch with each other's minds.

He stood for a moment in his dark briefs, his hand shading his eyes against the diamond glint of the sun, watching the birds shrieking in the distance. There was something to be said for Edgar Rice Burroughs and his Tarzan-man in the wildness of nature, she thought.

She moved in the sand, aware of her own primal urges awakening. Just watching him made her ache—the classic unclothed male. But not just any male: Gaines, sleek, lean-hipped, long-muscled. It was his legs that were long; they gave him much of his height, and now they were carrying him gracefully into the shallows.

Oh, God! She flipped on her back and let the sun burn her eyes. She'd weaned herself from this part of Gaines once. She was a fool to put herself in the position of having to do it the second time.

He was waist-deep in the river now, washing his hair. He bent to dip his face in the water, and he straightened quickly to spit over his shoulder.

She stood up. He didn't turn. He hadn't looked at her once, yet she guessed that he knew she was walking toward him. He was standing very still. Yes, he knew, though he couldn't hear her approach over the sound of moving water and fierce birds. His head was bent, water dripping from his hair.

She walked up behind him and stood, letting the water swirl about her waist.

"Did you like it?" he said.

"What?"

"Watching me."

"Did you mind?"

"I wasn't being caddish before."

April pressed herself to his back, to the back that she had loved more than anything in the world. Her nipples were cold and hard, and she knew he felt their invitation. She wrapped her arms about his waist and strained to press herself to the back of his hips.

"I want to say that I love you because . . ." She dropped her hand low to touch him. He wanted her. He wanted her to touch him.

"Because why?" he prompted thickly, moving his hand to hers, holding it there, curved about him.

"Because I do."

Gaines turned in the circle of her arms. He bent his knees and came up into her as she stood there—hard, quick, deep. He clasped her tightly to his chest and she wrapped her legs about him. Her breasts flattened between them, and the water swirled around them as if they were an island.

"I wanted to kiss you for a very long time," he said hoarsely, and bent his head.

"Then do it," she said, and opened her mouth to accept his eager tongue.

He withdrew himself to carry her from the river. He lowered her gently to the sand where his clothes were scattered. April was shivering from nerves. Too many years; too many inhibitions grown around the scar tissue.

She thought it would be a quick and savage release. She lifted herself up to him, reaching for him. He pushed her hand away.

"I know exactly how," he murmured, and stretched out beside her and drew her into his arms. "You taught me good, April."

"Oh, Gaines," she whimpered, urgency in her voice, demands in every move. Couldn't he tell? Couldn't he sense? She grasped his shoulders fiercely, her eyes wide and pleading as they plunged into his.

"Please!"

But he ignored her pressing hands and quick motions. His mouth found her knees and her legs and her thighs and pungent warmth as if it were yesterday, and she was gasping because of her desire for it and her nails were digging into his shoulders as she grew daring and bold and made love to him as much as he did to her, turning, reversing, thrilling as he watched her mouth close upon him and the love glistening in his eyes until the last possible moment that only she knew about, and then she eased herself quickly down upon him so that there was nothing left but the deep-thrusting center of it and her holding him so that it could come crashing down upon them both and wash them, spent, into infinity.

"I wish we didn't have to leave here," she said much later when they had eaten and grown accustomed to the sight of each other's nakedness again.

Gaines sat cross-legged, his back bent broadly to the sun, nibbling a piece of cheese he didn't want and reading from her book of poems. She was braced on one arm and was drawing abstract pictures in the sand with a twig as he read.

> "Witness thou
> The dear companion of my lonely walk,
> My hope, my joy, my sister, and my friend,
> Or something dearer still, if reason knows
> A dearer thought, or in the heart of love
> There be a dearer name."

He lifted his head. The lights of her skin were warmly pink where the sun touched it, but the shadows of her breasts, her arms, were darker—coral, promising. Her detachment disturbed him, as if once her satisfaction had been reached it was total and permanent and now she no longer needed him.

Male egocentricity, he mocked himself; still clinging to the selfless sacrifice of the female when it came down to the conflict of "your way or mine." He felt fresh stirrings deep inside him and put his finger in the book and closed it.

She looked out at the hills. "It's going to be a long walk to al-Qunay."

He smiled. "I doubt we'll have to walk. Out of the hills, yes. But there'll be farmers on the plateau."

"You're a scrounger, Gaines Southerland." She came back to him, pleased him by lifting the backs of her fingers to his lips for a kiss. "I didn't know I'd once married a scrounger."

Gaines picked up her twig and scrawled her name in the sand: April. Then he drew a heart and wrote his own name below hers.

"You forgot the arrow," she said. "There're always arrows."

He drew a wobbly arrow projecting from both sides of the heart. Very casually he said, "Why do you call me a scrounger?"

"Why?" She threw him a glance. "You scrounge up Marek and a room. You scrounge up a truck. All in a strange country. Impressive talents, Gaines."

"If you'd known what you were getting," he asked, "would you have married me the first time?"

She was absorbed with the drawing again and made a series of smaller hearts all around it. "I don't think anything could have kept me from marrying you."

"Could it now?"

She didn't answer the question. Then: "Were there other women, Gaines? After we broke up, I mean." A flush spread over her throat and up to the crests of her cheeks. "I don't know why I'm embarrassed to ask that. We're divorced, for pity's sake."

Gaines didn't want to answer. There had been a few women afterward. Mistakes of bitterness. A male outcry.

"They were nothing."

"Tell me about them." She showed no signs of jealousy.

He felt mildly piqued. "What d'you want me to say? That they weren't as good as you? That I couldn't 'perform'?"

She flipped onto her stomach. "I went out with a few men. Nothing. I mean, there wasn't any . . . you know what I mean."

The gulls had grown friendly and were walking along the river, preening and looking for tiny tidbits of food.

April finally broke the silence. "A while ago you used the expression 'when I married you the first time.' "

"And?"

"The first time implies a second time."

Gaines lay the book open on the sand and stared at it a moment. "I was a little fragile when I said that. Would you give me an answer if I asked the question?"

A small smile curved up her mouth. She shook sand out of her drying hair and it silted over her hands. Sand clung to her buttocks and the backs of her legs, and she reached back to brush it off. She had no idea, he thought, of how it aroused him to see her touch herself so abstractedly.

"Would you treat me the second time like you did the first?" she said.

He'd known this question would inevitably find its way to the surface. "I never meant to hurt you then."

"Back at the room," she pressed on doggedly, "you told me there were things you wanted to say."

"There are."

"Are they connected to why you're here? In Orban?"

Gaines made a flourish on the border of hearts. His reply was not a lie, yet it was a lie. An evasion, of which she'd had too many.

"Everything about a man is connected. And connected to all of it is that I love you. That I've never stopped loving you."

April's face was a collage of disappointments, and Gaines knew a moment of anger when he saw it—as if she had had a mental list of suspicions and had checked them off, one by one, memorizing, entering in the computer, cross-referencing. And his love couldn't balance the equation.

With a violent movement of her arm she swept the hearts and arrows away and scrambled up, walking away with an ironic naked beauty.

The sting reached to the marrow of Gaine's bones. How little it took, he thought bitterly. Old ghosts. Unexorcised.

He came to his feet and went after her. He grabbed her arms, an equally sudden movement, and in its way just as violent.

"I'm sorry," he said, and caressed the places his fingers had bruised. "I didn't mean to do it like that."

The sun was dipping in the sky. It caught April's eyes as she turned, two shimmering seas in the reproach of her face.

"It's a battlefield again," she whispered.

"No. No force."

Her face was full of confusion. "Gaines, I don't know what to do anymore, what to believe."

He took the risk that he always took with her, for she was the only woman in existence who could hurt him. He drew her down to the sand until they were kneeling before each other. He ran his hand over her belly, felt its flesh quiver. He parted her legs, touched the silk.

"Don't judge me," he said, making himself totally vulnerable to her. "Want me. Just want me."

She whimpered when he sank his fingers into her and took her mouth at the same time. When he realized that she already did want him, that she'd been lying there desiring him even as she judged him, he knew a moment of self-hatred.

"I have never deserved you," he said against her mouth, for she was lifting herself up to his hand, moving against it with a slow, moaning rhythm.

He sought the place that would bring her release, and she took his thumb and placed it there. It was immediate —short, intense, gasping. Then again with her face buried in his neck.

"Shh," she said after a time as she pulled him down upon her. "I'm not judging you now."

Chapter 6

IT REALLY HADN'T SOLVED ALL THAT MUCH, APRIL thought, amazed, disappointed. She had lain in Gaines's arms and known that she loved him above all living things. There had been moments when she'd been certain that he returned that love. She had thought that at last he would take her into his heart fully and they would "have love"—no secrets, no private, isolated places.

Yet, here they were again, twenty-four hours later, looking down at the light-studded bowl of al-Qunay, and she was thinking that she must have been crazy to expect him to give that much.

In the beginning of their relationship Gaines had been the center of her life, the object of that deliriously new marriage experiment: Her Husband. She had given everything, content to revolve around him. Somehow, it hadn't worked. And now, after the disillusionment, the past had somehow flown over her head to dangle mysteriously in front of her as the future. Gaines was not the center of her existence anymore. He was, or could be, the Matching Half: Her Man. Equal billing? That was even worse. How much easier to sacrifice oneself to another person than divide equally.

Yet she was willing to do it. He, evidently, wanted only to be the center: a selfish ninety-ten split. They sat beside each other in another ancient truck that he had "borrowed" up in the hills. Neither spoke because neither understood exactly what was happening. It was as if, now that they had returned to civilization again, their love had been a trick of the mind, something very nice but that should be put in a proper perspective with reality.

"From here it looks so deceptively peaceful," she said because she wasn't brave enough to remain silent.

Gaines fit his hand to his mouth in the manner of a hawker. "Al-Qunay, folks, step right up. A modern city with modern pleasures. One day's journey from the Mediterranean. Never be lonely again. Buy a friend. Laugh with strangers."

Depression laced through his stark, overcontrolled irony. April measured his tension by his hands' opening and shutting upon the steering wheel.

"What next?" she said with studied detachment. "What will we do now?"

He'd done a great deal already, of course—leading her out of the hills, bargaining with peasants for food, getting the truck and hot-wiring it and driving them back to the city. She guessed what his answer would be.

His hands tightened about the steering wheel. "*We* won't do anything. *I've* got to go back down there."

"I want to go with you."

"Forget it."

"Now that we're here I wish you wouldn't go."

"Bruce will get himself killed if I don't."

"I care about Bruce."

"Then understand."

"I can't. You're not going just for Bruce."

"You're imagining trouble."

"I'm afraid. Please . . ."

"I have to!"

Round and round and round she goes, and where she stops . . . everybody knew but her.

It was a very hot night. Clouds had shut off the stars and were massing in gigantic banks in the west—heavy, full of humidity, choking off the slightest breeze. Gaines rubbed at the gray film of dirt on the windshield, then unconsciously wiped his fingers down the side of his khakis.

She waited for some gesture from him that he at least sympathized, but he remained immersed in his own thoughts. She slid a cautious look at him.

"When we were still married and you left me," she said evenly, "was it to see this man, Marek?"

He groped for the gun beneath the seat and became absorbed with making sure it was in good working order. She wanted to slam the thing to the floor, throw it out the window.

She caught his hands. "Gaines."

Gaines looked down at their clasped hands as if they amazed him. He still refused to face the issue, didn't he? It had felt like this when she'd suspected him of being with another woman, except that she knew now that wasn't true. What was it with him?

She tightened her hands about his with a harsh little shake. "Tell me."

He took a deep breath. "When things quiet down, I'll—"

"Not when things quiet down!"

His eyes were a blaze of anger. Then, instantly apologetic. He searched for nonexistent words and finally sighed, "I can't talk about it now."

April jerked around and shrank into the limits of her body. "None of it meant anything to you, did it?"

He tried to touch her face, but it was too late. She cruelly shrank from him and made herself even smaller.

"Don't do this, April."

"I was honest with you."

"And I was honest with you."

"You touched the magic places. You said the magic words, one of which was 'marriage.' Forever this time."

"And I meant forever."

"You said things would be different."

"They will."

"No they won't. You'll go on the same as before, and I'll get hurt and leave you again. And then I'll hate you and hate you and hate—"

Gaines's helplessness was galling to him. He slammed his foot on the accelerator and started the truck. He drove along the ridged edge of the bowl and parked in a large thicket of cypress trees that were pearled heavily with dew.

He killed the engine and closed his fingers painfully into her shoulder. "April, listen to me."

"Do you know what I regret the most, Gaines? We never had a routine, you know? None of those little unimportant daily rituals that keep people's lives from running around."

The truth in her words stung him. "We had enough. More than most."

She turned on him with the wifely bitterness of years. "Enough? Do you call living in constant worry enough? Have you ever once put yourself in my shoes? I love you, yet I can't live with you because of this great folding screen between us. I wanted to plant a tree, Gaines. A plain, ordinary little tree."

Gaines blinked as only a bewildered husband could blink. "What?"

April knew her display was based on selfishness, but she wanted it all. "I wanted to plant a tree in the backyard and put a notch on it every anniversary." She buried her face in her hands. "I imagined myself taking your hand and us walking out together to see how we'd grown. It would be tall, and by the time we were old it would be so big around . . . it . . ."

He pulled her to his chest in a rough despair. "Oh, April, this will be the last time I ever leave you. I swear it. I do want to marry you again. I want it more than I wanted it before."

His lips grazed her jaw as he crushed her in his arms. "Trust me," he whispered, "just this once more, and please, if you love me, just . . . don't . . . ask. I have to go now."

Before April could tell him anything, he reached between them and thrust the .45 into her hands, a violent intrusion of steel. He closed her fingers hard about it.

"I don't think you'll need this, but . . ."

Her eyes widened at the sight of the gun. She shoved it back at him. "I don't want it."

For that one instant Gaines was not her husband or her ex-husband, not even a man she knew. In that moment he gripped her with both his stranger's hands, and his lips curled back dangerously over his teeth. He was, she thought, capable of anything.

"Take it!" he ordered. "I'll be back as soon as I can. Don't move an inch from this truck."

His mouth came down hard upon hers and he released her abruptly. He was out in one discreet motion. She saw him for an instant before he disappeared into the shadows. He moved so swiftly and so soundlessly that she wasn't sure if she heard the grass or his swift, light tread.

Whispering his name like a lament, she leaned her head back upon the seat and closed her eyes. Oh, what a fool she was. She'd thought she was so very, very clever: rousing him as he slept, tempting him so shamelessly, annoying him, prancing, posing until he took her without preliminaries—quickly and with the relentless purpose she'd wanted. And then she had tormented him more.

"It was not enough," she had said.

"It has to be. I can't do it again."

"You must."

He had loved it. He had watched her touch her breasts and arouse him as he said he could not be aroused. He had said things to make her bold, embarrassing her, making her more and more bold until she lifted herself brazenly, offering herself with a look. He took her, with his mouth, his fingers. He took more than she wanted to give, and then he had moved deep inside her. And then again in the river when they bathed.

And now? What? She was a moth whose wings had been singed badly once and, knowing the danger, had flown headlong into the flame again. She was burned, and nothing was really changed. Gaines was very little less the mystery than he had always been, and she was a cinder jostling about on the ground, prey to the first fanciful breeze that took the notion. Kismet? No, insanity.

The noise that intruded upon her tortured musing was hardly a noise at all—a sensing, an intuition.

April opened her eyes and sat perfectly still, trying to hear it again. When she couldn't, she sat up, tilting her head and straining. Had she imagined it? Had something moved in the trees? Or was the hot wind ruffling the cypress branches?

She leaned her head out the window and let the breeze blow across her face. She tried to see, but the darkness was too thick, the curtain of trees impenetrable. A fox, probably, or one of those foraging, furry creatures of the night.

She lay back down in the seat and told herself to go to sleep; it was nothing. Then she popped up as if pricked with a needle. There was no mistaking it this time. Whatever it was, man or beast, it had come decidedly nearer.

Moistening her lips, clutching her bag and feeling vaguely grateful that there was a weapon in it even if she had no intentions of using it, April knew that it wasn't Gaines. He wouldn't come back without having done what he'd set out to do, and he certainly wouldn't let himself be heard doing it.

Slowly she opened the door of the truck. The hinges cried out, and she froze for a moment, half expecting a blinding flash of light and the order to stop or be shot. But only the trees whispered and sighed. Far in the distance a truck strained to climb the switchback road up the hill. She slipped her bag over her shoulder and remembered, grimly, Gaines's warning not to leave the truck.

Telling herself that it was only a precaution, she picked her way through the trees. The undergrowth was wild and difficult, the humidity stifling, but at least she wouldn't be sticking out like a thumb if someone was roaming about.

She waited for a long time, wearying of pressing against a tree with her senses honed to the snapping point. Everything seemed to take on a different texture out there in the trees, she thought; especially the quarrel she and Gaines had had. Out there it seemed impossible that two adults couldn't behave like civilized human beings and give a little. Sighing, resolving to change her way of thinking, she began retracing her steps toward the clearing.

When the sound came again it was much closer than before; a voice this time, and not one but two, both male. Dear God!

April fell back against the nearest tree and flattened herself until she was melting into the rough bark. She inched her head around only enough to see the men when they emerged from the trees. They wore dark clothes, camouflage fatigues. Rifles were slung over their shoulders. They spotted the truck and exchanged remarks and walked over to investigate, circling it warily, almost comically, as if it were an animal baring its fangs at them.

"What do you think?" one said in Arabic as he ran the beam of his light over the hood and then inside from top to floorboard.

"Probably stolen."

"Call in and see."

Static hissed through the night air as one used a two-way radio.

Fear had a remarkable ability to clear the head, April decided as she trembled in her hiding place for the next ten minutes. Someone had once said that you have to hear the angel wings before you change. Perhaps she'd heard them; as she stood unmoving, listening to her heartbeat and knowing that disaster was only a few feet away, all she could think of was escaping this and repairing her bridges with Gaines. Was that a cop-out? she wondered. The presumption of bargaining with destiny? I give up; I'll revolve around you if you'll just let me stay?

The radio finally squawked again. The men murmured together when they learned the truck was stolen. What now? April grew rigid as the beam of light glanced off trees all around her. Two brilliant amber eyes gleamed at her, then disappeared in a quick scurry.

"If anyone was here, they've been gone a long time," one of the men said.

"Put the beam over there."

Footsteps echoed through the trees like the Giant of

the Beanstalk. *Fe, fi, fo, fum*, April thought on a note of hysteria. *I smell the blood of a stupid little American girl!*

"There is nothing," a man finally called out. "The thief is probably in town by now. We're wasting time."

"Might as well drive the truck."

"It'll save a trip back for it."

By the time the engine fired, April felt as if she had been holding her breath for hours. The gears complained as the truck inched back in reverse, then groaned forward. April glanced around just as the headlights slashed across the cypress branches.

When the truck finally crept down the incline, she nearly collapsed. Bending from her waist, she let her elbows come to rest on her thighs. The blood felt drained from all moving parts of her body. She wanted nothing more than to drop to her knees and just go to sleep.

But she couldn't, and she couldn't stay there. What would Gaines think when he returned and found her gone? He'd be horrified, and she felt more distress over what he would feel than what she had just gone through. He would, however, after he thought about it, figure out what had happened. Then he would look for her. The logical place would be the embassy. That, then, is where she must go.

Clutching everything about her—the remnants of her tired courage and the fresh knowledge that one isn't promised a second chance if the first is squandered— April began tediously picking her way down the hillside.

"It is all my fault!" Bashir mourned as he paced his small room at the embassy. He held his hands out from his kaffiyeh as if it were a real possibility that he would fling it off and tear his hair.

"Madame should have my tongue cut out. She should have me shot. No, that isn't bad enough. She should have me drawn and quartered for my criminal act of calling Ali Jassim! Agh, how stupid!''

"How could you have known?'' April waved away Bashir's lavish self-abuse. ''What madame should have you do is fetch a pot of hot tea. I feel a hundred years old.''

They had both shared their stories—Bashir with enormous fervor and much self-condemnation, and she conveniently omitting the interlude that she and Gaines had shared beside the river but accurate in everything else. Bashir called himself a dozen more unflattering names.

He lifted his sad, myopic eyes. ''This Gaines Southerland tries to protect madame.'' He bowed his head. ''Fanatics are everywhere. It is dangerous to be an American in this country.''

At least he hadn't inferred that Gaines was a criminal, she thought. He went on about how he was sure it would all work out in the natural order of things.

April hardly heard what he said. She was imagining Gaines in trouble. She pictured him trying to find Marek. Perhaps he was in some office at this very moment, burning incriminating business records that could send him to prison.

She came to her feet and looked around for her bag. ''Curfew or not,'' she said, ''I have to get home.''

The small man was up in a flash, hurrying about the room, turning back his simple bed, lowering lights, spreading himself over the door as if defying her to take one step toward it.

''I will not hear of it. Madame will eat now. Then she will get a good night's sleep on my bed where it is safe.''

She looked from the bed to him. ''Oh, no, I can't take your room.''

''It is too late to return home. The patrols pick everyone up.''

"Well, I'll sleep on one of the couches then. Really. Tomorrow you can go to my apartment and bring me some clean clothes."

His arguments were too complex. Deciding early on that it was safer—definitely quicker—to give in, April agreed to sleep in Bashir's room. After she had eaten, he placed her feet on the hassock and covered her legs with a shawl. He selected some music on the radio and hovered over her until her wine glass was empty. Then he gathered the tray and dishes.

"I don't even know what to do next," she confessed as she slumped back in his chair. She was very tired. "Here I am at the embassy again, and there's Bruce to think of. And Gaines. And Ali Jassim." Her brows flew together. "Won't Jassim find it strange that I've reappeared just as suddenly as I disappeared?"

Bashir smiled and straightened to his complete five feet five. "Of course. There is only one thing to do."

She smiled her query.

"Lie."

She laughed. "To Ali Jassim? Oh, Bashir, I'm afraid I'm not very good at that. I—"

"But I tell wonderful lies. I made this terrible . . ." He didn't know the right word.

"Mess," she teasingly supplied.

"Exactly. I will get madame out of it. I will tell the Stupid One that madame was kidnapped by a counterterrorist, and that by an exceedingly wonderful act of cleverness she has escaped and has just made her way back to the embassy. I will tell him now."

Without giving April a chance to debate the wisdom of such an outrageous strategy, Bashir telephoned the same Captain Nadal he'd talked to before.

April was flabbergasted. Bashir spun out his lie with the skill of an artist who has long prided himself in his craft. Every inflection of his voice was calculated to win trust, every subtle intonation. She would have believed him herself.

In the end, Jassim was very gracious. He waived April's having to appear before an interrogation committee and said that he would accept her invitation to the embassy for coffee the following day. They could talk about it then.

When Bashir replaced the telephone, April, not relishing an encounter with Jassim but knowing it could have been much worse, shook her head. "All I can say is, I'm glad you're on our side, Bashir."

He gravely agreed that it was the best thing. Then begging her forgiveness several more times for all the trouble he had caused, he took his leave and paused outside her door. At least Gaines Southerland was only passingly in her affections, he consoled himself with a shake of his head. There was still hope when it was only an ex-husband.

Chapter 7

BRUCE CALLED THE MINUTE HE GOT WORD OF APRIL'S return. The phone rang at the embassy at half past eight o'clock, and April dragged her way up from a deep and exhausted sleep. She felt as if someone had taken a rod to her back. And she realized, upon clearing her head, that Gaines had not come to the embassy.

"How did you know about me?" she sluggishly asked Bruce.

It was all in the morning papers, he told her. Jassim was making a big thing of it to draw upon American goodwill. He also told her that Jassim had dragged him in for questioning in connection with her abduction. They had all been out of their minds. Was she positive she was all right?

She assured Bruce she was safe. Nothing that a little rest wouldn't cure. How was life treating him? Then Bruce told her about Amalgamated Textiles.

It had happened while she and Gaines were bouncing

about in the old truck. Bruce had taken a minicam into the American-owned textile plant. He interviewed the spokesmen for the employees who had publicly accused the Amalgamated administration of everything from poor working conditions and bad wages to discrimination.

Before the day was out the workers called a strike. Amalgamated offices were broken into and the administration was threatening to close the plant. There were three law suits presently being filed, plus another three countersuits. Ali Jassim was furiously talking about having Bruce arrested.

April realized it was going to be a terrible day.

After she hung up the telephone, she sponged herself with tepid water and sent Bashir to her apartment for the coolest dress she owned—a sleeveless pearl gray georgette with a scooping, embroidered collar. She also had him bring some proper shoes and her pearls. It was ninety-four degrees when she met Bruce and Cynthia on the portico, and it wasn't even ten o'clock.

Bruce looked like Clark Gable on safari. His short-sleeved bush jacket had a host of flaps and buckles and streaks of sweat running down the sides and back. Belted over duck slacks, and given the added flamboyance of his stick, it was striking.

Hugging him, April told him so.

Bashir took one look at Bruce and excused himself with the muttered announcement that he would bring something cool to drink.

"By heaven," Bruce laughed, and waved for Cynthia to come in off the portico, "I think I've psyched out that little man."

"Bashir's nervous," April said. "A tall American man with a stick is too much out of *Uncle Tom's Cabin* for him."

Since it was too hot to go out into the courtyard, April

seated Cynthia—who was sensibly dressed in a pair of shorts and a sleeveless top—beside an ashtray.

"Better a tall man with a stick than a tall terrorist with a baton," Cynthia dryly observed. She picked up her ashtray, stood up and perched on the windowsill, crossing her legs and putting a cigarette lazily between her lips. "The heat is killing me. Tell us about your adventures, Ms. Southerland. You're an item with the AP, UP, and women everywhere."

Laughing, April looked at Bruce, then realized that Cynthia was serious. "Oh, no. I absolutely forbid it. I couldn't stop the newspapers, but I absolutely forbid the television or *Time*. I'm serious, I mean it."

"Don't be modest," Bruce said. "Do you know how many people would kill for publicity this good?"

"What do I want with publicity?"

Cynthia couldn't imagine anyone not wanting publicity. She coughed raspily. "Don't you know what this kind of story could do to that viper over at the House of State? Give us a description of the man. You say he broke into this very office?"

What irony, April thought; if Bruce only knew that he and his camera were innocently searching for Gaines.

"I'm sorry," she insisted. "I'm going to have to be hard-nosed about this. No interviews. Now, tell me everything Jassim said."

Hobbling to the window, Bruce anchored his stick into the carpet and turned as if he were preparing to deliver a treatise. "The idiot accused me of staging a show. Can you believe that? As if I would deliberately kidnap my own sister-in-law . . ."

At first, when Bashir glided into the room with his tray of drinks, April paid him no mind. She followed his movements absently: the ritual of the napkins, the protocol of the bow, the lowering of the tray with its silver-rimmed glasses. But when Bashir looked over Cynthia's head, April sat very still. Something was wrong.

She arranged her smile as Bruce accepted his drink. When he lifted the glass in a brotherly toast and continued spinning his tale, she came forward in her seat until Bashir had finished with his choreography and glided across the room.

"Madame?" he murmured as he bent over her with a glass.

"What is it?"

"Trouble."

"I can see that. Where?"

"Outside, please."

April stopped Bruce in midsentence. "Would you mind if I left you for a few minutes?" she asked smoothly. "Something's come up."

The old reporter's nose twitched. "Really? Can I help?"

"No, no. It's nothing. But I do have to leave for a minute."

His hazel eyes narrowed. "I smell something in the wind."

"It's the dust. It affects everyone like that." Smiling, she walked past Cynthia toward the door. "Be right back."

Neither Bruce nor Cynthia believed her, of course. She preceded Bashir out of the room, and all her woman's intuition warned her what he would say.

"He is here, madame."

Her stomach turned.

"The courtyard. Hurry, madame."

They both hurried, down the hall and out the big doors, into the blinding sun and along the vine-covered alcoves and the rose-bordered walks. Bashir stopped before the door of an aged wine cellar, which wasn't really a cellar at all but a storage room for fruits and canned items, plus a few bottles of vintage Rothschild.

"Here?" she said, her heart pounding.

"He refused to come inside, madame. I could not think of another place."

Stepping into the wine cellar from the brilliance of the courtyard was like going blind for a few seconds. A bright slash of light divided the room in half. A heavy dankness clung to the air, and the smell was so overpowering April wanted to sneeze. She felt for the light switch. The hand that came down over hers was not Bashir's.

"April?"

Her gasp sounded like a thunderclap in the small room. "What has happened?"

Before she could move, Gaines stepped from the darkness into the white shaft of light. He was no longer wearing khakis but a business suit of lightweight linen the color of cream. A vest was buttoned about his waist, and his shirt was freshly laundered. The knot of his tie had been loosed and the top shirt button undone.

"You're hurt!" she cried, and clapped her hand over her own mouth.

Sweeping his inspection over the courtyard, Gaines shook his head in a warning and flipped on the light. Bashir shut the door at the same time.

Hardly had April's eyes adjusted when Gaines began shrugging out of the suit coat, his injured arm remaining straight at his side as he favored it.

"What happened?"

"Don't ask. It just needs to be set, that's all."

"Oh, Gaines," she whimpered, and carefully helped him draw off the sleeve.

The fracture was a fairly simple one and, if such a

thing had to happen, in a relatively convenient place several inches above his wrist.

Gaines met Bashir's eyes over her head. "Whatever you've got," he said. "Bandages, something hard enough for a splint. Something to drink, too, if you don't mind."

"Yes, sir."

Bashir pushed his glasses up on the bridge of his nose and, for the first time since April had known him, left the room without addressing her.

The emotions that descended upon April were too many. After all her self-flagellation the night before, her realization that Gaines had been hurt and that she hadn't been there was replaced with an anger in direct ratio to her worry.

"Oh, what have you done now?" she berated him. "Can't I trust you for one minute without you running out and trying to get yourself killed?"

"God, woman, what a tongue you've got."

"Consider yourself blessed that I don't say what I'd like to say. How did this happen?"

The break hurt Gaines more than he was willing to admit. April pushed him down onto one of the crates and brushed his hands from the shirt. She removed his vest and unbuttoned the shirt. When she peeled it off over his arm, he sucked in his breath between his teeth.

"How *did* this happen?"

"I ran into something."

"Idiot," she said, and gave a great sigh of despair. Cupping his face in her hands, she shook her head. "Gaines, something's got to give between us."

He knew it was over. There was a point when a thing began to backlash; his protection of her had reached that point. He circled his good arm about her waist, needing her more than he'd ever needed anything in his life.

"Oh, love," he said, and dropped his head upon her shoulder, "you win."

"When did it happen?"

"Very early this morning."

"Was it Marek?"

"No. In a way, yes. I talked to his wife. Last night after I left you in the truck." He leaned back in her arms, his scowl threatening. "By the way, I nearly had a stroke when I went back and there was no sign of that truck."

"They confiscated it. Don't tell me about your strokes; I thought I would have one out there in the woods. And don't change the subject."

Shrugging, he went on with his story. "Some anonymous person called Marek's wife late the day before yesterday and told her that Marek had been picked up and had then escaped. She didn't hear from him all that night or all the next day. She was beginning to think everything was all right when she was told he was being held at the Colony."

April's eyes closed. The Colony was the Devil's Island of Orban.

"It's not her fault. She broke down and confessed to me that it was all a trap, that someone was in the bedroom that very minute. Could I just get her out? Well, I couldn't leave her there. There was a bit of a scuffle with the man in the bedroom. Oh hell, you've seen enough movies to imagine what it was like."

She knew, and she didn't want to hear the words. "And I had your gun," she managed to say.

"It wouldn't have made any difference. When you're outnumbered twenty to one, you don't hang around taking potshots."

She lifted her head and, as a mother would take an erring child into her arms, drew his head to her breast. She stroked the back of his neck.

"I knew you were in some kind of trouble. I think I always knew, but I never guessed that—"

He coughed hard, and she nearly buckled under the weight of his big body. "Don't try to talk anymore," she said. "You're safe here, at least for a while. We'll get a doctor."

He tried, without much success, to smile. "I am a doctor, April."

"You can set that fracture?"

"You can."

"Me!" She bent over him until her nose was level with his. "I won't do it. I won't even think about doing it. Forget it."

"I'd tell you everything."

She cut him off with a look. "Listen to me, Gaines Southerland; this isn't the pioneer days. I'm not touching that arm or giving you a bullet to bite or any of that stuff. You're having a doctor and antibiotics and . . ."

By some means she was not quite sure of, Gaines had drawn her into the space between his legs and was holding her close while she was talking.

"It's all right," he said, and stroked her back, as if for once he was content to let her take care of him. "Everything's going to be okay. Just hold me for a few minutes."

Her love was far beyond the halfway mark now, and April knew it. Even if he gave nothing, she would give everything. She held him until Bashir came.

Bashir seemed to know a good deal about injuries, which didn't particularly surprise April. He also seemed to understand a lot of Gaines's delicate predicament, and that did surprise her. Had Gaines told Bashir something he hadn't told her?

They talked over her head as if she weren't even there. Gaines wanted to know the proximity of the embassy to the rest of the town and what Bashir knew of the schedule of patrol units through this sector. The embassy had a four-man guard, night and day, Bashir said.

"I know a man who can set this for you," Bashir told him after he had answered the questions. "He is not a doctor, and he costs much money."

"We want a doctor," April declared emphatically. "Get him quickly. I don't care what it costs."

"I care," growled Gaines.

"Shut up," said April. "Gaines can't stay out here in this storage room, Bashir. We'll have to get him to my apartment."

He shook his head. "But after dark, madame."

"For the time being I'll put him in one of the reception rooms."

Gaines gestured at one of the bottles on Bashir's tray. "Is that for drinking?"

The younger man grinned. "Much better inside than out." He sloshed some of the liquid into a glass.

April placed the glass into Gaines's hand. "Before you go, Bashir, have some food sent to the reception room."

"Yes, madame."

"And get your medical man as quickly as possible."

"I will go for him myself. He will want his money in advance."

She thought a moment, but before she could reply Gaines fished for his wallet and withdrew a number of bills. "He gets the rest when this bone is set."

Bowing to them both, Bashir slipped out the door.

It wasn't until April draped Gaines's suit coat about his shoulders and stood him up that she realized how much the ordeal had wearied him. When they passed the room where Bruce and Cynthia waited, she held her breath for fear one of them would come out.

She put Gaines in the same reception room where

she'd received Bruce the first time. She immediately drew the drapes shut and returned with a pillow. He winced as he lowered himself.

Kneeling, she arranged his jacket about his shoulders. "How long has it been since you slept?"

He pulled a face. "Forever."

"Whatever needs to be done to straighten all this out"—she held his gaze meaningfully—"we'll do it together. From now on we're a team. You got that?"

Grinning, he nodded. "You won't like it."

"I'm not a child."

How well aware of that fact he was. She never stopped taking him by surprise. Beneath all her impatient demands that sometimes drove him to distraction was a woman that would surpass any concept of femininity he would ever have. She had spoiled him for anyone else with her relentless pride, her sudden unpredictable tendernesses, her unyielding eccentricity for fair play.

"Marek is deeply involved in Nahrhim's government," he told her. "Very high up. If he hadn't been so quick on his feet, he would have been arrested when Jassim threw everyone else in jail. Could you give me another drink of that stuff?"

She placed a glass in his hand and poured the liquid in a swirling stream. Behind them the door opened.

"Just place the tray on the table," she said without turning around. She stooped beside his waist and placed her hand upon it. "There's something I have to tell you before you get started, Gaines. Bruce is here."

Gaines lifted his head from the pillow. "In the embassy?"

"He's waiting for me to come back. I have to tell him something."

"Oh, truth would be just fine, April," Bruce said evenly from the doorway. His laugh was mirthless. "In fact, I'm beginning to think it would be novel."

As April slowly straightened to meet Bruce's accusation, she guessed she looked like a thief caught going through the window, one leg in, one leg out, goods in hand. Cynthia Hymes didn't help matters any by stepping from behind Bruce and flicking her sharp journalist's scrutiny from Bruce to Gaines and back to Bruce.

"My sainted Aunt Agatha," she said drolly. "Another Southerland."

April walked to the door and peered out into the hall to see if any more surprises lingered there.

Bruce folded his arms majestically across his chest and gave them the benefit of his unforgiving Southerland chin as April shut the door.

"Aside from trust," he said, glaring at Gaines and refusing to look at April at all, "which is obviously not a pertinent matter here, I have very little to say. Succinctly put, Gaines, do you have any idea of what you're doing to Mother?"

Gaines heaved himself up on the divan to sit, keeping his injured arm cradled to his side. April guessed that he was in a good deal of pain. She placed her hand on his shoulder to keep him from rising. Bruce limped over to brace his weight upon his stick.

"Gaines, I have to tell you something. For the past three years Andrew and Tremaine and all the rest have been calling you a low-down, good-for-nothing bum. I have stood up for you until I'm blue in the face. Frankly, when I get home I'm going to apologize to Andy and give him a medal. You ought to be shot."

Gaines swore under his breath.

The fraternal crossfire was bad at any time, but now it was dangerous. April stepped directly into it and narrowed her eyes at Gaines.

"Lie down," she ordered, and turned to the eldest Southerland. "And you, Bruce, I know things've been strained between you and your brother lately. I honestly would rather you hadn't found out he was in the country. But since you have, you might as well know that he's been hurt.''

Bruce's expression was incredulous. He thumped nearer and bent over Gaines. He lifted the suit coat and peered down at the swollen and discolored arm. ''Good God! She's serious!''

''Don't look so shocked, Bruce.'' Gaines's mockery came with a smirk. ''Without violence, you'd be out of a job.''

With shaking fingers, Bruce dived into his pockets for his pipe and tobacco. He packed his pipe and tamped it. ''Unbelievable,'' he said, gripping the pipe in his teeth and patting his pockets for his lighter. ''What headlines this is going to make.''

Gaines hiked himself on an elbow and pointed a finger. ''No, I'll tell you what's unbelievable. You and that television camera are going to start a civil war over here, Bruce. That little stunt at Amalgamated Textiles was stupid. Take my advice and go home while you can.''

''That happens to be a credible report. John Brannigan has violated every ethical—''

''John Brannigan is about as pertinent to the issue as my big toe,'' barked Gaines. ''You're probably running a close second on Jassim's hit list as it is. One more bit of purple journalism like yesterday and—''

''Purple journalism!'' shouted Bruce. ''Look here, you—''

Bruce's hands were balled into fists, and Gaines's neck was stained a dark scarlet. Bruce bent forward without the aid of his stick, and Gaines looked as if he were about to lunge off the divan. April caught him with the heel of her hand, her eyes furious.

''I don't think the civil war is out in the streets!'' she slashed across Gaines's anger. ''You don't have any room to talk about stirring up trouble, Gaines. *Now sit down!*''

Gaines dropped his head back wearily against the divan and let his heavy lashes come down.

Swinging around, April pointed an irate finger at Bruce. ''Bruce—''

''In case everyone's forgotten,'' Cynthia interrupted, her cigarette burning dangerously near her fingers as she assumed a cynic's slouch above Gaines's head, ''this man is in pain.''

With an enormous look of gratitude, April heaved a sigh of relief at Cynthia.

''Thank you,'' she said fervently. ''I've sent for someone. He isn't a doctor, but he's supposed to know what he's doing.''

Cynthia found an ashtray and extinguished her cigarette. She waved at Gaines's arm. ''D'you mind if I see?''

''Be my guest,'' growled Gaines.

As the shaggy head bent over his arm, Bruce finally found a light and encased himself in a great cloud of pale blue smoke. He paced the room with a shambling gait, puffing and mumbling. Presently he accused his brother with the pipe stem.

''Okay, Gaines,'' he said grudgingly, ''I'll admit I stirred up more of a hornet's nest than I meant to at Amalgamated Textiles. But, dammit, everyone's so anxious to sweep everything under the table.''

''For the time being it's got to be swept under something,'' Gaines mumbled.

''All right, I'll back off. But that still doesn't explain how you turn up here hugger-mugger with a broken arm. What're you really up to in Orban, anyway? You can tell us. Manufacturing for the military? Armaments? Or something more simple? Black-market commodities?''

Gaines didn't answer. He leaned back and scowled up at Cynthia's platinum punk hair. "Who are you?"

Cynthia gave him a grin and jerked her head at Bruce. "I'm with him."

"A reporter," April calmly supplied. She poured some more of the wine into a glass and held the glass to his lips.

"We have a right to know," demanded Bruce. "The police could be down on our necks at any moment."

"No they won't." Gaines tossed down the whole glass of wine in one shot and wiped his mustache with the back of his hand.

Bruce swore a particularly unattractive oath. "Trouble with the law of a foreign country. That's just great."

"Mercenaries are not the law," said Gaines.

Bruce snorted.

April placed her hand on Gaines's forehead. It was glistening with beads of sweat. She lifted her brows at Cynthia. "I hate to involve you, but would you? Please?"

"Some ice?" Cynthia was eager to help.

"But don't intimate that Gaines is here. No one knows. Tell them—"

"I'll handle it." With a narrow-eyed disapproval for Bruce, Cynthia murmured, "Be ashamed of yourself," and slipped out the door. She shut it soundlessly behind her.

Bruce stared after Cynthia. "What did I do?"

"What you always do," Gaines mumbled.

Stomping to the window, Bruce waved his pipe at April, who was standing over Gaines's head, her arms crossed with frustration.

"Oh, go ahead, April. Pamper the wretch. Can't have him dying on us. How would we explain a corpse?"

Gaines seemed oddly content to let April fuss over

him while he waited for the "doctor." When she bent to plump some pillows behind his head, he circled her waist with his good arm and drew her down beside him.

"Don't worry about me," he said as he nestled his head in her lap and cuddled her waist. "No one ever died of a broken arm."

She tried to disguise her concern with lightness and fondly combed through his hair with her fingers. "If you know so much, why are you lying here?"

He grimaced. "I've been asking myself that very question."

"You ought to get into another line of work, Gaines."

He pulled himself up onto an elbow. The teasing was gone. "Now that you mention it," he said softly, "I was thinking the same thing."

April caught a breath. "Highly advisable," she murmured, which meant: *Don't promise me anything you can't keep.*

He didn't seem to watch her as he spoke, as if he were musing to himself. "Maybe I'll go back to med school when I get back home. It wouldn't take much for me to finish, you know."

"That would make your mother very happy."

He rubbed a place on her arm, and they both watched his long brown fingers play upon her skin. "I might open up the house," he said. "Might even do some work. The trim needs painting. And the guttering's a mess."

"The house has been closed an awful long time." April was beginning to shiver, and not just from his caress.

"Too long?" His eyes found hers.

She shrugged self-consciously. "Well, I mean . . ." She ducked her head.

"You know, when I went back for that truck and you weren't there . . ." He lay back. "I wished I had done a lot of things different. I wished I'd . . . planted a tree."

"A tree?" exclaimed Bruce.

April narrowed her eyes at Bruce, and he turned swiftly back to the window.

"If I ever get another chance," Gaines murmured, "I'm sure I will."

April didn't move.

Gaines cleared his throat. "What kind of tree do you like?"

The pause dangled between them like something fallen that needed to be picked up.

"A strong one," she said in a thin voice. "One that lives . . . a long, long . . ."

"An oak, maybe? But there are maples, don't forget. They can take a lot, and they live practically forever."

Bruce's gentle puffing on his pipe filled the room. Gaines took April's hands in his and stroked her fingers with slow, thoughtful moves. He didn't look up. "What d'you think?"

April could hardly speak. Gaines was asking her forgiveness in a way he'd never asked for it before.

Pulling her hand free, rising, turning in a small, disoriented circle, confused by the violence she'd seen in him and the unspeakable tenderness and sensitivity, she wanted to say yes—yes, yes, yes!

Before she could, a knock sounded on the door. Three pairs of eyes met. April didn't have time to reach the door before Cynthia slipped through and motioned behind her.

A small brown-haired, brown-eyed man stepped into the room, hardly taller than Bashir but much more finely boned. He walked with womanish precision and offered April a small hand with grave formality. He looked as if he had received the death sentence by being brought here.

Behind him, Bashir stood prodding him forward. "Henri Detaille, madame," he announced breathlessly, as if he'd been running. "But I have news of a very extreme calamity."

April's first thought was that Henri Detaille could not or would not set Gaines's wrist. "Can't he do it?"

"Oh yes, madame." Bashir removed his glasses and began wiping the perspiration from them. "Not that. It's the commandant. He is arriving at the embassy this very moment. It will be ghastly. Very much ghastly."

"What?" choked Bruce.

Gaines slumped down on the divan. "I'll be damned."

Though April knew that Bashir was commonly given to excesses when he spoke, she didn't doubt that he spoke the exact truth this time. She placed a restraining hand on Gaines's shoulder and looked up at Bruce with desperation wide in her eyes.

"What'll we do?" she asked.

The embassy was protected by diplomatic immunity, but that immunity was only as good as the honor dealt it. Ali Jassim could post men to watch it day and night. He could arrest everyone who came in or out if he wished to do so. He could, if he really wanted to, search the place or tear it apart brick by brick. Did he know Gaines was here?

Quickly—blood was thicker than water, after all— Bruce stepped forward and took both of April's hands in his own. She remembered another time when he had done the same thing, at Saint Michael's.

"April, listen to me. If this man isn't to wind up in the Colony"—he indicated the prone form of his brother— "we must have time. You're the only one who can buy it."

He was right, of course. Though what she would have to do to buy time might be less than ideal: lie through her teeth; sell her soul. April gazed at the small brown man bending over Gaines's arm.

"Ouch!" snapped Gaines, rearing back and glaring at the man. "Who are you?"

"Henri Detaille, monsieur. I have some experience. Please, do not wiggle so."

"Wiggle? I'm not wiggling. What're you doing there? Wait a minute." He jerked away from Henri's probing fingers.

Henri Detaille lifted his eyes to April and helplessly implored her. He, too, was unnerved. When he'd realized that he and the boy had been seen by Commandant Jassim, he had nearly lost the contents of his stomach. He wished dreadfully to be relieved of this job.

"Madame?" he pleaded.

Bruce was smiling maliciously at his brother. "Oh, Gaines, do be still," he said. "For a doctor, you make a terrible patient."

Henri's eyes widened at the elder Southerland, and he waved his thin fingers at Gaines. "This man is a . . . doctor? Of medicine?"

A grumbling sound came from Gaines's chest. "And if I am?"

Henri let out a great sigh of relief and smiled. "The problem is solved, monsieur. Set your own arm."

Gaines held up his hand. "Are you crazy?" His mouth curled downward. "I'm paying you good money. You'll do it, and you'll do it right."

He indicated the case Henri had set on the floor beside his feet. "What have you got in there for pain? Novocaine? Meperidine?"

The Frenchman threw his hands to the ceiling. "What do you take me for, monsieur? Someone who can go in to the chemist and give him a list? Narcotics are reported to the government. Ali Jassim would know within a half hour if I bought narcotics for this embassy." He rambled off in a French tirade about the enormous ignorance of foreigners.

April had not counted on a temperamental medic. The seconds were slipping hopelessly through her fingers.

"You think this is Johns Hopkins?" Henri was demanding of Gaines. "Let me tell you something, monsieur. I do not wish to come here. I do not wish to doctor a doctor." He stepped to Bruce. "You, monsieur. I will tell you what to do. You set the arm. You are an American. Jassim will think twice before he shoots you."

"Please." She smiled her prettiest and placed a hand on the Frenchman's arm. "You will be extremely well paid. Gaines is a little noisy, but he's harmless. I'm going now to talk to Commandant Jassim. I can almost promise you that he will not bother anyone."

Gaines was rifling through Henri's case, mumbling to himself. ". . . got to have some novocaine in here."

Grossly insulted, Henri grabbed the case out of Gaines's hands, clutched it to his chest and threw back his head in offense. "If you don't mind . . ."

Gaines held up his hands. "Demerol? Got any of that?"

Henri's brown head turned from side to side in the negative.

"Codeine?"

Another shake of the head.

Gaines's lips thinned. "Marijuana?"

The angle of Henri's chin shot up. "Monsieur!"

Glumly turning, Gaines moved away, cradling his arm to his side. He paused. "An aspirin?"

"Voilà!" Henri's face cracked into a smile.

Groaning, Gaines sat back down on the divan.

April implored Bruce with a whimper. "Can you take care of this?"

Bruce strode quickly forward. "He'll be all right, April. It's something they learn in med school. A few stiff drinks, and he'll never know the difference. Go do . . . whatever you can.''

Bashir was waiting by the door. April straightened her shoulders, smoothed back her hair and stepped to an etagere, where she studied her reflection. She was giving the collar of her dress an adjustment when Cynthia hurried across the room.

''Here.'' She extended a lipstick that she obviously never used. ''Knock him dead.''

So the feminist knew how to conduct war, after all, did she? April flashed a grateful smile and applied the coral tint to her lips. ''Gaines, will you be okay?''

Gaines's lip curled. ''At the hands of Jack the Ripper, here? Of course.''

Cynthia fell into step as April and Bashir moved into the hall. ''What will you do?'' she whispered from the corner of her mouth.

Pausing, her hands shaking a little, April exchanged a woman's look with her. ''What we've done for centuries, Cynthia—whatever is necessary.''

Cynthia touched her shoulder. ''Right on.''

Chapter 8

"THIS IS VERY MUCH DANGEROUS! TERRIBLE, TER-rible!"

Bashir's distraught whisper echoed down the empty hallway as he and April hurried to the office where Commandant Ali Jassim would be received.

"Ali Jassim is very angry at Bruce Southerland," he reminded her. "He saw me with the Frenchman, running. He has the teeth of a crocodile, and now he is suspicious."

"I realize that."

"Madame must put him off. Talk to him tomorrow. Talk to him next week. Perhaps God will have mercy upon us and let someone assassinate him before next week."

"Bashir!"

"I will talk to him myself. Lying is my talent. I am the best. I will tell him that—"

April cut him off with a look. "You have one concern right now, Bashir, and that is to see that Gaines and Henri are not interrupted while that arm is being set."

"But madame," he wailed, "Ali Jassim could bring an army into this embassy."

Did he think she didn't know that? April came to a stop outside the door and almost let her head thump down upon the facing. She would do anything to help Gaines. He had come into this country and risked himself to get her out, and he was trying, without much success, to save Bruce from his own folly.

What if she couldn't help? What if she couldn't lay Jassim's suspicions to rest and he did bring an army into the embassy? He could do it today. Before they even got Gaines out.

She forced iron into her spine. "If Jassim violates this embassy, then all our worries are over, Bashir. Permanently."

Bashir's olive face paled. "Let me stay. Madame will need me."

"You don't think I can pull this off?"

His face looked like a sad clown's. "It is true madame cannot lie very well."

April brought the edges of her teeth together. "That's what you think," she said grittily, and sailed into the office and straight to the window.

Beyond the fence one of the guards was saluting as Jassim passed him on his way through the embassy gate. The embassy guard snapped his heels together and fell into step a few paces behind him.

She let the drape swing back into place. "Now . . ." She rubbed the pearls as if they were worry stones. "If you don't want us both to be shot, Bashir, meet the commandant at the door and stroke his ruffled fur.''

"Oh, madame, it will be a calamity."

"Hush!"

With a helpless shrug, Bashir started out the door. He was so distressed that protocol was forgotten. As he passed through the opening, he stopped, turned, implored.

"Go," April said.

"It's all in the eyes, madame," he said as parting advice. "Remember to lie with the eyes."

April shut the door in his face and slumped against it to gather her wits. It was a deadly gamble she was about to take, the most serious game of poker anyone could imagine. She was terrible at cards.

First off, she must be certain of her hand. One: Even if Jassim knew that Gaines had been at Marek's house, he didn't know Gaines's identity. And he didn't— she hoped—suspect that Gaines was actually there in the embassy. Two: Jassim would know that Bruce was in the embassy; the guards would have told him that. She thought she could help there, and she would be very vocal about it. Three: Ali Jassim had a certain attraction to her because she'd once stood up to him. As much as possible, she must capitalize upon those feelings.

She felt the hot kick of adrenaline and glanced about the room. The divan sat against the wall opposite the two desks. Arranged at right angles with it were two chairs and two end tables. The red carpet in the center was thick and plush.

She bent over one table and checked the silver case containing American cigarettes and the box of Cuban cigars. Quickly she moved to her desk and glanced at the papers there—steel-plant administrators and their families who were being processed for the return home. She scooped them up and tossed them into a drawer. As a last-minute precaution, she glanced at herself in a mirror. She smoothed her hair into place and adjusted her pearls. If only she had just a little cleavage!

Bashir's tap sounded at the door.

"Commandant!" she exclaimed as she opened the door and gave him a smile that she prayed did not betray the thrill shivering up into her throat.

Ali Jassim filled the space. He wasn't wearing fatigues today but a dress uniform. Insignia were pinned to his epaulets, and medals rode across his chest. His aura of power was so strong that April wouldn't have been surprised if he had carried a whip instead of a baton.

"Madame," he said with measuring black eyes, "I think you forgot I was coming."

She touched her pearls with what she hoped was feminine chagrin. "I thought about it all morning, Commandant. I must confess to getting waylaid. Won't you come in? It's terribly hot. Will it storm, do you think?"

Jassim walked into the room and over to the window. He clasped his big hands behind his back and peered up at the burgeoning clouds. "Undoubtedly."

Turning, he lifted his brows. "Are you afraid of storms, April Southerland?"

She smiled. "Storms have never frightened me too much."

"No human frailties?"

"A number." She flushed slightly. "But not storms."

"And now you have piqued my curiosity."

Bashir bowed and stepped forward to take Ali Jassim's hat. Jassim pulled one hand over his gleaming mass of hair, waved the small man away and gave the hat to April instead.

He was testing her, she thought, forcing her to accept a familiarity. She walked to her desk and put down the hat. From the corner of her eye she saw him watching her. She sent Bashir a look to leave the room.

"I saw your man as I was arriving," Jassim said as Bashir made his exit. "He and his companion were in great haste. I said to myself, Now, what could make Bashir Id-Nasaq hurry so? Another abduction of Madame Southerland? Foul play afoot again?"

April refused to nibble at Jassim's bait. "Bashir tries to keep me from making a fool of myself. He was afraid I'd forgotten you were coming, and he was hurrying in to tell me so I could freshen up. As you can see, he didn't make it in time."

"On the contrary. I hadn't expected you to look so . . . What do you Americans say?" His black eyes teased. "No worse for the wear? Am I making you nervous?"

She laughed. "Actually yes, you are. Please sit."

That obviously pleased him. He walked across the carpet with an arrogance that would have made some women swoon and lowered himself to the settee. He took care with his creases and, smiling, touched the baton to the opposite cushion.

"Beside me, madame. Sit where I can see your eyes."

April arranged herself on the opposite end of the settee, wondering now if Jassim had some card up his sleeve. She lifted the top off of the box of cigars.

"Please smoke if you like."

"Ah." He accepted and drew the cylinder back and

forth beneath his nose. "I don't often indulge myself. A matter of morale. I don't like to ask my people to sacrifice something I'm unwilling to sacrifice myself."

"Smoking a good cigar is going over to the enemy?"

"Samson yielding to the charming temptations of Delilah, perhaps."

She laughed. "Well, that cigar came from Castro, not Delilah."

He cut off the tip and replaced his knife in his pocket. April lifted the silver lighter from the table. John Strakes's name was engraved upon it. Discreetly covering the name, she held the flame to the tip of the cylinder.

Jassim drew the flame into the tobacco and held her eyes with the vise of his own. April knew a moment of fear, but he smiled, then leaned back on the settee and crossed one ankle over his knee.

"Now," he said, and gave her a look that said: *You may interest me, but things will go badly for you if you lie.* "Tell me why Bruce Southerland is such a stupid man."

Relieved, for it was a question she had been prepared for, April explained how Bruce's motives were innocent in themselves. "He has no axe to grind," she concluded. "He only wants the American end of it to be ethically correct, no matter who's in power, you or . . . Nahrhim."

"I don't care about his motives. Some of my supporters are not as generous to Americans as I am. They would like to send you all back home."

"Bruce is only doing what any dedicated reporter would do. He's impartially reporting the facts."

"Tell him to stop."

"You're assuming he will uncover American fraud."

Jassim's brows sparred with hers for a moment. "If he does, he will force me to take action I have no desire to take."

"I don't know if he will stop."

His look was openly irritated. His words came with an underlying promise of retribution. "Don't try to use this trouble as a weapon against me, April Southerland."

Until he said the words she hadn't realized that she'd been hoping, far back in her consciousness, to back him into a corner. One round for the commandant.

"I will do what I can," she said meekly.

She walked to a small cabinet and removed a bottle of fine Russian vodka. She removed heavy crystal glasses from a shelf. If Jassim was attracted to her because of her fighting spirit, she thought, she was taking the wrong approach. She turned abruptly.

"Why did you really come here today?" she said suddenly. "You don't really need me to play intermediary between you and Bruce. You might like the convenience of it, but you don't need it. And I don't think you're particularly interested in how I survived my ordeal. What do you really want, Ali Jassim?"

Whatever the reason, the tactic worked. Jassim came slowly to his feet and closed the distance between them. His gaze was more admiring than it had been on the portico steps; it lowered to her breasts, her waist, her hands.

She spun the top off the bottle and attempted to pour. It staccatoed on the rim of the glass.

"Your hands are shaking, April Southerland," he said mockingly. "Here, allow me."

He took the bottle from her hands and poured some

into each glass. Without thanking her, as if her familiarity were something to be taken for granted, he placed a glass into her hand and lifted his to the light. He swirled it thoughtfully for a few seconds.

"Why do you suppose someone would kidnap you, madame?" he said easily. "I have been puzzling that over and over in my mind ever since it happened."

She moved to the window and sipped the vodka. She hated straight vodka. "To strike at you, perhaps."

"Me?"

Her laughter was uneasy. "You surely aren't unaware that people exist in this country who would do anything to make you look like a savage, Commandant."

"Oh, you do have nerve, April Southerland." He moved directly behind her and forced her to turn. His eyes roamed more boldly now, over her hair and her mouth. He reached with a fingertip and lifted the pearls level with her nose. "Not many women would say that to me. Tell me, do · you think I'm a savage?"

"I think, Commandant Jassim"—her throat threatened to seize at this new danger—"that you will do anything to get what you want."

April could feel his breath upon her forehead. It was sweet and laced with tobacco. "And what is that?"

"Everything."

Black brows lifted. "But that would include you, madame."

The moments that he stood towering over her, his small, subtle eroticisms enmeshing her like invisible threads of a spider around its victim, were the longest April had ever lived through. At one point she thought he would touch her. Yet he didn't.

Letting out her breath, she lowered her eyes. "Yes."

Jassim dropped the pearls and tossed back the vodka, grimacing as he swallowed. He forced himself to take a tight hold on his emotions. He had looked into April Southerland's clear green eyes and seen another pair of eyes—not so green as hers but just as innocent. She, too, had been ignorant of the terrible things in his past. He had loved her, and she had never returned it. She had held him at bay, as April Southerland was doing now. Yet, his attraction for this woman was very strong. She made him feel younger and, well . . . not so bad. With very little effort she could have him behaving like one of those sotted fools he despised—inspired to greatness, benevolent.

"Do you know what I think?" he said, watching her reaction carefully.

"No. What?"

"I don't think you were kidnapped at all."

April's head came up sharply, shock widening her eyes. Then she turned away from him, forced down some of the burning liquor.

"Do you really want to hear my theory, madame?"

No, she did not! "Of course."

"I think the man who abducted you was an Orbanian. But I also think he gave you to another man. An American. I think the American returned to this city and was seen in a woman's house."

An alarm shrilled in April's head. Fear began to drizzle through her veins like acid. "I'm afraid I wouldn't know about things like that."

"You wouldn't know? Well, I will explain. The man who abducted you from the embassy was an agent of former President Nahrhim. Marek Abdullah—very high on Nahrhim's intelligence force."

"Oh?" April felt her face stiffening. Marek, an agent?

"He was working with an operative from America. We do not know the American's identity, but we do know his reputation. He isn't heavy machinery; he is a courier of information. I have been told that he can spend a night with a computer and walk out with enough information to bring a country to its knees. Of course, I do not believe this. But he is a formidable man, this American."

All April's intentions slid out from under her like a rug. Things were adding up; the total was not what she had expected.

"I'll get word to him through Marek," Gaines had said.

"He's a friend of Marek's," Gaines had said.

"Marek and I conducted some business together once," Gaines had said.

She tried to smile, but nothing about her seemed to be working. "I, ūh . . ."

Jassim's eyes were the eyes of a falcon. "Marek Abdullah has told me this."

"He confessed?"

"What do you expect? It was the natural order of things."

"And you think—"

"I think nothing, April Southerland!" Jassim lashed out at her, his fury overpowering his attraction. "I know. *I know!* The American was seen coming out of Marek Abdullah's house with his wife. He and Marek Abdullah were agents, working together. I want this man, April Southerland. You spent time with him. You talked with him. It would surprise me very much if you didn't know where he is at this very moment."

And then, of course, she knew.

What amazed April was that it had taken so long for her to discover it. But it wasn't her fault, was it? No woman in her right mind would suspect her husband of being an agent. A philanderer? Yes. A criminal? It had crossed her mind. But an agent? Secret agents were for movies and books. Even now, in the split-second fragment when it all crashed down upon her—the hundreds and hundreds of signs that had cluttered her marriage, proof enough for a dozen wives—April could not blame herself.

She walked away from Jassim and placed her palms on her desk and leaned heavily upon them. She must be careful now. So very, very careful. It was Gaines's life.

"Your theory is correct, Commandant," she said guardedly, warning herself to stay as close to the truth as possible. "When Marek took me from this embassy, he did so at gunpoint. I had no idea who he was or that he was an agent. I was given to an American, true. He told me that he was returning me to the United States for my safety. Personally, I think I was making them a little nervous, being here on my own. But we weren't able to get out of the country. We parted company. That's all there is."

"Not quite, madame."

April let her eyes close. It wasn't going to work. Jassim knew too much. "What else, Commandant?"

"Face me, April Southerland."

It was all she could do to turn, to lift her head.

"You're lying," he said harshly. "You know it and I know it. Who was he? What was his name?"

"I don't know who he was," she lied desperately. "He was a tall man, rather good looking—"

"Six feet or over, a hundred and ninety pounds, black hair, full beard. Correct? *Is that not correct?*"

For the first time April saw Ali Jassim lose his control.

His face and his neck were diffused with anger. His hand came up and he stepped toward her. She braced herself for his blow. She closed her eyes and set her shoulders and did not move.

"Look at me!" he demanded.

"No."

He grasped her shoulders, his fingers cruel. "Damn it, you will!"

Her head went back, exposing her throat, but she still refused to look at him. In those stunning seconds, she felt herself lifted completely free of the floor. Her eyes flew open then. His face was nearly touching hers. His body was shockingly hard against hers and terrifyingly strong. He could have broken her in two.

"There are Americans in this embassy at this very moment," he said quietly through gritted teeth. "I want to know who they are."

Sweat beaded on April's upper lip. Her arms were numb. She knew he could feel her legs trembling. "This embassy is protected by international—"

His rage darkened. She thought he was capable of killing her. He held her for several seconds longer as if he were actually visualizing himself doing it; then he lowered her to the floor and his eyes slashed through her like blades.

"Don't ever throw that threat in my face again. I could tear this place down, and you could not stop me."

She wasn't sure her words would come out if she opened her mouth. She wet her lips.

"But . . . you won't." Like a child, she began shaking her head.

"Don't tell me what I won't do! Don't you know I hold your life in the palm of my hand?" He looked at her

in amazement and lifted his hand distractedly. "Don't
you know that I could make you beg?"

April's legs were moving now. They were carrying
her back against the wall. In her mind she saw Gaines,
sweat beaded on his brow as Henri meshed broken
bones. She must stand up to the man glaring down at
her.

"No," she said, and tried to stand taller. "You cannot
make me beg."

Jassim looked at April and knew that he would not
force her any farther. That didn't surprise him; he had
known from that first day he could not break her.

He walked to the desk and retrieved his hat and fit it
ceremoniously upon his head. Thunder was rolling in the
distance like a drum cadence. He waited until he was
certain his frustration would not show before he looked
at her.

"How is it," he said presently, his voice almost
normal, "that you, an American woman of no particular
importance, can embarrass me?"

April wished she were sitting down. She rubbed her
hands down her sides. "Because, Ali Jassim," her voice
cracked, "you are, beneath the terrorist, still a man. And
a man is human. He can be hurt."

"Not me."

"Yes, you."

He looked as if he would like to lift her off the floor
again. "How do you dare speak to me so?"

She said nothing.

He walked to the door. He put his hand upon the knob
and, on impulse, looked at her again. More gently he
said, "Tell me how you dare."

April saw the real man in him now, behind the
dangerous black eyes, behind the troop of armed commandos and the reckless rebellion against the world. As

bizarre as it was, in that moment she did not fear him. She almost smiled.

"Because you would like me to want you back."

He slipped his baton formally beneath his arm. He knew that she would escort him to the portico. He wanted to laugh; protocol never failed him.

Once they reached the doors and the guard outside opened them so that the humid heat flooded in, he drew himself to his full height. He said, as honestly as was in his power, "I don't want to arrest you, April Southerland. Don't do something that would force me to."

She didn't smile. The sultry wind lifted her hair and fluffed it about her face.

He clicked his heels. His back was very straight. "Good day, madame," he said, and descended the steps in perfect military form.

It was times like this that the word *fool* was invented for. As April walked back into the embassy with heavy, heavy feet, she thought any number of words would have sufficed for what she was: *schlemiel, sucker, nincompoop, ninny, dummy.*

She smiled at the embassy guard because he had no way of knowing how stupid she really was. And then the anger hit her. Didn't Gaines realize what he had done? In her ignorance she could've, could've . . . could have what? The old adage: What a person doesn't know can't hurt them. She had known nothing; she could have given nothing away.

But if she had known that Gaines was a spy—she still wasn't used to thinking about him that way—*that* could have tripped her up: a breath at the wrong time, a shift of the eyes, a fatal hesitation. And in giving Gaines away, she would have also ruined herself. Who would believe her innocence? Her, the ex-wife and on intimate terms, *very* intimate terms, with the agent. And that, of course, was why he had never told her. What loneliness had he suffered? Dear heaven, what pain?

She closed her eyes in a rush of grief. She'd made it so much worse.

Because she was returning to the room a different person than when she had left it, April was surprised when she entered. Bashir had restored perfect order. He was performing his passing-out-drinks rites. Bruce stood at the window with his pipe, having struck a thoughtful Prince Charlesean pose. Cynthia's legs were crossed, and smoke curled attractively about her punk-cut head as she argued over nuclear arms with Henri Detaille. Henri's confidence had been bolstered by the drink in his hand; he patted his mouth delicately with a napkin as he listened to Cynthia and glowed proudly at Gaines, who sat shirtless on the couch, his arm neatly splinted and bandaged.

Henri was the only one who rose to his feet when she walked in.

"Please keep your seat," she told him, and drew a chair near the couch. She accepted the glass of tea Bashir placed in her hand and looked at Gaines. "Are you all right?"

Gaines glanced down at his arm. "Don't I look all right?"

April didn't trust appearances now. She fixed Gaines with a stare that narrowed the universe down to the two of them. "I honestly don't know."

Bruce thumped across the room. "He's indestructible. Of course he's all right. Monsieur Detaille is a genius. Don't keep us in suspense, April. How'd it go with the terrorist?"

April smiled mechanically, answering Bruce but not looking at him. She was absorbed with the way Gaines was looking at her, the way his nostrils thinned slightly as he pondered her.

"For one thing," she recounted offhandedly, "Jassim wants you to stop reporting and go home."

"What?" Cynthia stabbed out her cigarette with a vengeance. "I expected something like this. Barbarian! We will do exactly as we have been doing."

"Who in hell does he think he is?" Bruce waved his stick.

"The man with the aces," said Gaines, also not looking at Bruce as he spoke, but at April.

The undertow between April and Gaines was moving swiftly now, strongly, and Gaines drew his tongue across the edge of his upper lip as his eyes narrowed in puzzlement. Gaines said: "He knows you're here, Bruce."

Bruce snorted. "So what?"

"He knows everyone is here," April amended. *How could you?* her eyes said to Gaines.

Henri's rosy glow subsided. He set his glass down with a clunk. *"Mon dieu,"* he muttered. "I am dead already."

"Not you, Gaines," April added, and her voice was so odd that Gaines cocked his head. His small frown said: *Tell me what you know.*

"He only suspects you are here," she murmured in response to his unspoken question.

"Suspects Gaines is here? Well, what of that? Unless . . ." Bruce paused and pointed his stick at Gaines. "Unless you're in this country illegally. All right, Gaines, I've about had it. You've been supplying arms to the pro-Nahrhim faction, and now we're all going to be arrested."

April abruptly broke the current between Gaines and herself by coming to her feet and walking to the mirror.

In its reflection she saw Gaines rise from the couch and, favoring his arm, walk to the window.

Gaines carefully drew the drape aside. He studied the street for a moment, then the massive clouds growing more water sodden by the minute. Ali Jassim's Land-Rover had pulled up beside the guards posted across the street, and the commandant was talking to them.

Bruce moved to look over his brother's shoulder. "What's he doing?"

"Posting additional guards, I would imagine," Gaines replied. "Within a half hour this place will be crawling in guards."

"Why, for pity's sake?"

In the mirror April could just make out one of the guards talking into his radio. He pushed down the antenna with his flank and made a sweeping motion at the embassy with the radio. Jassim talked a moment longer, and the men saluted him. They watched him stride majestically back to his Land-Rover and get in.

"They will do anything he says," Bruce observed softly. "Did you know that he had President Nahrhim executed? It went out on the wire services late yesterday."

Turning, Gaines abruptly met April's scrutiny in the mirror. "What else did you and Jassim talk about besides Bruce?"

April's eyes were the eyes of a wife. "He asked me about the abduction, and I told him. He explained in some detail that he was very busily involved in hunting down . . . agents."

For a moment Gaines just stood, running his fingertips over the bandage. "Then he must have told you about Marek."

"Who's Marek?" asked Cynthia.

Cynthia's question was ignored. "Yes," April said.

"And the man Marek was working with?" Gaines walked to the tray that Bashir had placed on a table. He turned his back and poured a drink. "I suppose he told you who that was."

A jagged finger of lightning streaked across the sky. Cynthia sucked in her breath. Thunder rolled in on a peal that rattled the windowpanes.

April felt a need to go to Gaines and put her arms around him. She wanted to kiss the back of his shoulder and tell him that everything was all right, that she understood at last. But she only watched him drawing a circle around and around the rim of the glass.

"He told me what he knew," she said gently. "The rest I deduced for myself."

Gaines was glad she knew. He regretted that he hadn't had time to tell her himself, but he was glad she knew. And he knew, too, that he had to get out of the embassy as quickly as possible. Every minute he lingered there endangered her.

Yet things were gaining in complexity, life and death complexities: Bruce's probe into dirty laundry, his own investigation for Wesley and the necessity of keeping things quiet, his life, their life, everyone's life . . .

He reached for his wallet and stuffed the rest of the money into Henri's hand. "The sooner you get out of here, monsieur," he said, "the better."

Henri lunged to his feet. Gaines thought that he would kiss him on both cheeks.

"Oh, monsieur! I will say nothing about this." He pressed his mouth to emphasize. "My lips are sealed."

April sprang out of her chair, cheeks flushed, eyes wide. "No!"

Everyone stared at her.

She held up her hands. "I mean, yes. Monsieur Detaille must leave, of course. Bashir will go with him in the embassy car. But"—she smiled—"if Henri is questioned, he must say that he was called to the embassy to treat a sprained shoulder for Bruce."

"Forget it," snapped Bruce. "I'm not getting mixed up in any of Gaines's shenanigans."

For the first time Cynthia wasn't on top of things. She pulled at a twist of white hair. "Will someone tell me what's going on here?"

Gaines ignored her. He smiled his compliment to April. Now he knew what she was thinking, and he saw his way out of the embassy. A Band-Aid for a mortar wound, true, but it would work. With a little luck.

He studied the massing storm. "Come here, April."

She moved to stand in front of the window.

"You've lived here for a year. Give me your opinion of the weather."

"It will probably be a bad storm. Telephones will go down. There'll be no lights for hours. The temperature will drop fifteen degrees in minutes; probably some hail, as dry as it is."

Gaines smiled. He removed several more bills from his wallet and waved them at the Frenchman. "Like she said, Henri, you came here to look at a sprained shoulder for Mr. Bruce Southerland. Right?"

Henri's frightened face was gray again. He looked first to Bruce, then back to Gaines, pursed his lips and whimpered, "If you say, monsieur."

Gaines grinned. "Bruce Southerland had an accident with some film he was shooting. A crate hit him on the shoulder. Bad bruise, some swelling, nothing serious."

The Frenchman nodded glumly. *"Oui, monsieur."*

"Good man. Bashir, take Monsieur Detaille home now before the storm hits. But before you go, do you own a razor?"

Bashir looked puzzled, then realized Gaines was stroking his beard. He glanced at Bruce's two-hundred-twenty-pound frame, then at Gaines's one-hundred-ninety-pound physique, at the stick, at the sling.

His small eyes crinkled behind the spectacles. He smiled. "Yes, monsieur, I have a razor."

"Bring it."

The young man swept open the door and hurriedly motioned the Frenchman out. The moment it shut, Bruce walked to his younger brother and squared off. The two Southerland profiles, practically nose to nose, would have been funny if lives had not been at stake.

Lightning laced the sky, and thunder rumbled.

Bruce wiped a hand across his mouth. "I swear, Gaines," he said, "if you're trying to make me angry, you're doing it. I didn't come halfway around the world to watch you shave. Now, are you going to tell me what's going on or not?"

Letting out his breath, knowing that nothing could save any of them now but the whole truth, Gaines placed his hand on his brother's arm. "Come sit down, Bruce. There's something I want to tell you."

Before Gaines began his story he walked to April and pulled her to his waist with his good arm and peered down into her eyes for a long, electric moment. He wished he could say everything that burdened his heart. He kissed her very tenderly, and his voice was low.

"I'm sorry," he said.

April didn't say anything. She didn't trust her voice at all.

Turning, glancing at his wristwatch, Gaines waved for Cynthia to sit beside him on the divan. "It's kind of complicated, Cynthia, but you look like a very bright woman to me. In fact, I think you're going to like this."

Amazed, Cynthia thought she probably would.

Everything went exactly as Gaines said it would.

At precisely ten minutes past eleven Bashir walked

through the embassy doors with Henri Detaille. The embassy limousine was waiting in its usual place beyond the fence. The driver stepped out and walked to the passenger side. He waited, as he always did, with his eyes straight ahead.

The wind rose steadily. Dead leaves scraped along the street, and loose pieces of clutter.

Bashir gave Jassim's two guards outside the gate a hostile look.

The guards stopped Bashir and Henri the minute they walked through the gate. They asked to see their identification.

Bashir reminded one of the guards that he knew exactly who he was. They had taken the same Chemistry II class at the university. It wasn't his fault one of them had gone over to the enemy.

The guard from Chemistry II gave Bashir a pained look. He explained that they had new orders. Absolutely no one was to go in or out of the embassy without being checked.

The guard checked Bashir's identification. Then he checked Henri's identification. He gave both to the other guard to see. The other guard said that Henri looked suspicious and wanted to know what he was doing at the embassy.

Henri quickly said he had been called upon to look at the shoulder of one of the American newspeople. His hands shook as he said it.

The guard looked at the shaking hands and said that Henri was no medical man, that he was a pervert.

Henri grew angry.

A number of minutes were taken up with questions about why Mr. Bruce Southerland had not called a medical doctor from one of the hospitals. Nothing was resolved.

The street grew very dark.

Bashir and Henri were released and told to go on their way.

The guards immediately reported to Captain Nadal at the House of State. Nadal agreed that Henri was indeed a suspicious man. He admonished the guards to be extremely careful.

The sky grew darker. The thunder was almost constant.

One half hour later Bashir returned in the limousine. He gave the guard from Chemistry II a hostile glance.

The guard looked somewhat regretful and asked to see Bashir's identification again.

At five minutes past twelve the two guards opened their lunches and began to eat.

The storm broke.

At the exact moment that the rain began, three people stepped onto the portico of the embassy. One was a tall, clean-shaven man wearing a pair of duck slacks and a rather baggy short-sleeved bush jacket with flaps. His left arm was in a sling. In his right hand he carried a black, brass-handled walking stick. The woman wore shorts. She had great legs but her hair was a mess. The other woman, whom they had all seen many times and knew was the attaché to the ambassador, hurried with them to the embassy gate. They all had umbrellas.

The guards, who had just stepped beneath a tree to eat, hurriedly replaced their lunches in their containers. They reluctantly walked out into the rain to check the identification.

The man in the bush jacket resented being made to show his identification. He slapped down his passport and said that he was Bruce Southerland. He extended his umbrella over his passport but not over the guard. He demanded in a surly voice that the guard get on with it.

The sky began to pour. The thunder was deafening. Rain was pouring off the helmets of the guards. It was sluicing down their backs and drenching their trousers.

The guard from Chemistry II told his companion to quickly get them some rain slickers. Over the thunder he yelled to Mr. Southerland that he had lost a good deal of weight.

Mr. Southerland yelled back that he didn't know what difference that made. His passport was getting wet, if he didn't mind.

The guard thought it was unkind that none of the three people offered to share an umbrella. And he didn't consider working for Ali Jassim as having gone over to the enemy; he looked upon it as being practical. They could have shared an umbrella.

He was about to say that to Mr. Southerland when the woman with the legs and hair smiled at him in a friendly way.

The guard was embarrassed. His clothes were sticking to him. Rain was drizzling into his ears. He knew he wasn't at his best. He asked to see her identification.

Unlike Mr. Southerland, she did not hold her umbrella only far enough to protect her passport. She extended it over the guard's head.

The guard, feeling grateful, smiled back. He noted that her passport said her name was Cynthia Hymes. He thought she had nice eyes. He told her he hoped she had a nice stay.

She replied in very bad French that he could drop dead.

The guard thought she said she would like to have a drink sometime. He smiled.

The driver of the limousine was standing in the rain waiting for his passengers. He did not look pleased with the guards.

The other guard now returned in a rain slicker and gave one to the guard from Chemistry II. He said he had just radioed Captain Nadal at the House of State about Mr. Southerland. He was waiting for a reply.

Mr. Southerland grew very displeased. Cynthia Hymes no longer smiled. She glared at the guard's bedraggled appearance and made him extremely uncomfortable.

The attaché to the ambassador peered out from beneath her umbrella and politely asked what on earth was the delay.

The guard from Chemistry II had grown rather fond of the American attaché these last days. He exchanged an uncomfortable look with his companion.

Lightning cracked with the explosion of a cannon.

What the hell? shrugged the other guard.

Mr. Southerland and Cynthia Hymes were waved on to the limousine. The attaché to the ambassador thanked the guards for their consideration and turned back toward the embassy.

As the limousine was disappearing around the corner, Captain Nadal finally came on the radio. He told them that they had done well to question Mr. Southerland so carefully. There was an American operative working the city. He was thought to be six feet tall. He had black hair and a beard.

The guards looked at each other. They had taken shelter beneath a tree. Rain still dripped off their helmets. They were cold and hungry. They congratulated themselves that no such person had come through their checkpoint. They promised Captain Nadal they would be very alert.

Nothing out of the ordinary happened for the remainder of the day except that the storm grew much worse.

Later in the afternoon the attaché to the ambassador

came out on the portico, put up her umbrella, waved cheerfully to the shivering guards and got into the limousine.

The guards were both glad when their shift was over. The guard who had radioed Captain Nadal said he was starving and that he was going home to eat dinner and make love to his wife. The guard from Chemistry II thought he would change clothes and drop by the hotel where most of the Americans were staying and see if he could catch sight of Cynthia Hymes.

Neither of them knew that a man six feet tall, having a game leg and wearing a pair of cream-colored trousers that wouldn't quite button about his waist was spending the night in the embassy. He was presently having a game of chess with Bashir Id-Nasaq. They were eating oranges. Beside them were two half-empty bottles of vintage Rothschild.

Chapter 9

APRIL FELT LIKE THE LAST PLAYER TO LEAVE THE locker room after a losing game, neglected and unloved.

She stood on the embassy portico beneath her umbrella and stared at the rain-shiny limousine beyond the wrought iron fence. She dreaded the lash of the storm, yet it had helped Gaines slip through the guards so she was grateful to it.

After being blessedly waved on by the guards, she took a deep breath and darted toward the car. In seconds her feet were soaked. Wet leaves stuck to her shoes. The driver, water sluicing off his slicker in sheets, helped her in. The leather upholstery smelled old and wet when she dropped back against it with a gasp.

How many more times would she ride in this limousine? she wondered as the car moved away from the curb in a purr of power. None, if she had her way about it. She wanted to leave Orban tonight. She was afraid for

Gaines, afraid for herself. She wanted them both to go home.

The limousine headlights probed through the sheeted gusts as the driver drove her through town. It was prematurely dark. Raindrops exploded on the windshield, and the wipers beat out a hypnotic rhythm: *clack, cl-clack, cl-clack*.

Her apartment was fifteen blocks from the embassy, the back three rooms of a very old house on a street lined with olive trees. The high wall surrounding it was badly in need of a new whitewash, as were many of the old places around. The courtyard was hopeless too, cracked and settling like an ancient old gentleman who was simply too tired to care any longer. But it was a respectable house. Many of the people in the neighborhood were members of the international diplomatic corps.

The limousine driver insisted on coming with her to the gate. April wished he wouldn't, but he stood drowning just inside the courtyard as she dashed up the flagged walk and ducked beneath the overhanging branch of an orange tree.

Turning, she waved.

He grinned through the flood, touched the bill of his cap and carted his bulk back to the car.

The door opened to April's touch. Though she expected it to, she still felt a prickle of apprehension. Gaines stepped out of the shadows and pushed the door shut. Sultan, her great striped cat, welcomed her with a purry stropping of her legs.

"Hello, pussycat," she said, smiling as she went willingly into Gaines's embrace. The prodigal son, she thought; lost and found. She hugged him with the nearest thing to elation she had felt all day.

Without saying anything, she stepped out of her wet

shoes and scooped Sultan up in her arms. Gaines was still wearing Bruce's loose trousers, and the bush jacket was unbuttoned. Its belt dangled from its loops, and his feet were bare. He kissed her, then pressed his mouth to her ear.

"Don't do anything to indicate that I'm here," he whispered, and placed his finger across her lips. "Someone has wired the place."

April leaned back in his arms, and Sultan leaped to the floor. "Wired? When?"

"Sometime after Bashir told Jassim you'd returned, I expect. A sloppy job but entirely effective."

She couldn't believe it. She moved past him into the wide, sparsely furnished living room, her stockinged feet whispering on the polished floors. Her three rooms were joined together by archways instead of doors. Richly embroidered hangings could be drawn together, and against the white walls they added a striking and ancient charm. But tonight they didn't afford much protection from hidden microphones.

She rotated in a circle. "Where?" she mimed.

Taking her hand, Gaines led her to the low divan with its Persian rug spread out before it. He pointed to the wooden frame. "Behind here."

Her brows went up.

He drew her to the kitchen and kicked a bare foot in the direction of the chrome grill at the base of the refrigerator.

She shrugged.

Taking her to the bedroom, which unlike the living room or the kitchen was delightfully cozy and feminine, he jabbed his thumb at her mattress.

April threw herself down across the bed and leaned her head over the side until her hair brushed the floor.

"Sultan," she exclaimed loudly, and peered underneath in a pretense of scrounging for the cat. "Come here, kitty, kitty, kitty. What d'you think you're doing? Come on, come on . . ."

She skimmed her fingertips along the frame of the bed, then exchanged a look with Gaines when she discovered it. A delicious malice darkened her pupils as she leaned even farther underneath the bed.

"Sultan, if you don't come out from under there . . ." She brought her hand down sharply upon the listening device and knocked it, clattering, to the floor.

Gaines immediately grabbed her. He pressed the laughter back into his chest; somewhere there was a man with a badly thrumming eardrum who was cursing a blue streak, but he shook his head in a warning to let the mike remain where it was.

"Jerks," she mumbled scathingly, and flung herself off the bed.

Gaines propelled her into the bathroom, a room almost as large as the bedroom and lined with gleaming white tile and appointed with antique brass. He pointed to the mirror that hung over the sink.

"Another one?"

He indicated the fluted gilt frame, then stepped to the shower and gave the spigots a twist. After a few grumbling complaints of the water pipes, a cloud of steam boiled out into the room. Between the rain pounding outside and the shower rushing on the inside, the small room roared like Niagara. They could at least whisper without worry of being overheard.

"Leave the microphones where they are," he said. "They can help us."

"How does he dare do that?" she fumed. "How—"

"He wants to catch you in the lie he suspects."

She stood on her tiptoes for a bright red towel and a bottle of shampoo. She placed them on the marble bench beside the shower and dropped down to sit. She remonstrated with him with her eyes.

"Why didn't you tell me you were working for the government?" she whispered, weakened by the truth all over again and tracing a line over his cheekbone with her finger. "Why did you let me find out that way?"

Gaines let his head thump back gently against the tile. His arm was throbbing. He pressed it against his ribs and closed his eyes. "I never dreamed it would come to this. I thought it would be just one time, and that you'd never have to worry."

"It cost us everything."

"By the time I knew that, the price had already been paid."

She placed her head near his. Gaines opened his eyes and brought his head down until their noses touched. His smile was weary, and his freshly shaved jaw seemed strange. They played a brief game of adoring and smiling.

"Jassim will crucify you," April said, and brushed back his hair.

"He'll have to find me first."

"Aren't you afraid?"

"Of course."

"Why are you doing this?"

He sighed. "I can't find a place to stop."

She supposed she understood that. Life was a circle sometimes, catching itself by the tail. "It's over now."

He only closed his eyes again, and her suspicions were too much a habit to let it go. She closed her fingers about his good arm and gave it a shake. "Gaines?"

He sat up. "I haven't finished the job I was sent to do, April. I have to find out some . . . things about American involvement here. Industrial things."

"Gaines, listen to me. I don't care about Marek. I

don't even care about this country, not really. I care about you, us. I want us to leave Orban. Tonight. We can walk out. Just leave, right in the rain. Please.''

Gaines let his eyes close. "I have to do this, April." I even think I've found a way to get us a way out. By boat. Tomorrow.''

"What about a plane?''

He shook his head at her naivety. "Sweetheart, Jassim would have you picked up for questioning the minute you walked into the airport. To say nothing of Bruce.''

"Tomorrow night then. We can leave.''

"If we're lucky.''

"You and Bruce and me?''

"Hopefully.''

Then it was done, April thought. It would all be over in a matter of hours. All over except for the worry. Now she understood why he hadn't told her what he was. A cruel form of mercy: ignorance.

She tested the water in the shower and reached behind her back for the zipper of her dress. "Don't give me any of the details,'' she said. "I don't want to hear.''

Gaines unzipped her dress and drew her back against his chest. His kiss found the side of her neck and his hands cupped her breasts.

"Oh, Gaines.'' She tipped her face up beneath his jaw. "I won't start whining. I promise. But don't lie to me anymore. Don't protect me. Don't spare me for my own good. Will you promise that?''

The bathroom was like a sauna, and they were both sweating. Gaines kissed the back of her head.

"I won't lie to you anymore.''

"Then I'd better get my shower before I grow mushrooms,'' she murmured, and stepped out of her dress.

She felt for the clasp of the pearls. Gaines released

them and let their length slither into the cup of his hand. The georgette dress was a filmy pool upon the floor. April unfastened the clip of her bra and dropped it. Bending, she drew off her pantyhose.

The ritual was so utterly devoid of coquetry, her nakedness so much a breath of artistry, that Gaines watched her without moving. He had many hundreds of memories stored in his mind, but none so precious as her at this moment: the disheveled hair and exhausted shoulders; the hollowed, weary back; the delicate cheeks that had, for lack of indulgent hours, dispensed with the bikini tan. He saw himself at fifty with age frosting his hair and lessening his own elasticity. He pictured how April would look then, and he knew she would be even more beautiful when age had touched her.

Without looking back, April caught the edge of the shower curtain and stepped behind it.

Gaines watched her silhouette for a moment, smiling grimly. He walked soundlessly through the house. He had told April the truth. Some of the information Wesley wanted, he already had. But there was the footage Bruce had filmed at the textile plant. It was a fuse to a very large keg of explosives. He hoped Bruce would be cooperative about putting it under lock and key. Discretion was the vital word here, as Wesley would say.

April was wearing a galabiya when she walked through the house, and Gaines was standing before a window facing the courtyard. He was watching the ritual of the lightning and the rain streaking the windows until he caught the whisper of her step.

Turning, seeing her, he felt a sharp, vivid sense of being cheated. It was unfair that mankind matured in such a backward process, that it never knew what it had until it was no longer there.

April walked to a sideboard near the windows and,

smiling, lit two candles in tall brass holders. She drew the drapes shut, and the room mellowed and grew warm—the storm outside and the promise within.

Gaines watched her turn on the stereo and flip through her albums to select one. The slim, shapeless dress—off-white with wide borders of old, loosely woven lace, unadorned with jewelry or even with shoes—made her look sixteen. She was such a collection of contradictions that he wanted to run to her, to smother her, to devour her so that nothing could ever come close to her but him.

The room suddenly felt too close. Despite her drawing of the drapes, he walked to a window that was sheltered from the storm and raised it. He was aware of her watching him.

She stooped as he turned, and her hips pressed against the cotton. He saw what he'd only guessed before; she was wearing nothing beneath the dress. He slowly let out his breath as she stood and bent and placed the stereo needle upon its vinyl groove. Over the sound of the rain and thunder outside, Ravel drifted through the room with evocative élan.

Gaines smiled. *Daphnis and Chloe* was a ballet they both knew well; they had seen it a number of times together, and, in their new house, they had even made love to it.

"Would you like something to drink before dinner?" she said.

He nodded and she padded quietly to the kitchen and fetched down two long-stemmed glasses. She filled the glasses half full of red wine and placed one in his hand.

"Do you know what's happening?" she said with a half-smile. "In the music?"

He listened. "Daphnis is dancing to win the contest. He is in ecstasy."

Her laughter was soft, lilting. "Treacherous male.

Letting the nymphs fawn all over him while Chloe, sitting there in a jealous stew, is forgotten.''

Gaines lifted his glass in a mock salute to Daphnis. "Every man's fantasy." He grinned. "Polygamy. Bliss of sheiks.''

"You're wicked.''

"I never said I wasn't.''

They smiled as poor jealous Chloe was brought by the music—hands bound—into the pirates' camp. She was their booty. She would be forced to dance for their drunken pleasure.

The look they exchanged was a knowing one, and April flushed. Chloe would dance, and in a moment Bryaxis, the pirate leader, would carry her away. The air would be full of lights and terror, like the storm outside.

"I know what you're thinking," Gaines teased her.

"I doubt that.''

"Every woman's fantasy. Treasures displayed. Men at her feet, lusting after her beauty, even to the death. In comes macho man, and he growls, 'You shall be mine tonight.' And he sweeps her up in his arms and carries her away to ravishment.''

She coquettishly tossed her head. "Pooh.''

Gaines laughed. "Seems I recall another woman who danced. On a strip of sandy beach, it was. She drove the poor man well-nigh out of his mind with her antics. Wore him down until he was only a broken shell of a man.''

April hid her smile by taking a sip of the wine. "If you don't be quiet . . . Are you sure they can't hear us talking over the microphones?''

"As long as you don't go near the divan.''

Her eyes twinkled, as if she knew exactly what she wanted and what she was doing. She lifted her glass. "To your health then, fair Daphnis.''

"And to yours, beautiful Chloe."

The musical score awakened Daphnis from his stupor where he had fallen in regret. Pan came to the rescue, and Daphnis found his Chloe and took her into his arms. Gaines leaned across April's shoulder and brushed a kiss across her cheek.

She blotted her lips against the light furring of curls on his chest. Slowly then, a whimsical sylph, she made a pirouette in the center of the room.

Gaines let his eyes warmly follow her moves. To whatever was going through her mind, he lifted his glass in salute. Her arms lifted in a *port de bras* that caught the glow of candlelight behind her. The outline of her body was a shadow, hardly there and as swiftly gone. Except upon the screen of his mind. He imagined her naked upon the thick rug that lay beside her bed.

She started to glide past him to the kitchen.

He set down his glass and caught her in a movement that sent pain stabbing through his arm. She turned. He lifted the glass from her fingers and placed it beside his.

"Forget dinner," he said thickly.

"Aren't you hungry?"

"Not for that."

She leaned back in his arms, her green eyes glistening and dark. "But your arm?"

His gaze moved over her, and his neck was hot and throbbing. "I daresay I can handle you with one."

"You'd better." Her taunt was low and husky. "Because I intend to fight."

A bright flash of lightning cracked through the room, and thunder followed immediately. The wind blew mist against the drapes and stirred the hangings that flanked the open archway.

Gaines threaded his fingers through April's hair and pulled it to tip back her head.

"Do your worst," he challenged and, laughing softly

over his pain, lifted her up and tossed her over his good shoulder.

The best part of it was, April thought in a daze as the uncontrollable cascade grew to its peak, that they were still in their clothes. Everything had been blindingly quick, telescoped from the moment that he had come to her at the embassy to now, when every second was too long a delay, every movement extraneous except the sensual thrust toward that human absorption with one's self, that incongruity of self-centered satisfaction. But shared. And shared. And shared.

It came quickly and violently to her. She clung to Gaines until she could breathe again, and she wanted to weep that it was good. But she was afraid to put a word to it for fear she would somehow lose it.

She wrapped her arms about his head until he relaxed against her, spent, exhausted, feeling the fresh pain in his arm until she, too, felt it.

"It's hurting you," she whispered. Daphnis and Chloe were finished, living happily ever after. His cheek was pressed to her breast, for he still lay upon her.

"The pain was worth it."

"No price too large?" She said it lightly, for she thought he felt it too—the dread of morning when they would face it as two different people because of what she had learned about him.

He grinned down at her. "No sacrifice too great."

She made him sit up, and she drew the galabiya down about her hips. "I really am hungry now."

"We might as well spare the time to eat. It'll take me a good ten minutes to recover."

Her laughter was high in her throat. She cuffed him on his clean-shaven jaw. "Follow me."

She made them a salad and fried a chop: only one chop, and a salad that was too small, for she hadn't shopped in days. Still a little hungry, they drank too much. They leaned back in the chairs around her tiny table and looked at each other for a long time. The storm was wearing itself out and so, too, this night.

"How do you feel?" she asked at length.

"Suspended," he said. "Waiting."

"Worried?"

"Perhaps a bit."

"For me? Us?"

"The future. What it'll be like now."

April placed her fingers on her mouth and looked away. He didn't know what it was like, did he? The waiting for him. What it cost her. The fact that he was bigger and she was smaller, he was older and she was younger, so he went and acted while she waited and prayed.

Feeling that if she didn't go to him now and put her arms around him she would have lost something that could never be retrieved, she rose to her feet. He was acutely attuned to her; they had once been able to nearly read each other's minds. Now she hoped that he could read her fear. Dear heaven, let him know how deep it went.

She wrapped her arms about him and drew his head to her breast. She stood there for a long time, listening to the wind and the rain and letting him feel her heartbeat beneath her breast. He didn't do anything foolish like pat her bottom or tweak her nipple. He simply let her hold him and stroke the back of his head, accepting her need to caress.

"Gaines?" she whispered.

"What, sweetheart?"

"Please don't die. Not now. Not when I've found you again. Please don't die."

He came to his feet and looked down at her for a

moment as if to say it was all right for her to be human and afraid. Then, leaving empty glasses on the table and mist collecting upon the windowsill and candles that sputtered in their holders, he took her to bed.

Gaines had hoped to leave April before she awoke. If Jassim had had her apartment wired, he had surely posted a surveillant outside the wall. The last thing he needed was to get caught trying to leave.

He turned carefully on the bed. April lay with her face nearly buried in the pillow. Her fingers were curled against her cheek like a little girl. He didn't dare touch her for fear she'd waken. He'd been so selfish, loving her for most of the night, kissing her for hours.

The pain in his arm was worse, but he dressed himself. He had just finished in the bathroom and was tying the sling about his neck when he heard April's light footsteps on the bare floor.

She turned on the radio on her bureau. The music was mixed with static left over from the storm. She came to stand before him with reproachful eyes.

"You were going to leave, weren't you?"

"I didn't want to wake you."

She turned down her mouth. "Your courtesy is commendable, Gaines."

"The truth is, I have to get out of here before daylight. I suspect we have friends waiting outside the wall."

Sometime during the night April had changed into a filmy gown of apricot silk. Its tie caught just below her breasts, and its length swished about her feet as she disappeared into the bathroom. In a moment she reappeared, sleep washed from her face, her hair brushed.

Gaines was putting Bruce's identification papers into his pockets along with his wallet, his coins. He drew on his wristwatch and tightened the belt of the bush jacket.

Bending his knees before her mirror, he ran her comb through his hair. He saw her walking back and forth on the rug.

"You okay?" he asked.

Her smile was a failure. "Sure."

Grimacing, he slipped his injured arm into the sling.

April perched one hip upon the dressing table and watched his simple toilette. "Why don't you let me help you with this?" she suggested.

He chuckled. "It's not my apartment they wired. No, I'll do my thing, and then I'll meet you."

"Not at the embassy."

"You know the city better than I do. Name a place."

April thought for a moment, then walked to her bureau for a paper and pen. She wrote down the address of a café. "This place is crowded most all the time. It's off the capitol square about three blocks. What do you think?"

Memorizing the address, Gaines folded the paper and tore it into several pieces. "You can do one thing for me," he said.

"Anything."

"When you see Bruce this morning at the embassy, tell him I've got to see him. He's going to balk at leaving, but maybe hearing your apartment was wired will convince him. I'll give him back his ID, and I should have the particulars about a boat."

She nodded. Her heart felt as if it would burst.

He switched off the bathroom light and walked to the bedroom window. Unable to stop herself, she hurried after him. She touched his back. He paused.

"I know I said I wouldn't interfere," she whispered, keeping her head down, "but . . . stay here. We'll get you some new clothes and have Bashir find you a passport. Then we can—"

He bent down to interrupt her with a quick, hard kiss. "I've got to go, love."

"Let me make you some coffee."

"I don't have time."

Her smile was the most difficult of her life. "Then, I guess this is it."

Gaines hid his depression behind a thin smile. "At the café. At noon." His fingertips hovered above her knuckles, mothlike, dreading.

She looked at the floor. "Noon."

"And you're not going to worry."

Her nails were cutting half-moons into her palms. She shook her head. "I won't worry."

The storm was over. Outside everything was fresh and wet; rich darkness, no moon, no stars. Gaines picked up Bruce's brass-handled stick.

"Kiss me then," he said lightly.

Her fists were rigid by her sides. She didn't want to kiss him. She wanted to punish him, to scream out in her rage. She obediently lifted her lips.

"I love you," he whispered.

He hesitated a moment before he swung his foot over the windowsill. April watched him climb the orange tree. He made it to the top without breaking any branches; then he disappeared over the wall. It had taken him less than two minutes, and even with his injury and Bruce's stick he'd hardly made a sound.

She did reach her pillow before the tears broke down the dam. Burying her face so the microphones wouldn't pick up her weeping, she cried for all the times she had misunderstood Gaines. And then she cried because this time she did understand, and she wished she didn't.

April arrived early at the café. The morning had been unbearably trying. Bruce had left the embassy after

Jassim's guards had changed, but not before he and April had a terrible argument over the film he had shot at the textile plant. He did agree to leave Orban, but he vowed he would not turn over his film. He wanted his passport and his stick back as soon as possible. He said he would meet Gaines at the café if he could.

Bashir returned to the embassy with the report that Bruce had left his hotel with Cynthia and Phillip. The three of them had gotten into a taxi together. He thought they were going to Amalgamated Textiles.

Furious, April had been unable to work. In a fit of nerves, she finally canceled her last appointment and called for the limousine.

She had the driver drop her off at another café several blocks away from their meeting place. There she went to great lengths in placing her order with the waiter. As soon as he left she went to the ladies' room. After slipping out the back way, she walked the five or six blocks to this café.

The table she selected was deliberately near the back and close to the bar. The music and service of this café catered to Anglos. It offered a somewhat limited view of the street, which would have been, except for the storm the night before, dusty and unbearably hot.

Today traffic was worse because the day was beautiful. More women's faces decorated the café than usual. Men in European suits crowded around the bar and watched the women, some of whom were dressed in the latest fashions, some in long black skirts and exquisite handmade veils.

April felt underdressed in her slacks and muted beige blouse. She sat listening to the Beatles and stared at the glistening jars of olives and the sparkling wine bottles behind the bar.

Bruce came after all. Smiling with relief, April waited as he passed through the crowd at the entrance and spoke to a waiter. The waiter directed him to her table. Watching him stride toward her, no trace of a limp, April's face fell. He looked ghastly.

He fell into his chair, out of breath, as if he'd been running. He fished for his pipe. "Is it all right if I smoke in here?" he said on a rushed breath.

"What's wrong?"

His hands shook as he filled his pipe. "What d'you mean, what's wrong?"

"Well, look at you. You're shaking all over." April had a horrendous thought. Her hand came down hard upon his, almost sending the pipe skittering across the table. "It's Gaines."

"No, no." Bruce let out his breath and left his pipe unlit. "It's . . . oh, damn it, April, some crazed arsonist set the textile plant afire. It's a bad one. Cynthia went up as close as she could get. She said they're blaming me for it."

April lowered her head. What next?

"That's not all."

Her head came up. "What?"

"I think there's a warrant out for my arrest. Or whatever they call it in this damned country. God, where is Gaines? I want to get out of this place."

In the face of all that had happened to him this morning, April didn't have the heart to remind Bruce that he'd brought it all on himself, that Gaines had warned him over and over. Bruce was an intelligent man; he knew what he'd done. Glancing about, then at her wristwatch, she motioned to the waiter. While Bruce lit his pipe, she ordered coffee. They both waited, nervously glancing from their hands to the door, back to each other.

It was one o'clock when Gaines entered the café. April guessed that he'd already spotted them, for his eyes flicked coolly to hers, then away. He found a place at the bar and ordered a drink. He slouched on a stool for about ten minutes, until April felt hair rising on the back of her neck. Did Gaines think he was being followed? Or that she was? He must have heard about the textile plant.

Presently Gaines made one last reconnoiter of the café and tossed down the last of his drink. He walked toward the table with a jaunty stroll, using Bruce's stick and the sling to advantage. Dressed as he was in the slacks and bush jacket, if he'd had a pince-nez he would have looked like a British army officer on leave from Burma.

Bruce took one look at him and groaned. "Oh, God."

"Well, old chap," Gaines said as he flamboyantly swept out a chair. "I heard you've been very busy this morning."

"You know."

Gaines smiled, but April guessed that beneath the blasé exterior he was stretched like a wire. "My dear fellow, the whole city knows."

Bruce colored. "Well, sit down, old stick, and don't rub it in."

"Have you ordered?"

April shook her head. "We waited for you, General." Gaines laughed.

They gave their order for lamb, which in al-Qunay was prepared with a simple seasoning of cumin and other herbs. It came served on a small mountain of rice. The salad wasn't quite so exotic and was floating in dressing. April managed to get it down between bites of black bread and butter, along with the usual goat cheese. Dishes of yoghurt followed after that, and fresh oranges along with their coffee.

It was while Gaines was negotiating with the waiter for the check that April glimpsed the uniformed guards enter from the street. Her fingers gripped Gaines's wrist with such violence that even Bruce lifted his head.

Gaines took one look at the front of the noisy restaurant and twisted back around. Without betraying any alarm, he said quietly, "Bruce, don't turn around." He nodded briskly to the waiter. In Arabic he told him to bring the check as quickly as possible.

When Gaines slowly met April's eyes it was with a look she had seen before. The mask: unemotional, calculated, a stranger's. April saw, from a swift sidelong glance, that the guard was elbowing his way through the crowd. He was the same man who had stood arguing with them in the rain.

Gaines placed his napkin beneath the edge of his plate. "Bruce, I want you to get up and very quietly walk to the back of the café and leave."

Bruce was breathing hard. His danger was as clear to him as if it were painted on the walls of the building. He shook his head. "Perhaps he'll leave."

"He won't leave. He's looking for you right now."

Fear blanched the tan on Bruce's face. He knocked the dottle from his pipe, and his hands were shaking when he slipped the pipe into his pocket. The guard was speaking with the proprietor now, leaning over the bar. His companion was wandering through the array of tables, unobtrusively studying the diners.

"No," Bruce said. "This is my doing, Gaines. I won't leave."

A muscle knotted in Gaines's jaw. "Don't argue with me, damn it. You too, April, get up and leave. Do as I say."

When the proprietor's arm came up and extended to point out Gaines to the guard, April suddenly felt very old, very useless. She also saw in the proprietor's brief gesture the reference to Gaines's sling. The guard from Chemistry II stepped away from the bar and looked straight into her eyes.

"I can't leave," she said under her breath. "He's seen me."

What passed between the two brothers was one of those wordless exchanges that could never be described. April didn't think she would ever forget the battle Bruce had with his pride. She thought, in that moment, that he implored his younger brother for forgiveness but was, in his inadequacy, grateful for a way out. Gaines had identification on him that said he was Bruce. He was dressed in Bruce's clothes. He carried his stick. Gaines knew—the irrefutable bottom line—how to handle himself in a situation that Bruce had absolutely no equipment to cope with.

The decision was made in the lowering of an eyelid. In that singular, irrational moment April hated Bruce. How could he do it? But hatred was wasted, for the guard was almost upon them.

"Go," Gaines said quietly.

With the turn of a shoulder, as if he wanted to say something to the waiter, Bruce rose from his chair. And in that same fateful moment, Gaines turned his profile so that the guard could not miss it.

April felt life slipping away from her.

"Mr. Southerland?" came the guard's voice. "Mr. Bruce Southerland?"

Please no! she implored Gaines with a look. No!

But Gaines turned and gave the guard a cold smile. "Yes?"

The guard motioned to his companion. The second uniformed man came to stand by the table. They both recognized April and they politely inclined their heads.

April's heart missed a beat. Her eyes sought Gaines, but he was once again that strange man she did not know.

A hush fell upon the people who sat nearest. As if a tray had been dropped, heads began turning to see the cause of the lull. It spread like an epidemic, and soon everyone was watching.

The second guard touched his pistol in its scabbard. "Everyone remain seated," he ordered. "No one will be hurt. Please remain calm."

A foolish grin turned up one side of Gaines's mouth. "Were you speaking to me?" he drawled, and slowly came out of the chair.

"We'd like to see some identification please, Mr. Southerland."

Gaines glanced around himself, letting his eyes lightly graze the top of April's head. He tossed a laugh at one of the women sitting at the bar.

"Excuse me, dear," he said, "but I think you shouldn't be standing so close behind me. Confidentially, I don't know how good a shot this man is. If he tries to shoot me down while I'm getting my papers . . ."

Snickering flitted along the bar, and the guard's surly scowl darkened. "Stay where you are," he ordered. "I'll get the papers."

As Gaines stood still, smiling and making eye contact with the woman, the guard nodded for his companion from Chemistry II to frisk him. The process drew a few uncomplimentary remarks from Gaines. He fished out a passport from one of the pockets and handed it over. From where he stood he glimpsed Bruce hurrying across the street outside, his search for a taxi.

April had never wanted to attack another person so badly as she did the guard. She placed her coffee cup down in its saucer, and it clattered so loudly that the guard leveled his black eyes upon her.

She gave him a sick smile.

The guard from Chemistry II studied Bruce's picture and narrowed his eyes at Gaines. He noted the same loss of weight as before. "Let me see something else."

The guards considered the identification and were

obviously satisfied with it. "Mr. Bruce Southerland," he said, "you are under arrest."

"No!" blurted April.

"May I ask the charge?" Gaines said in a monotone.

"Come with us, please."

"I want to call the American embassy," Gaines protested loudly. "You tell me the charge of the arrest."

"Come with us, please."

"Where're you taking me?"

Slowly April followed the two guards and Gaines to the door. Gaines was playing the role of a frightened man. She realized that he was feeding information to her as best he could. Gaines leaned toward the bar and spoke to the proprietor.

"You saw what happened," he said as if panic-struck. "They just walked in here and started threatening."

The proprietor shrugged in dismay. The second guard, growing exasperated now with a jabbering American man who was making them look bad, brought the side of his hand down upon the wounded arm.

Gaines went white from the pain. "I demand to talk to my embassy!" he yelled. "You're not taking me to the Colony until I've talked to the embassy. And I demand to see a doctor. I'm being arrested on false charges. I demand an attorney!"

As if she were another person, April turned to the nearest man at the bar. He was older—a European, she thought—intelligent, obviously appalled at such crass behavior.

"The man's asking for a doctor," she said. "What's so unreasonable about that?" She turned to the guard. "You know me. I'm the chargé d'affaires at the embassy. I request that you tell us the charges."

The guard was chagrined. "Madame, it is arson. We have to take him in."

"See how easily it's done?" Gaines said to the same man April had spoken to. "Arson, they say. And don't ask any questions. Where're you taking me?"

The second guard turned on him. "You don't hear very well, do you? I said, shut your mouth. You'll see a doctor at the Colony and not before. And you, lady, sit down."

The babbling American was suddenly transformed into a quiet and dangerous man; he had gotten the answer he wanted, and in a voice of deadly calm, he said to the guard, "Leave her alone."

Across her head Gaines exchanged a glance with the older man. The man's nod was almost imperceptible as he placed his hand upon April's arm.

"Madame," he said quietly. "There is nothing you can do. Please. There is nothing."

Knowing that, yet hearing the sound of the guards snapping iron about Gaines's wrists, April wanted to die. If the older man hadn't forcibly pulled her away she would have gotten herself arrested as well.

"They are taking him to the Colony," he said, holding her so that she was partially shielded from the sight of Gaines being escorted out the door. "Perhaps there is something you can do."

She looked at the man as if she had never seen him before. Without a word, she picked up her purse and Bruce's stick. She walked out under the bright sun burning in the clear, azure sky. She didn't see people and she didn't see the traffic. She walked what seemed to her no distance at all. But it was, in fact, many blocks.

She waited for five hours in the House of State. Using her status at the embassy, she talked to four different officials. She was refused permission to see the man arrested as Bruce Southerland. The only thing that she knew at the end of those five hours was that the prisoner had been taken to the Colony after his arrest. She would have to wait until the following day, and even then she would have to obtain special permission from the office of Commandant Jassim to be allowed in.

Bashir had the limousine from the embassy waiting for her when she finally accepted defeat and walked down the steps to the street.

Chapter 10

ON THE DESK SAT AN UNTOUCHED TRAY OF FOOD. IT was visible in the shadowed light that spilled from the embassy hall. From the open window a wet breeze moved the drape. The air was clean and rinsed, and the only sounds were those gentler ones of the night—occasional traffic and water sluicing down the spouts from a tagalong cloud left from the storm.

April lay on the settee, her arm over her eyes. Her weeping was over; there were no more tears left. She was empty, scooped out with the keen scalpel of circumstance.

Pausing at the open doorway, entering with a silent tread, Bruce came to stand over her. His desire to help was rough in his voice for he blamed himself for everything. "April?"

She lowered her arm but didn't open her eyes. "I'm awake. What time is it?"

"Eleven."

Sighing, April tried to quell the tremors that ran through her legs. She stood up and smoothed haphazardly at her slacks and retucked her blouse. She must look terrible. She felt terrible.

Bruce drew out one of the chairs beside the settee and lowered himself down into it. They stared at each other briefly, and she finally took the chair opposite him and pulled her legs up tightly in a knot.

"I was told that Ali Jassim was the only one who could authorize me to get into the Colony," she said on a sigh. "They told me to come back tomorrow. I've been lying here, thinking. I don't think we should wait that long."

Rising, Bruce walked to the cabinet where the liquor was kept. He removed the same bottle of vodka that April had offered to Jassim. He poured some into a glass and tossed it down with a sharp intake of air. "Would money help? I will do anything."

April bent her head, pressed her eyes. She had talked with Bashir about the possibility of bribing someone at the Colony. At that moment, the shrewd little man was scurrying about the city, doing whatever mysterious things it was that he did.

"Could you get it?" she asked flatly. "Now? I mean tonight?"

"If it will help, I'll try."

"Ali Jassim is a radical, Bruce, with a terrible history of violence. But he's growing older. He took Nahrhim's office, but he wants the continued support of his revolutionaries. Still, he's not a stupid man. He knows he needs American money."

As Bruce considered, April moved to the window, pulled the drape aside. Through the wet panes the lights of al-Qunay ran together like watercolors. She touched the place at her throat where her pearls usually lay.

"How much?" he said.

With eyes that said she would do anything, ask anything, April gazed up at him. "Two hundred thousand dollars?"

Bruce wasn't able to come up with two hundred thousand cash in the middle of the night, but he got security for it. After a hectic hour on the telephone he reentered April's office. Bashir had also come through. He had talked to people who knew people who knew people who knew people. The guards who controlled the entry and departure at the Colony were incorruptible, he said, but there were men on the inside who were less so. If April could get into the compound itself, there was a chance.

Placing an envelope into April's hands, Bruce looked at the woman who had once married his brother. She was different from the hollow-eyed grieving girl of an hour earlier. She had changed clothes and made up her face. She was beautiful and unsmilingly determined. He glanced at his watch. He, too, felt renewed and edgy with determination.

"Bashir says that you're expected at the Colony," he told her, and folded her hands about the envelope. "This will speak their language."

April peered down into the envelope, looked up and smiled. "Well, I guess I'd better go then."

For a moment Bruce considered the danger of what she was doing. Then he took her into his arms and held her close. "Gaines is very lucky," he said into her hair.

From the door came Bashir's discreet knock. He was no longer wearing European clothes. He wore the galabiya of the natives. "The car is ready, madame."

Bruce pressed her hands together and kissed April lightly upon her cheek. "Good luck."

"He'll be all right," April reassured him, and prayed

harder than she'd ever prayed in her life that she was right.

April insisted on going into the House of State alone. Bashir waited in the embassy limousine while she spoke to the guards at the entrance. Once inside, the guards detained April for some minutes. They couldn't remember a visitor from the American embassy ever coming to the House of State at two o'clock in the morning.

"It is an emergency," April explained, and politely but firmly refused to say more.

The guards looked at her black silk dress and expensive black shoes. They saw the luster of her pearls and her green determined eyes. They exchanged uncertain glances.

"Wait here, madame," she was told. She was deposited in a reception room.

April sat very straight and laced her hands together as she waited. She tried not to think about what Gaines was doing at that moment. She tried not to picture what would happen if she couldn't get him out. Stop it! she screamed inside her head. Just . . . stop it!

In several minutes one of the guards returned. "Will madame please come with me?"

He did not say if Jassim would see her or not. April was careful not to look at him. He led her past a group of offices, down a long tiled corridor, past another length of official rooms to an elevator. They ascended three floors. He guided her down another long hallway—quiet, carpeted, wallpapered and discreetly lit, a crimson runner skimming down the center of it. Plants were potted in strategic areas. There were several lovely antique tables with silver bowls.

"One moment, please."

She took the chair he indicated and waited for him to

use the telephone. Before he returned the telephone to its cradle, a door opened some distance down the hall.

Another uniformed guard stepped out into the hall and turned to look. "Madame Southerland?"

Her heart was in her throat. She came tremblingly to her feet. "Yes?"

"This way, please."

The suite, when April was escorted into it, gave the impression of being luxurious: dark with shadows, lavishly spacious. Somehow she didn't connect physical opulence with Ali Jassim, and then it dawned on her that these had been the living quarters of the assassinated President Nahrhim.

A gilt mirror was in the small entrance, and umbrellas hanging from a tree. She looked at herself in the subdued light, at her paleness, her apprehension. The door clicked shut behind her.

She stood shaking in the foyer until she heard the deep velvety roughness of his voice.

"Madame, please enter."

The large room was in deep shadows. At first April thought Ali Jassim wasn't there. Then she saw him standing before a window that faced the street. He was peering down at the movement below. April received impressions of steel-framed posters and lots of glass and wood surfaces, hallways veering off to the right and left. She wondered if she would be photographed. Or recorded.

Her fingertips turned icy when Jassim turned from the window. She tried to feel for her tongue, but it was heavy and glued to the roof of her mouth.

"So," he said, not walking to her or inviting her to sit, "you have exhausted your resources. You have done all you can do."

"Yes," she said in a low voice.

"And you have turned to me."

"Was I wrong?"

She thought he paused to chuckle to himself, but she could not be sure of that. "You once told me that you would never beg, madame."

He would know everything by now, of course. He probably had a complete dossier on Gaines. Pretensions would not only be futile, they could ruin any breath of a chance she had with him.

"I once said a lot of things," she admitted meekly.

The violence in him was more tangible than ever. Clear across the room she felt it, pulsing just beneath his surface control. She let her intentions slither to the floor as a woman drops a garment.

"I'm sorry it's so late," she said. "I suppose you know—"

His words cut like a razor. "I know who he is, madame. I know everything. You lied to me."

His hand passed in front of his face then, as if he were willing himself to cordiality. He shifted his weight to one foot. "I had not retired. There is not much sleep in this business."

Not saying more for fear of saying the wrong thing, April stood very still. Somewhere she heard a clock chime half past the hour of two.

He moved toward a liquor cabinet and poured two glasses of some colorless liquid. Without asking her if she wanted any, he walked to where she stood and placed it into her hand. He leaned back upon a chair covered in fine morocco leather.

"Thank you," she whispered.

He lifted his glass and gave her a wry smile. "To success, madame."

April lifted her glass and heard their clink. She looked up at him over the rim of the glass. He was still in uniform, though she guessed when he stepped nearer that he had been trying to sleep. His weariness clawed its way down his face and into the creases beside his eyes.

Suddenly she lowered the glass and, walking quickly, replaced it on the cabinet. Her plans to seduce Gaines's life from Ali Jassim seemed a folly. The hopelessness of it knocked the breath from her.

"Sir . . ." She couldn't keep her head up, and her hair fell about her face. She couldn't cry in front of him, she swore to herself. Not tears.

Ali Jassim looked at her drooping shoulders and knew that he had found the vulnerable spot in her at last: an American, an agent, a man whom he would like to turn his back on and leave to fate. And a man, though he had never seen his face, whom he was envious of.

He took the necessary steps that brought him behind her. He set down his glass. "Why did you really come, April Southerland? To bargain for his life? To buy it?"

There was a heavy despair in her voice. "What would it take? If I can, I will pay it."

The big hands came down upon her shoulders, turned her, clasped her face and forced it up beneath his own. "You really do beg me, April Southerland?"

The fear was thrumming in her skull, turning her bones to liquid. She was almost standing on tiptoe, he had forced her head up so, and she had images of herself in Jassim's bed, his mouth upon hers, his body moving upon hers, for even in her fear she knew that he desired her enough to do it.

"Yes," she said on a dwindling breath.

Mockery was in his eyes as he raked them over her face. His palm relented its harshness and slid down the side of her neck. He did not lose control enough to actually touch her breast, but she knew that he wanted to. She saw the hard discipline in his jaw, in his temples.

"You disappoint me, madame." He slurred his words. "I once thought I saw steel in your eyes."

She wanted to slap his face for that. "When you saw that, Commandant, I was the only one you could kill!"

She knew, the moment the words were out, that they were a mistake. The lapse of his control was in the curl of his lips. His arms were like iron about her, pulling her to him. There was the hot urge to struggle, the impulse to fight and scratch and kick, but April forced herself to be docile.

His breath was rougher than normal when he stared down at her. "Perhaps in another lifetime, I would be in his place, waiting for you to save me."

His power was a drug. "Perhaps."

It was a bizarre interlude—masks down, understandings primitive—Jassim, wondering how this quiet American woman had affected him so and knowing that he would never forget her; April, realizing that her acceptance of his passion would be honored and that he had probably never let anyone see this part of him, ever.

"And then," he said very softly, "perhaps I would be happy."

He released her abruptly and April had to catch herself to keep from stumbling. He turned hard on his heel and walked to a lamp and turned it on. The moment of intimacy was dispelled with the light. He pulled out a chair and sat.

April heard her own breaths as she watched him write on a piece of formal letterhead stationery. She couldn't read what he wrote, and he didn't read it to her. He folded it and placed it in an envelope.

"This will get you in to see him," he said as he came to his feet. "I want you to know that I am not unaware of what I am doing. I know everything about this American. I know his name; I know his past."

"Then you know my past."

"As much as I want to know. I cannot authorize his release, madame. You must surely realize that. I am controlling this government with the most fragile of reins.''

Without considering the audacity of giving him her back, April walked to the window. She ran her fingers over the heavy brocade of the drapes.

Ali Jassim moved up behind her. In an act of easy familiarity he unclasped her bag and placed the envelope inside and snapped it closed again. He looked down at her for some time, and April guessed that it would be the last time she would see him.

''If Gaines Southerland can get out of the Colony,'' he said, his voice thick in his chest, ''I will not interfere. It is the best I can do.''

Tears stung her eyes. There was an impulse to touch him, but she knew he wouldn't want it.

''Thank you, Ali Jassim,'' she said. ''Perhaps in another lifetime.''

His hand came to his mouth, and he coughed lightly. He averted his head enough that she could not see him clearly and, with a curtness, said, ''Now, you really must excuse me, madame. I am very tired.''

He walked her to the door and waited until she collected herself enough to pass in front of him. She moved out into the entry and groped in her mind for something to say, but she didn't know what it would be. ''Thank you'' was not something he would want from her.

So she hesitated at the door for one brief moment. Then, forcing herself not to look back, she lifted her head and made her way past the guard and down the carpet runner to the elevator. She knew that his door had not shut. She guessed that he was watching her go.

The Colony was not a real prison. Until the late fifties it had been the capitol building of Orban. However, with the arrival of modern al-Qunay and the dream of becoming a viable political entity, a new capitol had been built that would blend more with the steel and glass of the skyscrapers.

The streets surrounding the Colony had kept their attractive little shops and restaurants and hotels, and though a wall had gone around the old capitol building, it still looked quite innocent sitting there. Strangers to the city might think it was a convent, or a wealthy eccentric's home. It was anything but; it was a human dump for people that the state didn't know what to do with— political prisoners, primarily. Most of President Nahrhim's deposed government were residents of the Colony. It was six blocks from the House of State, where Ali Jassim had temporary living quarters.

It was at the Colony that April's hope finally reached its limits. All the way through the complicated checkpoints she kept Gaines foremost in her mind. That strengthened her walk beside the thick-chested guards. It kept her chin erect and her eyes valiantly ahead. She had come to this place with safe passage from Ali Jassim, the highest authority in the land, plus Bruce's bribe, which washed any number of sins. It was nearly over, she told herself repeatedly. Gaines would soon be released.

At the final checkpoint the guard read Jassim's memo and looked her up and down as if he suspected her of forging it. He didn't speak. He waved her escort away and jerked his head for her to come with him.

She followed him through an underground tunnel whose floor and walls and ceiling were a threatening gray. The sound of their footsteps echoed down the cement shaft like doors closing upon reality. She stared at the guard's holstered gun. If she never saw the outside world again, who could prove anything, one way or another? A knot of fear tightened in her chest.

She followed the guard to a metal door, also gray. His keys rattled as he searched through them. He inserted one into a slot. Without looking at her, he thrust his left hand out, palm up.

"The money, please," he demanded, as one would say, "Pass the salt."

Trembling, she placed Bruce's envelope into his hand. She wasn't surprised when he didn't look at it. He knew exactly what it was, what his share would be.

"Follow me," he said.

The heavy door slid into the wall. Past the opening was a space the size of a large gymnasium. Hundreds of men sat about on the floor in various states of semidress, some bandaged, their heads resting in their hands. Some slept, and some were obviously ill. They were buried alive. It smelled bad. A half dozen guards wandered among them, all heavily armed.

April shuddered, her eyes searching in panic for Gaines. But he was not in this place. The guard led her along the outer perimeter, past another door and into another corridor, not so long this time. There he motioned for her to stay as he spoke to another guard.

The envelope with the money changed hands. Then, without a word, her guide left her and walked back in the direction he had come.

The remaining guard shrugged at her. "Outside."

She tipped her head at him. "Outside? You mean out of the building? Out of the Colony?"

"You cannot remain here."

He led her to a door. Keys rattled again. The bolt of the lock shot open and he jabbed his thumb at the darkness.

Beyond the exterior walls of the building was a cement alley. At the extremity of that was the brick wall that surrounded the Colony with its deadly strands of wire strung across the top. The only exit through the fence was a pair of iron gates that were chained together in the center. He surely didn't mean to leave her there alone!

"Go," he said, and shut the door in her face.

She stumbled out into the night and crouched against the outer wall of the Colony.

She waited for an hour. Every fear magnified itself. Every horror assumed gigantic proportions. Finally despairing, realizing she had been duped, that Bruce's money had been taken and she would undoubtedly be dragged back before Ali Jassim as a militant against the country, she covered her face. Her back raked against the wall and she rose slowly to her feet.

Alone, cold, deserted: that is where her hope died. When, long moments later, she lifted her head from her hands, seeing Gaines materialize was like viewing a mirage. At first she didn't believe her own eyes. She blinked, balanced herself and willed her legs to support her.

Two figures, Gaines and a guard, were moving soundlessly along the back of the building, keeping in the shadows. Gaines was handcuffed, and he still wore Bruce's clothes. He—or someone—had discarded the sling, and his injured arm pressed against his side.

April started walking, hesitantly at first. And then her breaths were coming in rapid little gasps. Her feet seemed to sprout wings. She flew to him and flung her arms about him.

"Oh, Gaines!" she whispered, holding on, weeping quietly. "Oh, Gaines."

Gaines embraced her as much as his bonds would allow. He pressed his face into her hair, caressing her forehead and her ear with his lips and murmuring, "It's all right, darling. Everything's going to be all right now."

He gently detached himself. "Get these things off me," he said to the guard.

The uniformed man glanced around them. He unlocked the cuffs and slipped them into a pocket. "I will unchain the gate and leave," he said. "You must go through, and I'll come back and lock it."

The instant the cuffs came off, Gaines drew April to his side and kissed the salty tears. He pushed back her hair and raked his eyes over her. "It's okay now."

"Every bad thing, I thought it."

"I'm sorry. There was another interrogation."

"Did they hurt you?"

Some unidentifiable emotion passed through his eyes: lethal, deadly. "Not where it shows."

The guard was impatient to leave. "Time is important."

April clutched Gaines's hand tenaciously as the guard walked to the gate. He looked up and down the street, pretended to inspect the chain, then shook it. Swiftly unlocking it, he gave the impression that he had satisfied himself. He moved on.

For the next minutes, Gaines and April waited. They looked at each other. April pressed his fingers, her love an ache that had no beginning and no end.

Gaines drew her close into his side. "Once we step out, April, keep near the wall. If there's trouble, don't stop for anything." He smiled, and nothing existed for her except the knowledge that he was there.

"Tell me you love me," he said.

"I want to 'have love' with you," she said over the knot in her throat.

His embrace took her breath away. Then he said, "Keep close." His body was taut, like a wound spring. "Ready?"

Lips numbly compressed, she nodded.

Gaines moved across the cement alley and flattened himself against the inside of the wall. He made another survey of the street. There was little traffic. The side-walks were deserted. Only two hours of darkness remained.

He motioned for April to come beside him. She did. The gates were open only enough for a person to duck and slip through.

"I'll go first," he said. "Give me a few seconds. If nothing happens, you follow."

April's heart was beating like a trip-hammer. She watched Gaines turn sideways and slip through the opening. Every nerve in her body was prepared for a shot to ring out. After several seconds she began to breathe again. Then she lowered her head and slipped through the gates. The heels of her shoes clicked lightly upon the cement.

Once outside the Colony, Gaines grabbed April's hand and held it tightly. They didn't run but moved swiftly alongside the wall.

The car seemed to come from out of nowhere. From a side street April saw it. It was a dark-colored car. It didn't have its lights on.

"Gaines?" Whimpering, she pulled back on his hand.

The door to the limousine swung open. Bashir poked his head out the window on the passenger side. Time seemed to stand still as he squinted through his glasses.

"Madame," he said happily, "it is nearly four o'clock."

In those first few moments of slumping back against the familiar leather of the limousine, April didn't know what she felt. She let her eyes close as Gaines crushed her in his arms. She was aware of him catching his breath, and she held on until the shivers finally subsided enough for her to talk.

"I can't take any more, Gaines," she whispered into

the front of Bruce's bush jacket. "I love you and I just can't."

Gaines knew she couldn't. He had never wanted her to take this much. He spoke over her head to Bashir.

"Take us to the embassy," he said. "We'll pick up Bruce. It's over."

Chapter 11

But of course it wasn't over.

By the time April and Bruce returned to the United States, that particular truth had etched itself into her mind like a bath of acid. Gaines remained behind: Bruce's film to be retrieved, the added complication of the fire at Amalgamated Textiles, a few more loose ends for Wesley, life changing by accident.

Love was an accident, she thought; it was left monstrously to fate. She wasn't inclined to be generous with her love. She didn't want to look back and say, "At least I had that much of Gaines. Better to have loved and lost than never have loved at all." She wanted it in her hands—all of it, greedily. She wanted Gaines to come home.

High above her worry was one sustaining strength: Robert Humphries. Her father showed his concern in such quiet, unobtrusive ways when she returned—having her car serviced and putting fresh linens on her bed and asking why she didn't move in with him until Gaines came back.

While she lowered her eyes and protested that it could be weeks, inside she hoped desperately that he would insist. He did insist, and when Benson Paletto called to see if she would come back to work, Robert tactfully suggested that she take a rest and organize his cupboards instead. She repapered them all and shampooed the carpets and cleaned the windows and sent the draperies to the cleaners.

Wesley Durant, as it turned out, was like a clergyman seeking a new convert. Now that she knew about Gaines, he spoke with her almost every day. She imagined men like Wesley taking a course: How to Deal with the Beloved of the Agent. He didn't realize, of course, that he only added insult to injury, saying he wanted her to be happy while doing everything he could to deprive her of the one thing that would make her happy.

She appeased him in her best John Strakes voice, "I do appreciate your concern, Mr. Durant." And added the lie, "I'm sure things will work out for everyone."

Bruce called every day. "When everything settles down," he told her in an effort to give her a fresh sense of purpose, "I have a job offer for you."

She explained as politely as she could that she had had one already.

"You can do that anytime. Come with me to Central America. Do some translating, help me with the script. You'll love it."

"Work for you?" She laughed. "No way."

"That thing in Orban? Forget it."

Bruce's ability to forgive himself was beyond belief. She said, "Well, I might, but I doubt that Ali Jassim will."

"You know what he did, don't you?"

Jassim? April gripped herself in a moment of silence. "I'm afraid to ask."

"He returned John Strakes's body. It just came over the wire this morning. And he's releasing some of the political prisoners. Isn't that a shocker?"

No, she thought some days later on a biting October morning. She leaned back in her chair at the breakfast table and absently stirred artificial sweetener into her coffee. Jassim's release of the prisoners didn't surprise her. But what of Gaines? Did Jassim know Gaines was still in the country? Would he continue to turn a deaf ear and a blind eye? For her?

The jangle of the telephone at her elbow made her start. Bruce, she thought with a wry shake of her head; it was his time of day.

"Take a hold of yourself, sweetie," his voice cheerfully boomed when she answered. "I called you with good news."

"I can use it. I feel terrible today."

"Mother wants to see you."

Ah, the royal summons. April set down her cup. "Is that so?"

"Don't be like that. She knows she's got some bridges to mend. I mean, everybody hasn't exactly agreed with her over the years—a remark here, there . . ."

April glanced up as Robert walked into the room, knotting his tie as he came. She pointed to the hot coffee that had perked and the toast that was about to pop up.

"She's giving a big to-do next week," Bruce went on. "A mob of the medical people, some of her political friends. She says she wants you to come."

"Me?" she said, trying to sound surprised.

"Yes you, goose."

"Does she know? About Gaines, I mean?"

Bruce's voice lowered a couple of discreet notches. "Hell, April, I've started a dozen times to tell her, but if Gaines had wanted her to know, he would've told her, wouldn't he? Things were pretty tense the last time they were together."

"Well, I'm sure you did the right thing."

"You'll come then?"

"I think I'll wait until she calls me, Bruce."

A small tension clawed at the line. April pictured herself talking to Mary with stiff smiles and clenched fists.

"She'll probably call today," he said. "Oh well, behave yourself. Maybe you-know-who will call from the airport and ask you to pick him up. He's long overdue."

"Six weeks," she said, and rubbed at a spot on the table. "Maybe you're right. Maybe today."

"Talk to you tomorrow then."

"Of course. Goodbye, Bruce."

"Bye, love."

Robert Humphries brought his coffee to the table as she replaced the receiver into its cradle. He looked at her, wrapped to her chin in a pale cream robe, her eyes as glistening as emeralds because she'd been crying again. Being due in early surgery was a good excuse not to pry into her affairs. But it was only an excuse; her heart was breaking and he didn't know how to help.

"How are you feeling this morning?"

Her pretense was laced with a small smile. "Fine."

"I wonder why I don't believe that."

She smiled at him again and bumped the table gently as she rose. She walked to the glassed-in wall that looked out onto the backyard. She'd grown up in this house, she thought fondly—she and the trees. They were tall and brilliant with crimson and rust and burnt-gold leaves.

The wind caught them and spun them free to waft gracefully down and be blown against the fence as if they needed that one last huddling contact.

"Have you talked to Mary yet?" Robert asked.

She laughed, then fell silent. She studied her hands. "Bruce said that Mary wants to talk. I saw Andrew yesterday and he mentioned it. Everyone's told me that Mary wants to talk except Mary."

His daughter's tenacious pride always baffled him. Robert set his cup clattering into its saucer and stood behind her. He awkwardly cleared his throat.

"April, this thing with Mary will work out. She's let me know, in so many words, that she feels very bad about what happened. I know how you feel about the past, but—"

Her eyes struck his with an impact. "Do you, Daddy? Do you have any idea how that hurt me back then? All that talk about my trapping Gaines?"

"But you weren't pregnant."

"That doesn't matter. The fact is, he did marry me because we thought so. All right, so I had it coming, but Mary shouldn't have talked about it like that. Not to her children." She shook her head. "Not to her children."

"Your love for Gaines can transcend all that. You said he wants to get married again."

The mist of her breath collected upon the window-pane. She drew a line through it. "Sometimes love is only a small part of it."

"Well." Not knowing how to solve the problem, Robert began buttoning his vest. "You know how I feel about the two of you."

Smiling, April turned to him, walked up and straightened his tie and adjusted the collar of his blue shirt.

"Isn't it crazy?" she said with a transparent cheerfulness. "How a person doesn't just marry another person."

"They marry a family."

"It all seemed so simple when Gaines and I talked about it in Orban. And now . . ."

She returned to the window. There was the sound of his pocket change, the clink of his car keys. She finally said, "I guess what I'm trying to say is that I'm frightened."

"Of what?"

Her shoulders came up, lowered. "There were times in Orban when I watched Gaines . . . There was something about him—an anticipation of the danger, every minute wired with energy of the unknown, sensing that he was doing something very few men could ever do. He . . . looked forward to it as much as I hated it."

"He would stop if you asked him to."

"And that's my problem." She touched her forehead with a half-obstinate, half-wondering touch. "He would. He would turn his back and walk away from it."

"Then you should be happy."

She didn't reply.

Robert walked to the door. He turned in the space. "April, look at me."

When she did, the morning sun at her back silhouetted her slender shape. She looked as fragile as the frost melting on the windowpanes.

"Love costs a lot, April," he said clumsily. "Don't try to be the one who does all the giving. I made that mistake with your mother. Wanted to make it perfect, give her the world. There's an old saying—you get what you pay for. Don't cheat Gaines out of his share of paying."

Robert's honesty sent April's mind tumbling back to the infinities of that day on the river with Gaines. She could close her eyes and remember his body moving upon hers, the feel of the warm sand at her back, being filled with him, possessed by him. Was that when it had happened? she wondered. Or the other time? That stormy night when they were both so tired, so needful of each other?

She tried out new words in her mind and wished they could flow from her to Robert by some magical osmosis. "Daddy . . ."

Robert lifted a hand as if he were offering a gift he was uncertain of. "I'm going to make an appointment with Dr. Haddis today, April. I want you to keep it."

She wished—only for a second—that she had kept her secret. When she peered up at her father through the veil of tears, she guessed she looked like that little girl again: needful and too fearful to ask. "There's no question in my mind, Daddy. I know."

He smiled. "So do I. But go and get the official word anyway."

April couldn't bear his kindness. It burst a dam inside her. "It's just like the first time," she wept bitterly. "How can life give me the same problem again? How can I give myself the same problem again?"

After her sobbing had subsided, he said, "Perhaps it's not a problem that *you* need to face as much as one that *others* need to face."

"Mary?" Sniffing, she wiped her eyes on her sleeve.

A shrug was in Robert's tone. "She's older now. Believe it or not, some of us learn a few things over the years."

He touched his tie, threw down a last swallow of coffee. Before he walked out the door, he grazed a knuckle across her cheek. "Haddis will make room for you early. Get dressed. I'll call you from my office."

April stared at the place where he had been until she heard the front door close and the car start and drive away. Then she turned back to the window and resumed her study of the trees. The house was in order. All the windows were clean, all the baseboards dusted and all the light fixtures polished.

"Oh, Gaines," she whispered in an attempt to find comfort for the one thing that wasn't in order. "Please, please come back to me. This time I really am going to have our baby."

After April had dressed and returned to Dwayne Haddis's office, he gazed across his desk with an expression that said, *It's a good thing this happened before you got any older.*

"We can wait for the results of the test if you want to," he said, and peered over his glasses with a question arching his brisk brows.

Ever since she'd first known this untidy, middle-aged bachelor whose face looked as if someone, somewhere, had made a tragic mistake, April had thought that he cared more about women and how they felt than anyone she knew. "You're sure now, aren't you?" she said.

He smiled comfortably. "Yep. Now, answer me something. Do you want it?"

As if he'd just knocked the breath out of her, April slumped. She laughed. "You don't pull any punches, do you, doc?"

"That's not my style, and you know it. How are you and Gaines getting alone?"

It was impossible to take offense with a teddy bear. She shook her head. "I didn't say this was Gaines's baby."

Dr. Haddis leaned back in his chair and rested his elbows on his girth. He pressed the tips of his fingers together. "Don't con me, girl. When did you get back from . . ." He waved the fingers of one hand. "Wherever it was?"

"Some weeks ago. Why?"

"You didn't pick up any fevers or anything over there?"

She shook her head.

"Good. Now all we've got to worry about is Gaines's family."

Not caring if she had known this nice man for years, enough was enough. April came to her feet and began putting on her coat. When the doctor moved around his desk and helped her on with it, he laid his big hands upon her shoulders.

"She may be my chief-of-staff, April, but Mary Southerland is a hellcat. I don't want this business making you sick, do you hear me? I care about one thing, and that's you. Anyone who lifts a finger, says a word . . ."

Feeling lighthearted for the first time in days, she hugged him. "You and Daddy. Do you think I can't handle one ex-mother-in-law? Why, I'll have you know, Dwayne Haddis, that I've gotten to be rather a hellcat in my own right."

"With those pussycat eyes?" Haddis motioned lavishly to his nurse, who had poked her head in the door. "Here's April's chart, Lois. Set her up for an appointment in a month."

"Going to get out the old knitting needles, eh?" Lois gave April a knowing wink.

"Forget it, Lois. I'm going to Central America with Bruce."

The doctor sent her out the door with a fond shoo. "You do, young lady, and I'll put another Southerland name on my hit list."

April left both of them tossing worn-out mother jokes and maternity ward witticisms after her. She walked through the waiting room in an easier frame of mind and glimpsed a girl crouched in the corner with a magazine opened on her knees. Her fingernails were bitten to the quick.

Disturbed, April smiled. The girl flicked her eyes away, drew her body into a more self-protective huddle. April hesitated for a moment, then walked on with saddened steps. What quirk of circumstance kept her from being the one with bitten nails? Robert? Gaines? Her own strength, which she didn't even believe in?

Once out in the corridor, she bent over the water fountain, then gazed around herself with a decided determination to improve her outlook, no matter what it took. Things had changed at Mercy, hadn't they? Or perhaps it was she who had done most of the changing. Here's to change, she thought, and punched the elevator button with fervor.

An elderly man held open the door. "Nice day," he said with an old-fashioned tip of his hat as she got on.

"Why, yes it is," she replied as the door swished shut. Smiling, she surprised herself by honestly meaning it.

A number of feet from the water fountain, in the open doorway to an area restricted to the public, Mary Southerland stood with her hands pushed deeply into the pockets of her green smock. She didn't move as she watched April step into the elevator and speak to the old gentleman.

What was April Humphries Southerland doing on the fourth floor of Mercy General Hospital? Robert's office was on the second floor, and to her knowledge April hadn't been there in a very, very long time. Fourth floor was . . . Mary felt the quickening tingle of understanding. Fourth floor was obstetrics and pediatrics.

She clicked her pen shut officiously and clipped it to her pocket. She kept her silvered head erect as she glided to the reception area of obstetrics. Opening a door, she walked back behind the desk.

"Hello, Dr. Southerland." The receptionist was swift to smile and even more swift to throw an eye about the office to make sure everything was in order.

"Hello, Grace. I'm wondering if you would check on a lab report for me."

Glancing at Mary Southerland's empty hands, Grace said: "Of course, Dr. Southerland."

Mary reached across and ripped a page from a scratch pad and scribbled down a patient's name whose lab report was presently lying on her desk. She held her chin at an irrefutable angle. "I appreciate it, dear."

"No trouble at all, Dr. Southerland."

Grace pushed back her chair and walked across the hall with a whispery squish of her shoes, and down two doors to the lab that serviced OB and pediatrics. As Grace's back disappeared around the clean white facing, Mary removed her bifocals from her pocket. She fit them about her ears and leaned ever so casually over the appointment book open on Grace's desk. She scanned the slotted spaces with an expert eye and found precisely what she was looking for—10:00; April Southerland; Haddis.

Smoothly removing her glasses and flicking her critical administrative eyes over the adjoining examination room, Mary made sure she was not at the reception desk when Grace returned.

"Oh, there you are," Grace exclaimed breathily. "Henry said to tell you those reports had already been sent down to your office."

With a small nod, Mary accepted the news. "I see." She walked serenely toward the door that opened onto the waiting area.

"There is a bottle of disinfectant sitting beneath the

sink in the examining room, Grace," she said with terse efficiency. "See that it's put away immediately."

Behind the chief-of-staff's back Grace glared for the briefest second. "Yes, Dr. Southerland," she said sweetly through her teeth.

Snarled traffic on Constitution Avenue made April run later than she had expected. After enjoying a quick soup-and-salad and then indulging herself by browsing through the baby department at Fox's and scanning a book by Dr. Benjamin Spock, she ended up getting caught as the children were coming home from school.

All the way to the house she stopped and started her little Datsun behind school buses. She smiled as the bright nylon windbreakers flashed at the windows. Children tumbled down the steps with shrill cries and waved lunch boxes with Kermit the Frog and Miss Piggy on them. Down the block mothers were waiting at front doors. Garages had those single snaggletooth spaces waiting for paternal cars to come sweeping up the driveway and reunite the family at the end of the day.

Pregnancy had a way of changing brain waves, she thought with amusement as she parked in front of the house she and Gaines had bought. Last year she was translating in a foreign country; now she was washing windows and noticing lunch boxes.

She turned off the engine and looked at the house for a long time. She placed her hands across her abdomen and tried to picture herself as one of those mothers bending down and placing the lunch box in a daughter's hand. She saw herself waving goodbye and blowing a kiss. But when she searched in the fantasy for Gaines hugging her and driving off to work, it cruelly refused to come into focus.

She climbed out of the car and shut the door. Inside

her, safe within its warm human cocoon, was all the weapon she needed to make Gaines quit the Agency. All she had to do was use it.

She walked up the twisting sidewalk that skirted the house. It was a gracious old two-story brick that had been painted a dove gray. The trim was intricate and clever, a darker gray. A tall boxwood hedge shut out the neighbors on one side. To the east a flagstone terrace ran alongside the French doors, which opened out onto the lawn.

Inside, furniture was shrouded with dust sheets. Doors were shut and blinds drawn. The water was cut off, as was the electricity. The telephones were disconnected, refrigerator left open, pipes drained. Everything waited: Sleeping Beauty in repose for the kiss of Prince Charming.

The wooden gate to the backyard squeaked when she pushed it open. The chyrsanthemums were in bloom! Dozens of bright petaled faces nodded at her as if to say, "You didn't forget us, did you?"

That first year she'd gone on such a spree, had planted great, luscious beds across the back with every season in mind. And look at them now, smothered with weeds. Everything suffered from neglect. The rose of Sharon trees needed trimming. The grass needed fertilizing. The windows needed washing, and the patio and the guttering and the creaking gate. It all needed attention.

With a stab of misery that she couldn't blame on her pregnancy, she leaned her head on one of the posts of the gate. She squeezed her eyes tightly shut.

Couldn't she just say it? she thought with a rush of self-pity that washed away all her new resolutions. Dear God, *she* needed attention.

Gaines's plane was an hour late in landing. Not that one more hour was going to bring the world toppling down, he thought wearily as he stretched out his feet and looked at his wristwatch for the hundredth time. He was six weeks overdue. He was depressed. He was nervous. He wanted to close the too-long distance between April and himself, once and for all.

Too edgy to eat, he trimmed his new beard instead. It was still quite short, but he shaped it and clipped his mustache. After washing and changing his shirt, he set his watch and returned to his seat with a sigh.

The stewardess kept looking at him. She'd asked him twice if there was anything she could get him. Smiling, he'd let her know in a nice way that he didn't want to talk. It seemed forever before he saw those familiar runway lights and felt the solidity of the nation's capital under the wheels.

Since all he had was a flight bag, Gaines was out of the airport and into a taxi in record time. It was all he could do to keep a civil tone with the driver. Everything the man did seemed to irritate him unbearably.

Finally, after a seemingly endless drive across town, he got out of the cab and looked over the top to find Robert Humphries's house deserted. No lights were on. The car wasn't in the garage.

Gaines stood rubbing his fist into his palm. Where could April be? Sighing, he had the driver take him to Bruce's condominium.

Damn it! After rapping three times at Bruce's door, he couldn't raise anyone. Where was everybody? He began imagining horrible things.

"Stop behaving like an idiot," he told himself. In a kind of incredulous despair, he proceeded to pick Bruce's lock.

A panel of pale blue light sliced across the carpet as Gaines pushed open the door. He let his senses take over from habit. He could hear the hissing bubble of the aquarium. Feeling about for a light switch, he stepped in and closed the door. He looked around at the familiar neatness of his brother's living room and walked through the empty, rooms. Swearing under his breath, he finally dialed the number of his mother's house.

"Gaines!" exclaimed Bruce in a near-shout, then lowered his voice to a harsh whisper. "Where are you?"

Gaines felt relief hit the pit of his stomach. "At your house, you dummy. What're you doing at Mother's?"

"Lawd, son, you're missing the party of the century. Everyone you haven't seen in the past ten years is here. How'd you get into my place?"

"I broke in," Gaines said dryly. "Have you seen April?"

"I'm looking at her right now." Music pulsed in the background, glassware clinked together, laughter bubbled and voices exploded with fragments of words. "She's discoing with Andy. She's got on this long slinky green thing, Gaines. She's a knockout. When did you get back?"

Gaines blinked to clear his head of an image of April—that subtle beat when she danced, that sophisticated little wiggle he could watch for hours and that turned him on to the point of . . .

"Just this minute." He pinched the bridge of his nose in frustration. "I can't find anyone."

"They're all over here. Listen, Gaines, are you okay?"

"Sure, I'm okay."

"I mean really okay."

With a flex of his healing arm, Gaines said: "I'm knitting back together. Look, I'm tired, and it's been hard. I've got to talk to a man; then I'm coming over there. Where're the keys to your Caddy?"

"On top of the refrigerator. Gaines?"

"What?"

Bruce cleared his throat, his hesitance letting the

sounds of the party leak through. "Look, Gaines, I never had the time to say thanks back there. I wake up in the night, you know, sweating. I'd be in prison if it weren't for you. I—"

"Forget it." Gaines had spied Bruce's car keys. He didn't want thanks; he wanted April's face, the feel of her holding him. "Look, don't mention that you talked to me. Okay?"

"Sure, Gaines. See you in a little while."

"Right."

For a moment, Gaines pressed the telephone against his jacket and held down the connection with a fingertip. He was tempted not to check in with Wesley. But that particular groove was engraved deeply into his gray matter; he knew he would. He looked down at his corduroy trousers and loafers and thought of Mary's spectacular parties. What the hell?

He savagely dialed the number of the CIA.

April wished with all the depressing wisdom of hindsight that she had simply told Mary no. When the call to court had finally come, all her rehearsed brush-offs had mutinously stuck in her throat. All she could think was that Mary was Gaines's mother and that, for his sake, she could afford to yield a little pride and bend the knee.

She hardly remembered agreeing to come, but she obviously had; she was shampooed, manicured, dressed, shod, and walking up the sidewalk on the arm of her father. She had worn green lamé—six hundred reckless-ly spent dollars' worth of it. But it brought out her eyes, she'd told herself when she'd written the check; and it heightened her color and lent her simply cut hair an added flair. It accentuated her small waist and flat stomach and, most importantly of all, it made her look very, very unpregnant.

She and Robert were late. The nearest they could park the car was a half dozen houses down the street.

"I feel like Anne Boleyn going to her execution," April grumbled, her steps growing slower and more heavy as they walked up the shrub-bordered walk.

Connolley Avenue was one of the wealthiest streets in town: impressive, snobbishly self-sufficient, no one knowing his neighbor. The entrance to Mary's house was guarded by huge mounds of dormant azaleas. Hedges reached window height, and clever stonework lent privacy in ways unique to turn-of-the-century houses.

Robert laughed. "Don't worry. Her axe is dull from all the guillotined members of her staff."

Giggling more from the jitters than humor, April stepped onto the lighted porch and let her stole slide down the slender, gold-shot sleeves of her dress. She sent her hair back from her cheeks with a toss of her head.

"How do I look?"

Robert pressed her arm. "Lovely."

"I mean, do I look like a pregnant lady?"

"Definitely not."

Suffering a dire need for Gaines—she'd never gone through one of these trial-by-fire ordeals without him— she gestured harshly to the bell. "Ring it, then."

Light spilled out of the house, along with delicious smells and the sounds of music and laughter. Behind the butler April glimpsed glittering dresses and masses of fresh flowers. Assuming stage front was Mary, gorgeously gowned in lavender chiffon.

How long had it been? April struggled to remember as she arranged her smile. The last time she'd seen Mary was when she'd attended a hospital function with her father, long before she'd gone to Orban. The divorce had just become final. Mary had looked at her with a perfectly bland face, as if she could not remember who she was.

Time missed a beat. Mary gave her a quick up-and-down perusal, and her lipsticked mouth smiled as if it were impossible that April did not want to be there.

"How lovely you look tonight, April," she complimented tranquilly. "How are you feeling?"

The question left April cold, as it was meant to do. There was nothing out of line in such a remark; it was a hackneyed, overworked phrase that rarely required an answer. Yet the undercurrent was alive with implications that both women understood.

April turned her head askance, as if to say, *Am I reading wrong, Mary Southerland? Do I feel you warning me?*

You have not misread me, Mary's perfect smile assured her. *I have, and always will, outdistance you.*

When Andrew strolled up like the Scarlet Pimpernel, winking extravagantly at April and reaching around his mother to shake Robert's hand, Mary cooed: "Dance with April, dear. Bruce has already been snared by Nell Hathaway. Robert, there's a heart surgeon here from Los Angeles who's been waiting anxiously to meet you. You will be absolutely fascinated with his new techniques."

So strong was April's sense of having been read her rights, she let Andrew maneuver her out onto the dance floor before she came to herself.

"Will you stop that?" she scolded as he led her in a sensual wraparound and leaned her back in his arms. "You'll enflame every spinster in this room."

Andrew laughed down at her and admired the plunge of her neckline. "If you weren't so hung up on that brother of mine, I might just enflame you. Tell me, April, what does it take for a man to catch your fancy?"

She played the game with the skill she had learned as attaché to the ambassador. "I refuse to answer. You intimated that I'm a spinster."

"Well, what are you then?" he groaned. "A married lady?"

"Would you mind if I were?"

"Married to me? Not at all."

"Silly. You know who I'm talking about."

He drew her into his arms and pressed his mouth to her ear. Chuckling, he said, "Are you sleeping with my brother, April? Has that dastardly Gaines gone and seduced you again?"

"You know Gaines isn't in town," she replied as she searched absently over his shoulder for sight of Robert.

"That's what everyone says. But you have a look about you, my dear. It gives me the uncomfortable feeling that I've missed something."

Mary's living room was high and two-storied. Rough stone veneer swooped up to join with a ceiling vaulted with dark oak. Upstairs, a spacious balcony looked down upon the guests. Lighting was soft, and fires blazed in the big fireplaces. Bruce and her father stood in a group near one of them, and someone had removed a screen to poke at the flames.

As Andrew guided her near the outer edge of the dancers, April signaled to a waiter, thinking that the excuse of champagne was exactly what she needed. She leaned back in Andrew's arms to ask him to fetch her a glass, then froze so suddenly that he stumbled over her feet.

He caught her by both arms. "Oops, I didn't see that com—"

Grasping the direction of her openmouthed stare, he followed it to a group of men clustered around the fireplace.

April couldn't believe what she saw. What in the world was Wesley Durant doing here?

"April?"

She raised her hand to hush Andrew and brushed a wisp of hair back from her cheek. "I'm sorry. I saw someone I thought—"

She didn't know that Wesley Durant was an acquaintance of Mary's! Or was he? Did he . . . *Gaines!*

Hardly realizing what she did, intent only in collaring Wesley, she breathed a hurried kiss upon Andrew's cheek. She didn't even look at him. "The dance was lovely, Andrew. I've got to . . . I mean, I'm sorry. I . . . I'll be back in a minute."

Andrew took a couple of dazed steps after April, but he had no sooner been stranded without a partner than a ravishing blonde sidled up beside him. She placed her hand on his shoulder and struck a modish slouch.

"May I cut in?" she purred.

He gazed down at her, back to the sight of April urgently making her way through the crowd of people. Shrugging, he twisted his mouth into a grin.

"Well now." He removed her hand and drew her into his embrace. "I guess you've already done it."

To Gaines's surprise, he blushed when he dashed up the back steps two at a time, slammed through the back door of his mother's kitchen and ran headlong into Robert Humphries.

Perhaps it was the shock of seeing him after so long. And perhaps it was because, in that one startled second, he felt destiny grabbing him by the collar; Gaines guessed that April's father knew everything about their love affair in Orban.

"Doctor," he said on a dazed breath as he reached behind to shut the door.

Robert was answering a page from his beeper. As surprised as Gaines, he covered the receiver and extended his other hand. "Why, Gaines, what a nice surprise. I'm—could you wait a minute?"

Leaving an instruction with the nurses' station at Mercy Hospital, Robert finished his call and quickly hung up the telephone. He wiped across his mouth and nodded awkwardly. "Well, you're looking real good, Gaines. Real good."

"Ah . . . thank you. I guess you know." He smiled vaguely, torn between the need to be cordial and his desperation to find April. "About me, I mean. My going to Orban."

Robert nodded. "Thank you for getting her out of there like you did. It could have been another story entirely."

"Don't thank me."

Gaines struggled to control his frustration by walking to the counter and pretending to browse over a tray of hors d'oeuvres waiting to be taken out. He extended the tray. "Help yourself."

Just to be polite, Robert selected something, and Gaines picked up a stuffed mushroom, lifted it to his mouth, then placed it down on the counter.

"Sir," he said, his agitation rising, "I don't know how much April told you. I . . . uh, I haven't even seen her yet this evening. I just got off the plane. I haven't . . ."

He glanced down at his cord trousers, then distractedly at the door beyond which was the party in full swing. They were two men loving the same object and knowing no way to articulate it, both having lost something they loved, both fearing to lose again.

Robert tried to clear a thickness from his throat. "Go find her."

"Thank you." Gaines lunged for the door.

"Gaines?"

Turning back, Gaines waited impatiently.

Robert smiled, brushed crumbs off his hands. "Gaines, I just wanted to say . . . Well, April's about the most important thing in the world to me."

"I know that, Robert."

"I've made my own share of mistakes with her."

As if he couldn't fathom anything as grand as his own errors, Gaines turned his hand. Robert traced over the design in the tile with the toe of his shoe.

"Before you talk to her, there's something I . . . What I'm trying to say is, life doesn't have a magic potion to make a man a good father instantly, Gaines. Up to now I've stayed out of April's life, tried to give her the freedom to make her own decisions. I never interfered in that trouble with your family." He sighed heavily. "Now I'm going to do something I've never done before."

A sharp needle of apprehension stabbed Gaines, but before it could focus itself into conscious reality Robert was speaking again.

"What I'm going to do," Robert said, "is what I've despised in other fathers." Their minds met—one exasperated, the other anxious. "She's carrying your child, Gaines."

Gaines had turned so that he was leaning heavily upon the edge of the counter. At Robert's words he continued to lean there, not moving, not breathing, as the realization settled deep into the marrow of his bones. He gave a little half laugh of surprise and pleasure. He wiped his hand over his beard, his smile handsome and pleased, while in his mind he saw wonderful images of the future—April in a snow white gown caught high above a belly filled with his child, April with an infant cradled in her arms as its mouth searched for her breast. And then it dawned upon him—Robert's distress.

His black brows were fierce as his head came up. "Something is wrong?"

Comprehending, Robert reached out to prevent Gaines's paternal fear from asserting itself any further. "No, no. Not that. It's only that . . ."

The Southerland eyes were intensely piercing. "Go on, man!"

"It's just that I . . ." Robert turned his head away. "I'm not completely sure she'll tell you, Gaines. What happened before, you understand. She doesn't want to trap you into anything."

Circumstances collected above Gaines's head with the threatening force of an avalanche. He was aware of two things at once: his desperation to see the mother of his child, and his need, by some means as yet unclear to him, to relieve her of a burden she should never have been forced to bear.

He hardly realized that he had taken Robert's hand and was pumping it up and down. "Everything will be fine, Robert. I give you my word it will."

He left Robert staring after him, bent with his own doubts. Robert sighed. He had broken his own rule. He had stuck his nose in where it had no business being. For the first time in years he felt like a real father to his daughter.

Wesley Durant didn't seem at all surprised to see April making her way toward him through the kaleidoscope of colorful gowns. And April got the distinct impression, as she caught his eye, that Wesley had been expecting her to discover him. With an unhurried manner, he lifted his hand near his jaw. He signaled her to meet him at a point beyond the crowd, a more secluded and quiet area behind a massive profusion of flowers.

He detached himself and walked toward it. "How very nice to see you, Mrs. Southerland," he said when she reached him. "Could I get you something to drink? Some champagne, perhaps?"

"Where is he?" Her whisper cut straight through the amenities. "I don't want to play games with you, Mr. Durant. Where is Gaines?"

Wesley walked April along the outer edge of the two-story room. He glanced about them without the slightest expression betraying what he thought. He pushed open a door. The room was dark, a long formal table stretching almost the entire length of it, flanked with the shadowed bulk of chairs.

"I had no intentions of playing games," he told her. "Why don't we step in here where it's not so noisy. We can talk."

The mistrust April felt for him made her draw back in resistance. "I don't want to talk. I want to know where Gaines is."

"Only a moment, please."

Grudgingly she let him guide her into the room. He motioned her forward through a high arched opening that led farther back into the house, nearer the kitchens— something resembling a den with bookcases and a desk and a fireplace that was lit and provided the only light in the room.

She said almost violently, "Has something happened to Gaines?" and twisted her fingers together until they hurt.

"Of course not. Gaines will be here in a few minutes. I'm to meet him here, as a matter of fact. Everything is perfectly in order, Mrs. Southerland. His plane was a bit late in arriving, I understand, but otherwise—"

Listening to Wesley's prattle was the last thing she wanted. "Then I'll go wait for him."

She started back in the direction from which they had come. He held up his finger as if something had just this second come to his mind.

"Before you go, Mrs. Southerland, there's one thing I thought I might mention."

Her look was guarded. "What is that, Mr. Durant?"

"Won't you sit down first? It's very pleasant here."

"No, thank you."

"Well . . ."

Shrugging, he moved nearer the fire so that he could see everything in the room. April moved about, her gown making a gentle susurrus upon the inlaid parquet. She wanted to go outside, to sit on the steps and hug her knees to her chest and wait for Gaines as she used to do long before any of this.

"You're a direct woman, Mrs. Southerland."

"Sometimes." She didn't look at him. "Not always."

"Gaines is very much in love with you."

"That goes two ways, Mr. Durant."

"Ah, April . . . May I call you April?"

Shrugging, she inclined her head in the affirmative.

"April, I've made no pretenses about wanting to keep Gaines as an operative if I can. He's a special man, your husband. Sorry, ex-husband; that confuses me sometimes. Anyway, you know what I'm talking about."

She wasn't sure she did, but growing uncomfortable beneath his stare, she turned slightly, dropping her fingers to toy with the edge of a book. "What are you trying to say, Mr. Durant?"

"That I know the things you want. But before you do anything, I want you to understand the kind of man Gaines is now."

"I expect I know Gaines a good deal better than you do."

He waved her to silence. "He's not the man you married before, April. This business is in his blood. Oh, he'll walk out on me if you ask him to. He'll go back to medicine and have the babies and pay the mortgage. But it won't be what he wants. Gaines has commitments to me, way down inside him. He's been torn between you and me for a long time now. Well, since the beginning, actually. If you really love him, April, I wish you would find it in your heart to step back and give him room."

April felt an outrage that went far beyond that moment. She looked at Wesley Durant and felt the rage of being violated. He was playing dirty, hitting her in her one Achilles' heel. She wanted to scream at him, *It's my turn now!*

She bent her head, fighting the angry tears. "Have you ever been in love, Mr. Durant?" she lashed out at him. "Have you ever had children? Have you ever done anything in your life besides manipulate other people's lives? Is that how you get your kicks?"

Wesley had never liked to get involved with agents who had women in their lives. It was always such a messy business. He moved nearer, and when he put one arm about her trembling shoulders he honestly wished that he could give her some magic solution.

"It'll all work out, Mrs. Southerland," he said softly, and withdrew a handkerchief from inside his jacket. Awkwardly he handed it to her. "I'm very sorry."

In her anguish April accepted the handkerchief and kept her head lowered so that Wesley, in his hovering, could not see her face.

The room was suddenly ablaze with light.

Wesley moved with a reaction that he was trained to, his hand coming to rest on his side where he wore his gun. April simply stood with her jaw slightly loose and looked guilty of everything.

"April," said the cold, calm voice of Mary Southerland from the doorway, "when I saw you yesterday at Mercy General, I wondered if it weren't something like this."

Chapter 12

WHEN APRIL SAW MARY IN THE OPEN DOOR, HER triumph almost incandescent on her face, she realized that what had begun years ago at Saint Michael's had finally reached its destined climax.

Mary had seen her at Mercy General; Mary knew she was pregnant; and Mary had just assumed, because Mary assumed the worst of her—always—that Wesley Durant was the father of her child.

Whether she was prepared to meet this moment of reckoning was immaterial. It was—and April knew a moment of hatred for Gaines and Bruce and all Mary's children who had never refused her this power—a thing she could not escape.

She watched Mary move into the room and position herself beneath her own portrait over the mantel. The blaze of the drooping chandelier kindled fire in the diamonds at her throat: a decree of power that April found menacing and terrible.

"You, sir," Mary said as she fixed her accusation upon Wesley Durant, "are not a guest here. I do not know you. How did you get into my home?"

Wesley seemed immune to Mary's authority. He gave her a CIA smile. "For that I must beg your forgiveness. It was necessary."

"A liaison? With this woman? In my home?"

"I am here to be of assistance to Mrs. Southerland." He replaced his handkerchief in his pocket with a slow choreographed movement and acknowledged April with a nod. "We were having a private word."

Distaste flared Mary's nostrils. "You have obviously shared more than a private word . . . sir."

"I beg your pardon?"

"You and she are cut from the same cloth, obviously."

The silence was much more threatening than speech. To April it seemed to focus and become hot: a ray of light through a magnifying glass until the intensity was fatal.

"Mary," she said with quiet dignity, her knees rebelling and a dryness filling her mouth, "I am your guest. This lie can do nothing but hurt both of us."

Not since Douglas's death had anyone dared to stand up to Mary. She gave a hollow, artificial laugh. "Well, my dear, that is a foresight you should have had before now. Years before now."

So, April thought sadly, life had indeed come full circle; it was asking her to stand up and be counted. If she cowered before Mary now, the anguish Mary had caused in the past would be as nothing compared to the future. She touched the pearls about her neck and felt much more helpless than when standing before Ali Jassim in the blinding Middle Eastern sun.

"Then I will say it." She formed her words with care. "I will give you the excuse you need. Take your

hands off me, Mary. Don't ever interfere in my life
again.''

Only Wesley moved after such a shocking declaration
of independence. He nervously brushed at his lapels
while resin bubbled in the fireplace and a shower of
sparks went hissing up the chimney.

''You can say that to me after what you've done?''
Mary said in disbelief.

April forced her head to remain erect; her only safety
seemed to be in impeccable good manners. ''What have
I done, Mary?''

''You mean besides carrying on your shoddy little
affair in my home? Or do you speak, perhaps, of how
you have insinuated yourself into my family and ruined
one of my sons? It has taken me years to build this
heritage. I have ordered my life beyond reproach and
have worked and fought for the best, the finest that life
has to offer. I have built my children a future. I've built
Gaines a future. And I've watched Gaines destroy it
because of a woman who is worth no more than a
passing fancy. And you have the gall to ask me, 'What
have I done?' ''

Any semblance of hospitality had disappeared from
Mary. Her anger distorted the elegance of her posture
and the angle of her careful hair. The light did merciless
things to her face and she suddenly looked quite old—
and very hard.

April felt a moment of weightlessness like being in a
fast elevator. She had to speak now; if she didn't, she
never would.

''It doesn't matter that you have hurt me.'' She forced
out the words. ''But in hurting me you have hurt Gaines.
Because he loves me, Mary. Make no mistake about
that. Nothing you can do to me will ever be just between
us. Not even the words we are speaking at this moment.

It will all hurt Gaines. And I cannot add any more to that hurt.''

Making Mary accept her was as futile as reasoning with a drunkard. How could love win against hate? And truth fight a lie? April wanted nothing more than to get out. She placed one foot in front of the other and didn't stop walking until she reached the center of the room. She turned back to find Mary watching, her face victorious.

''And you're wrong, Mary,'' she said on a final low breath, ''I'm worth a lot.''

Mary's laughter burst across the room, out of control. She lifted her arm in its gorgeously clad sleeve and her hazel eyes were dark with unforgiveness. ''Name one thing, my dear child!''

From the door came the sound of stirring. Mary and Wesley both turned to see, but April, in her pain, did not move. She heard the brass tip of Bruce's stick strike the parquet.

''What's going on here?'' his words lashed across the room. ''Mother, will you keep your voice down?''

''And will you keep yours down?'' snapped another voice as Andrew entered hard on the heels of his brother. ''What in hell is the meaning of this?''

''My question precisely,'' growled Bruce.

April's mind cruelly supplied her with versions of how this must all look to the two Southerland men. She saw a whole string of wrecked illusions of being accepted as part of the whole, of her child growing up and taking its place, of Gaines's pride in both of them.

Mary's lapse of control drained from her face. For one brief instant her eyes were flared and in the next she was once again the cool, composed matriarch. She lifted a beautifully negligent shoulder.

''April's small indiscretion,'' she murmured.

Bruce stomped forward, brows imperative. "April's what?"

As if he had struck her, Mary leaned back. She felt authority slip at its foundations.

"Indiscretion," she said less adamantly, and clutched the diamonds about her neck. "Indiscretion."

"What indiscretion, Mother?" demanded Andrew.

Mary groped for a way to be free of the alien doubts of her sons. Her accusation to April had started as just words, and now . . . She shook her head. "Must I spell it out? I mean, I could hardly believe it myself. Must I—"

"If you couldn't believe it, Mother," came an altogether different voice from the doorway, "then why did you say it?"

In the tension, no one had seen Gaines standing quietly in the portal, listening to everything. Now, with anger licking across the high, bladed planes of his cheeks, his black brows meeting above the bridge of his nose, his eyes glowed with a dangerous fury. Hard ridges stood out beside his mouth. His hands shook as he moved deeper into the room and shut the door. He didn't slam it; he shut it with the deadly determination of a man meaning to have justice, one way or another.

No one questioned his right to command the room. A tiny sound of gladness came from April's throat. And a look of deep alarm passed over Mary Southerland's; her mouth drained of color, as if she were seeing a ghost.

"Gaines," she whispered, fingering the clasp of her jewels. "I didn't know you were here."

"Obviously," Gaines said. He disregarded everyone as he walked straight to April and took her by the shoulders. He ran his eyes hungrily over her as if he must assure himself that no pinprick of damage had come to her. He lifted one large hand and gently smoothed back her hair.

"It's all right," he whispered tenderly. "Nothing's going to hurt you now."

April could not speak. Yet when she saw Gaines turn around, knowing that he would destroy everything to protect her, she lunged after him. She caught his sleeve to prevent him from going to his mother.

"Let it go," she said hoarsely. "Really. It's not important."

He pushed at her tenacious grip, and his voice cracked like a whip through the hushed room. Every eye fastened upon him.

"Not important?" He stared hard at Mary, at her paleness, at her agitated hands. "Anything that touches a hair of your head is important to me. Tell me, Mother, now that we're all here together, tell me about April's indiscretion."

"Gaines, darling," Mary said on a frail, hurried plea, "you must understand. You must try to put yourself in my place."

"Your place!" thundered Gaines. His chest rose and fell. "Your place is to be wise and kind and adored by your children and your grandchildren because of the breadth of your compassion. For us, Mother. For those of us who hurt when you have so quickly weighed us in your righteous, self-serving scales of justice!"

April had seen Gaines under unspeakable pressure, but she had never seen him like this. He filled the room with a dangerous presence, and, as if the very walls felt it too, the noise outside seemed to lessen. April pressed her cheeks. This kind of pain was passed down from father to son and its wounds never healed.

Mary stood starkly pale as if Gaines had struck her. Who would have thought that it would have been he, the roguish, laughing one whom no one really took seriously? For the first time in her life she knew she had gone too far. But it was done now, and there was no Douglas to help her repair it.

"I gave everything to this family, Gaines," she said on a thread of pleading. "It never mattered to you. Every dream you threw back in my face as if it were some rag beneath your contempt."

As if he, too, saw no hope of turning things around, Gaines pressed his eyes closed for a moment. He shook his head and sighed with a resignation of years.

"It mattered, Mother," he said, and moved April into his arms. "You just never saw it."

It was over, having come from nowhere and having gone nowhere—only a rubble of ashes to see where the burning had once been. Yet Bruce ached with the memory of Gaines being arrested to save him. He couldn't bear to see it end with his brother's life belittled again. He was the firstborn son, and he had never had the courage to call his mother's hand.

"Aren't either of you going to tell her?" he barked with a cock of his head at Gaines, then at April.

Gaines felt the gentle pressure of April's weight against him. He could smell the scent that never failed to please him, the heat rising from her body. He saw the violence that had filled his life for the past years and knew that salvation from it rested in the woman at his side and in the child within her body.

He straightened himself and drew April to his waist. With his family watching, he cupped her face between his hands until his mind melted into hers. She smiled up at him and thought that nothing mattered except that he was home. He touched her lips with the briefest, tenderest of kisses.

"It's over," he said to Bruce without looking at anything but April. "It doesn't matter anymore."

The dissonance, however, strained to be resolved like a classic theme demanding its tonic.

Mary's head jerked up. "Tell me what?"

Wesley Durant began moving across to Bruce in an attempt to prevent any damage to his plans. Andrew fidgeted.

"I love you very much," Gaines whispered to April as if the two of them were isolated. "Would you like to go somewhere and get married?"

She smiled. "As soon as possible."

"Tell me what!" Mary screamed to Bruce, her fingers grasping the diamonds with frantic distraction.

Heads came up and around.

"That Gaines is an agent for the United States government!" Bruce shouted, then forced himself to calm. "He has been for years. If it weren't for him, I would be rotting in some prison in the Middle East—if not buried in a cement wall. You don't know Gaines, Mother. You don't know him at all."

The hush seemed to go on forever. No one in the room was unaffected by the truth that came, if not too late, at least too unlauded. Wesley Durant took a breath of dismay. Andrew stared. Mary stood in a daze as the diamonds fell broken from her fingers to the floor.

It was in April's mind to look upon the scene and think with vengeance that Mary deserved what she was getting; and Mary did, much more than this. But as April stood in those ticking seconds of life's reversal, she thought of the child within her body and of its father who always saw a thing to its fair and just end. She thought of Robert and a mother whom she'd never really known. She remembered the loneliness upon a terrorist's dark face and of the day she had held John Strakes's body in her arms. And Gaines's taking her so lovingly beside the river. "I wish you loved me that way."

She detached herself from Gaines's embrace. She walked across the room without any glory for herself because she was a woman still; she would never forget this night as Mary had not forgotten that other night.

Stooping, she lifted the precious stones from the floor. She did not speak as she stood before Mary Southerland. She took the older hand in her own and placed the jewelry into Mary's palm. There was no need for words. She and Mary both knew; from this day forward, that which could not be loved would at least be tolerated. And that, with all of its problems yet to be resolved, was a beginning.

Turning, April returned to the side of the man she would marry. "*Now* it's over," she whispered so only he could hear. "Please take me home."

Gaines bought the tree the next morning while April was putting away the groceries. It was a thing he wanted to do by himself—a climax to something that had begun in him long before, by the river, perhaps, but a thing that needed tangible evidence: his sense of change in his life, the future with April, fatherhood. So, in the warmth of October sunshine, he simply got into the car, drove out on the highway and bought it.

The utilities hadn't even been put on. He had to run a water hose from the neighbor's house. When he returned, Ben came out into the backyard in an effort to be neighborly and also to get a closer glance at the house. It had been closed for over three years, and now its windows were open and the draperies were blowing in the warm fall breeze.

"Moving back in, eh?" he said.

Gaines smiled. "Yep."

"The missus with you?"

The temptation to say that that was a technicality— they had gotten a marriage license that morning, too— was on the tip of Gaines's tongue. But he just smiled. "Yep."

There had never been any question of where they would go after the ordeal with Mary. Even without any of the conveniences, they had come home. He had built a fire in the fireplace while she quietly padded about finding glasses, some wine. They had made love, then had searched for candles and made love again beneath the covers in the cold bedroom. They'd slept with their naked bodies fitted together like spoons in a drawer. But she hadn't told him about the baby.

When he'd awakened, he had suffered that uncanny horror of "What's wrong?"

April's breasts were warm against his back, and he turned. She murmured and lifted her head for him to kiss her, then furled her arms about his head when he slid lower to press his cheek against the safety of her breasts. In that one vulnerable gesture was as much pleasure as in all the desperate passion of the night before.

Purring, she wrapped her legs about his.

"Don't wake up," he said thickly, and placed a hand over her eyes. "Pretend it's all a dream."

Eyes closed, she stroked her fingers over the bones of his shoulder. "We've been together too long for dreams like this."

He laughed at her, and she reached down to touch him. He wanted to be enveloped by her. He came up into her with the easy carelessness of a lover who knows the other infinitely well. She opened her eyes and looked at him through sleepy lashes.

"I haven't brushed my teeth," she said, arching herself like a cat.

"What trials you burden me with." He chuckled. "What grand anguish."

The room was chilled, and gold with the sun's haze through the sheer drape. They talked, still coupled. Nothing seemed quite impossible in the early dawn.

Gaines wondered if she was thinking about the baby, forming a strategy of how to tell him.

After a time she threw the covers back, smiling as she ran her eyes over the way they fit together. He'd meant only to share a brief penetrating closeness before beginning the first day of their new life together. Yet, when he started to draw away, she clutched at him with a hand about his neck.

"Not yet," she said.

He smiled. "The neighbors will talk."

She rolled over until she lay stretched upon him. Smiling, he pulled down her head and kissed her. She snuggled for a moment in the curve of his neck as if content to feel their heartbeats complementing each other. *Tell me,* he wanted to say. *Tell me your secret.*

Yet she didn't tell him anything. And Gaines knew as he watched her sit up, straddling him with her eyes closed and her back arched, pressing tightly against him, that he couldn't put a price tag on her love.

"I was never unmarried to you," she said as if every word were a chore. She moved her hips as if she were lost in some inner center of herself. He could feel her tightening, concentrating.

He didn't tell her it had been the same for him. He forgot any intentions he might have had and lay passively beneath her; he watched the growing flush on her face, the way she opened her eyes to smile hazily down at him, then closed them again. As her strokes increased he felt an enormous satisfaction, an excitement that she could be this selfish, this selfless only with him. And when moisture glistened over her body and she reached for it—tightly, determinedly, finally finding it and bending low to let him hold her until the shudders stopped, and stopped again—he knew he wouldn't ask her about the baby at all. In her own good time, when it was right for her, she would tell him.

"Was it good?" she whispered roughly against his jaw, anxious now to think of him and make amends.

"Yes."

"But you didn't."

"I didn't need to."

He didn't want her to mar his happiness with a gesture of *noblesse oblige*. With an eccentric exhilaration, he dragged her out of bed. "Get up, lazybones." They ate doughnuts and coffee in a shop and went by all the utility companies and paid deposits. The act of doing common everyday things was enervating. They laughed and held hands as they ran up the steps of the courthouse.

"Your clothes and mine," he said. "We'll move them all this morning."

It had taken two trips in the Datsun. And another to the supermarket because April insisted on going down every aisle and poring over things at the produce counter. She bought firm fresh mushrooms and beautiful little snow peas. At the gourmet store he bought French wine and wild rice and cheese. On the way home with the back seat full of groceries, they laughed and sang "I Can't Smile Without You."

As she was putting things away—that was when he'd driven up to Myer's Plant World: "Trees, Bulbs, Seeds, everything for your plant needs." He watched the man count out his change into his palm and guessed with some satisfaction that Myer's Plant World had never sold a wedding tree before.

April nibbled cheese as she put the groceries away. She gave herself a minute so her morning queasiness would go away, and then she walked out into the backyard to see Gaines stabbing a shovel into the ground beside a stretched-out water hose. He hadn't heard her yet. He stood with his legs astride and hooked his thumbs beneath the waist of his jeans as he thought for a moment. Then he strode to where a leafless dormant tree leaned against the fence.

He caught her watching him, her green eyes twinkling.

"Actually, I was about to call you," he said sheepishly. "It's really a two-person decision. You have to vote."

She laughed and gestured at the tree. "What do I know about the finer details? I only know about notches."

"Well, how were you going to manage that?"

"How else? With the cuticle scissors."

Chuckling, he turned on the water to soften the ground a bit. In his jeans and polo shirt and Adidas he was the same unpredictable Gaines who had stolen her heart. You're such a crazy man, she thought happily; *I have never known a man who could make me like my life as much, or whom I could love as I love you at this moment.*

As if he read her thoughts, he turned and smiled. They stood looking at each other and both turned at the sound of a car pulling up in front of the house.

Wesley Durant pushed through the squeaking gate and walked across the yard, immaculate in a three-piece suit. Nodding at April, as if none of the business at Mary's party had ever happened, he shook Gaines's hand and looked about the yard, at the tree, at the open house.

Gaines stepped up beside April and closed his arms about her waist, pulling her back against him. "Darling, I take it that you and Wesley are acquainted."

April smiled thinly at Wesley, and Wesley straightened the lapel of his suit coat. "I would invite you in, Mr. Durant," she said, "but things are really a mess."

Wesley objected with his hand. "Oh, that's perfectly all right, Mrs. Southerland. I wouldn't hear of it. No problem. No problem at all."

Releasing her, Gaines moved farther out into the yard. Wesley shifted his weight. April thought they looked like two fighters, guardedly circling, searching for a vulnerable spot in the other to attack.

Gaines threw out an arm to indicate the entire back of the property and the house. "Well, what do you think, Wesley?"

The agent awkwardly looked around. "Ahh, very nice, Gaines. It's everything you said. Very nice indeed."

The ritual was almost funny, but April knew it was anything but. Gaines lifted his face to the sun and stroked his new mustache.

"If you were going to plant a tree, Wesley," he said solemnly, "where would you put it? About right here, do you think?"

Wesley studied Gaines through narrowed eyes. He flicked a glance in April's direction, but she only smiled nervously and placed her hands upon her abdomen. Wesley wiped a hand over his face.

"Well, I don't know, Gaines. That's pretty good, I suppose. You'd probably want to be careful about the water lines so the roots wouldn't grow into them. What did you have in mind?"

Gaines squinted. "Have you ever seen a sugar maple in the fall, Wesley?"

Shrugging, Wesley dragged a finger uncomfortably beneath his collar. "I guess I don't really know."

"That's the trouble with things, Wesley." Gaines nodded as if he savored the wisdom of his own words. "It all tends to slip by you. You wake up one day and you're fifty-five years old, and you don't know what a sugar maple looks like in the fall."

Thin lines of frustration edged Wesley's mouth. He looked at April in mute apology, then stepped closer to

Gaines. He was all business now, the CIA agent in command. "I get the drift, Gaines. You don't have to beat me over the head with it."

And Gaines was all business too. With implications buried in every word, he said, "Then you know what I'm saying."

Wesley said nothing for a moment. Gaines's calmness made him fish for a cigarette. He held it, then pointed it at April. "Why don't you ask your wife what she thinks. I mean, your . . . ahh . . ."

"Wife will do nicely."

"Well, ask her. Ask if she's ready to make the big decision for you. Ask if she's going to stand between you and your duty. Go on."

April had always known that the time would ultimately come when the decision—unfairly so—would fall upon her. But she had thought it would happen in degrees, a natural evolution. She wanted to grasp Gaines's love in both hands, like a child, and clutch it tightly: *It's mine; you can't take it away.*

Unsmiling, feeling more uncertain than before, she took a step backward. Her words came slowly, and with a cost she could not begin to grasp.

"I love you, Gaines," she said, listening to herself. "I'm . . . I'm saying it in front of this man. But I couldn't love myself if I kept you from doing something you felt in your heart you had to do."

With his head tilted at an odd angle, Gaines looked across the distance separating them. "What are you saying?"

"That I won't stop loving you if you stay with the Agency."

Wesley let out his breath in relief.

April's voice grew low and rough. "I'm saying that I'll marry you and try not to cling. I won't make you feel guilty when you have to go."

The words were too hard to say more. April didn't know how she'd found the courage to speak them out loud, but she felt a great burden lifted off her back. And an enormous weariness that took its place.

Wesley stirred. Sincerity was deep in his voice. "She's a very special lady, Gaines. I mean that. There are lots of ways we can make it easier for you two. I've got this friend, a plastic surgeon. He works miracles, they say. We—"

Like a blade, Gaines's voice cut through Wesley's monologue. "April?"

She'd ruined everything, hadn't she? After all her courage with Mary, why hadn't she just stood up for her rights to Gaines? Made a few demands? April lifted her head with considerable effort. Tears battled to force past her lashes. One spilled and she wiped it savagely away.

Gaines was smiling at her, with those straight, white Southerland teeth. Not for a second did he release her eyes as he walked toward her and directed his words to Wesley.

"I've done all I can for the Agency, Wes," he said, and smiled down at her. "I've neglected too many things. The best things."

April's lips parted. A surge of something wonderful pressed against her heart. She embraced Gaines with a trembling smile.

"But, Gaines," protested Wesley, "if you'd just apply a little discretion here . . ."

Gaines moved a thumb across April's lower lip. "I'll see you later, Wesley. Right now I think I'm going to treat my wife to a late lunch. She's looking a little peaked to me."

Even from where Gaines and April stood drowning in unspoken words and breathless looks, Wesley's sigh was audible.

"You really do look a little pale, my love," Gaines

murmured, and wondered if he would ever tell her that he'd known about the baby all along. "I think you'd better have a thorough physical before very long."

April thought of her secret. She wanted to laugh. She wanted to throw her arms about Gaines's neck and laugh up in triumph at the sun. But she mustn't tempt the gods, not when her hands were overflowing with everything she'd ever wanted.

She slipped her arm about Gaines's waist as he pushed open the gate. The hinges scraped.

"I wish you'd fix that thing," she said happily.

Gaines chuckled and signaled a haphazard goodbye to Wesley Durant over his shoulder.

"It's on my list," he replied, hazel eyes warm and glowing, "but nowhere near the top."

If you enjoyed this book...

Thrill to 4 more Silhouette Intimate Moments novels (a $9.00 value)— ABSOLUTELY FREE!

If you want more passionate sensual romance, then Silhouette Intimate Moments novels are for you!

In every 256-page book, you'll find romance that's electrifying...involving... and intense. And now, these larger-than-life romances can come into your home every month!

4 FREE books as your introduction.

Act now and we'll send you four thrilling Silhouette Intimate Moments novels. They're our gift to introduce you to our convenient home subscription service. Every month, we'll send you four new Silhouette Intimate Moments books. Look them over for 15 days. If you keep them, pay just $9.00 for all four. Or return them at no charge.

We'll mail your books to you *as soon as they are published.* Plus, with every shipment, you'll receive the Silhouette Books Newsletter absolutely free. *And Silhouette Intimate Moments is delivered free.*

Mail the coupon today and start receiving Silhouette Intimate Moments. Romance novels for women...not girls.

Silhouette Intimate Moments

Silhouette Intimate Moments

─ Coming Next Month ─

A WOMAN WITHOUT LIES
by Elizabeth Lowell

•

DISTANT WORLDS
by Monica Barrie

•

SCOUNDREL
by Pamela Wallace

•

DEMON LOVER
by Kathleen Creighton